Bailey Jacobs

First Series
Episodes 1 to 4

Isn't that a dog's name?

VJ Barrington

23 Feb 19

VJ BARRINGTON

First edition, paperback, 2019.

ISBN 978-1-9160201-0-8

Published by VJ Barrington
www.vjbarrington.com

For Bailey, Jacob, Cricket and Duke.
We miss you all.

Contents

Bailey Jacobs and the Disappearing Dogs

Prologue

There was room in his van for at least one more.

Having singled out three potential targets, he considered each one before selecting the blonde.

The women seemed unaware of his interest.

That was good.

He wet his lips, wrapped a chain around his fist, and closed in.

Chapter One

She didn't know how the day was going to end, but it hadn't started well. Having woken with tear-crusted eyes and a desperate knot in her stomach, Bailey Jacobs had missed breakfast, skipped lunch and headed into the park to contemplate events of the last twenty-four hours.

Sitting on a bench with knees tucked tight to her chest, she covered her face and cried.

Why?

A dog stopped to sniff her boots and she glared at it between ring-covered fingers. It cocked a leg, peed and moved on.

Why did he have to be such a dick?

A middle-aged couple strolled into view, their arms locked and hips swaying in time as they followed the path towards her. She could tell they were in love. They were so tightly wrapped you couldn't get a breath between them.

I can't believe he would do that to me *again*.

'Excuse me, Miss.'

She looked up to see an old man smiling at her. He had a walking stick in one hand and pointed to the space beside her on the bench with the other.

'May I have this seat?'

His small, wrinkled face topped a pale-blue jacket with matching trousers hitched high above his waist. She shrugged and collected the flow of her dress to make room for him.

'Thank you,' he said as he shuffled to the bench and sat. 'Do you know your laces are undone?'

Bailey grunted and covered her boots with her dress, then turned back to the lovers who were floating ever closer.

Paul hated cuddling in public. He'd happily fool around after a couple of drinks, but to show real affection … it would never happen.

'Margaret Baxter.'

She wasn't sure the old man had spoken to her until she felt his hand on her leg. 'What the—'

'Sweet sixteen,' he said. 'Danced until morning.'

He leaned closer and she prepared to slap the smile off his face.

'We were married forty-two years.'

She'd expected bad breath or that musty, medicinal smell you get with old people. But instead she noticed a hint of mint and a pleasing flash of spice. He had an infectious grin and grey eyes that twinkled fun.

'Peas in a pod, Margaret and I. Inseparable.'

A small dog appeared in the hedgerow, its patchwork face poking between a clump of early nettles as it foraged like a snuffling pig. When a jogger ran by, the dog disappeared after him.

'I wish my bones were so well-oiled,' the old man said with a sigh. 'When I was your age …'

Bailey drifted. Paul stood at the front door of his flat, face red with anger and spit flying as he cursed her for walking away from him. He wore Levis with the top button undone and his pot-belly catching the light. No shirt, no shoes, just jeans and a mop of scruffy brown hair. At one time that would have been an arousing sight, but not so much anymore. Not since he cheated on her.

Twice.

'Perhaps we'll meet again, young lady.' The old man kissed two fingers and lay them gently on the bench. Then he got up and turned his shiny brown shoes towards the car park at the end of the path where a woman stood waiting. Her yellow dress, bare arms and white-gloved hands were enhanced by the side of a black van parked ominously behind her.

The old man hobbled along, his walking stick prodding the ground with every other step. When he reached the woman they embraced and kissed, and Bailey's heart squeezed a little tighter. She couldn't remember the last time Paul kissed her, but guessed it was neither as gentle nor tender as that.

She stood, wiped her nose and followed the path in the opposite direction, disguising her derision with an acerbic cough as she passed the lovers.

It was early May and a recent spate of warm days suggested summer was going to be a hot one. Bailey removed her leather jacket and folded it over one arm. With her free hand she hoisted the front of her dress and traipsed though the park towards home.

Paul had asked her to move in with him a few days ago —a desperate attempt to save their relationship. At seventeen she was almost three years younger than him, and while that didn't put her off moving in, his promiscuity did.

Paul Thacker: cheat, liar and her first true love. She cringed. How could she be so stupid? The initial three months of their relationship had been a dream come true. Even the most mundane chores were new and exciting and so much fun. They were never apart in that time and hardly came up for air. But the last three months had been a nightmare that unravelled too quickly for her to comprehend. It wasn't just his inability to stay faithful—although it had hurt terribly the first time—she became the brunt of his jokes and he made her feel so stupid in front of his friends.

From start to finish, the whole thing had lasted just under six months. Whether that was good or bad for her first real relationship, she didn't care. All she knew was that she felt crap and wanted to die.

Life was a mountain of shit and she was stuck at the bottom wondering if it was worth the climb. Something had to change, but she didn't know what. In the meantime, she resigned herself to living at home with her mother and younger brother—which had its own challenges.

She didn't hate her mother—she actually admired her for surviving a shitty marriage and singlehandedly raising two fairly well-rounded kids—but she nagged constantly and it was so tiring. Her appearance, her job, her relationship … whatever Bailey did was never good enough. Paul had teased her about her failings often enough, so why did her mother have to do it as well?

From the pit of her stomach—where impulsive emotions and impetuous decisions often surprised her by erupting without notice—a realisation surfaced. Something she'd been ignoring for weeks but knew was inevitable—a decision that she welcomed and dreaded in the same breath: she wasn't going to be Paul's girlfriend anymore. That was final.

She sighed and pushed back a tear.

Life hadn't worked out the way she hoped and it frightened her to think what lay in store for a seventeen-year-old failure with no friends and fewer prospects.

Would she get over Paul? Would she get another job? Would life ever prove interesting enough for her to want to continue living it? Based on her experiences to date, she didn't hold out much hope.

At the ridge of a small hill, where the path descended into a vale peppered with trees and bushes, she stopped. Down below a woman walked through the long grass, waving a stick as she shouted. Bailey couldn't be sure at first, but as she closed the distance between them, she realised the woman was calling her name.

'Bailey.'

Bailey edged closer, her laces dragging behind as she placed each boot hesitantly in front of the other. The stocky woman had short hair and a scrunched up face. When she saw Bailey, she raised her stick, shook it angrily and marched towards her.

'You, girl. Stop there.'

Bailey had stopped but was now considering running.

'Have you seen my dog? Big. Tricolour. Bernese.'

Bailey's eyes darted between the woman's gnarled stick and intense scowl. 'What?' she said, stepping backwards.

'Are you simple, girl?' The woman let out an exaggerated breath. 'The dog in question is a Bernese Mountain Dog. His name is Bailey. He is waist-height, black and white with brown markings on his legs and chest. And he has two large brown eyes that are simply adorable.' She pulled a curt smile then let her face fall back into place. 'Now tell me, do you think you might have seen him?'

The woman spoke with a nasal timbre and her mouth half open as if sucking a sweet. Bailey didn't like snobs. She'd not met many but those she had always spoke down to her. This one was no different.

'Well have you?'

Bailey blinked, shook her head and said, 'No.'

'Very well, but keep your eyes open girl, just in case.' The woman turned and paced away, raising her stick in the air as she shouted, 'Mrs Chatterington's the name. Everybody knows me.'

Bailey followed the path through the trees and up another hill until she reached a row of houses lining the park. A narrow alley with high fenced walls led through a maze of back gardens to a quiet road at the front of the properties.

Her mother's house sat on the bend of a cul-de-sac. Brampton Road was a no-through road that consisted of detached houses built in the seventies. Number 10 had been Bailey's home for the last fourteen years—not including the summer she spent with her aunt after setting fire to her brother's bedroom.

As she slid a key into the lock and pushed the front door open, the rich smell of cooking preceded a voice from the kitchen. 'Is that you, sweetheart?'

Previously distracted by Mrs Chatterington and her missing dog, the reality of Bailey's tragic life came crashing back. She groaned, slammed the door and ran up the stairs, making sure her boots thumped every one that got in the way. Collapsing onto her bed, she pushed her face into a pillow and let the tears flow—wishing thoughts of Paul would piss off and take the pain with them.

When someone knocked on her bedroom door a short while later, Bailey squinted through a clump of matted hair as her mother entered the room carrying a tray. 'Leave me alone,' she yelled.

'Did you take a tablet?' her mother asked.

Bailey wanted to scream.

'Do you want one now?'

'What?' She heard a *whoosh* and the room filled with light. 'Go away.'

'I brought you biscuits.'

Bailey huffed, rolled her legs over the side of the bed and sat up. She grunted her thanks as she took a tray with a plate of biscuits and a can of Coke.

'Paul called again,' her mother said.

Bailey levered the ring-pull and the can hissed open.

'He sounded upset.'

She chewed on a biscuit.

'He asked if he could pop over tonight.'

Crumbs sprayed from Bailey's mouth as she blurted, 'What did you say?'

'I told him to wait until you were stronger.'

'What?' She scoffed. 'Stronger? Now he probably thinks I'm some kind of emotional loser locked away in a bedroom.'

Her mother frowned but said nothing.

'I don't want to see him. Do you understand? Not now, not when I'm *stronger*, not ever.'

'Yes, dear. Have another biscuit.' As Bailey dismantled a custard cream, her mother rubbed her knee and said, 'Whatever you do, don't rush to grow up, darling. You've got your whole life ahead of you and there's so much to enjoy.'

'But it hurts, Mum.'

'It'll get easier, I promise.'

'When?' Bailey felt a new tear crown and begin its journey down her cheek. 'I'm a failure. I'm crap at everything and nobody likes me.'

'Don't be silly, darling. I like you.'

'He cheated on me.'

'I know.'

Bailey rubbed the tear away. 'We couldn't even make it to six months.' Her voice cracked mid-sentence and she wished it hadn't.

'It happens, darling. It hurts, but it happens.'

'I'm trying to think what I did wrong.'

Her mother squeezed her knee. 'It's not your fault. He was the one who cheated, not you. Understand something, if this boy isn't the right one then don't try and make him.'

Bailey reached beneath the pillow and removed a photo frame that had seen better days. The picture was of a handsome man with thick black hair. He sat astride a motorbike while holding a baby wrapped in a pink blanket. She circled the man's face with her finger. 'Was Dad the right one for you?'

'No, but that was different.' Her mother's voice had an edge that Bailey hadn't heard since Aunt Liz phoned last Christmas. 'Tell me, did Paul hit you?'

'No.' She lied.

Her mother sucked in a breath and held it before speaking. 'Promise me something. If a man ever lays a finger on you, don't do what I did. Don't bottle it up. It's not normal and it's not okay. I'm always going to protect you, Bailey. So find me and tell me. Will you do that?'

Bailey nodded, thinking she probably wouldn't.

Chapter Two

Just after three o'clock as the afternoon sun found the edge of Bailey's bed, she woke to a high-pitched sound streaming through the open window. Wondering how her day could get any worse, she buried her face in the pillow and screamed for it to stop. Surprisingly, it did, but it was quickly replaced by a bank of noise that reminded her of a primary school playground at break time.

Bailey's bedroom overlooked a modest rear garden with a forty-foot strip of grass, a willow tree in one corner and a flagstone patio big enough for a hammock and barbecue. A six-foot fence shielded it from the surrounding properties and although most of the garden was overlooked in some way by a neighbour's upstairs window, there was a single spot beneath the willow tree where Bailey could sit unseen and untroubled.

Except that is, for the ever-present pollution of noise. If it wasn't the monotonous hum from a neighbour's busy lawnmower, or the out-of-tune whistling from the person pushing it, it was number 16 playing drums, number 24 hammering in his shed, or the general commotion of children clowning around in a nearby street.

Bailey hurled a pillow at the window and dragged herself to the edge of the bed. She scraped back her hair, massaged her temples and stretched her face into a yawn.

Bastards.

She stomped across the landing and stood on tiptoe to peer through a dormer window at the front of the house.

Sure enough, there were children everywhere. Swarming around an ice-cream van like ants on a toffee. Screaming and wailing in their excitement for sugar.

She wasn't sure what she hated most, the piercing pitch of their incessant wails or their boundless manic energy that tired her out so quickly. Either way, she had very little patience for the monsters.

At the entrance to the road, a shiny black van pulled over and parked. The driver sat watching the clamour of kids and made no move to get out. She didn't blame him.

In the bathroom she hardly recognised the person staring back from the mirror. A mass of tangled black hair crowned a listless face smeared with makeup. Paul always liked the way she did her face—pale skin, black eyes, black lips—he said it made her look mysterious. She scoffed. The only real mystery was why she hadn't seen through his bullshit earlier.

The sink discoloured as she washed and when she'd finished, the mirror reflected quite a different person. A fresh face with fleshy cheeks and blue eyes topped by a set of thick brows. She rolled her head as she inspected her teeth. Everyone said she had perfect teeth, but sometimes she wished she didn't. Sometimes she wished she could try the dentist's drill just to see why it made her brother cry.

Her cheeks glowed like shiny red apples. She hated how they made her look so young and unsophisticated. Paul's friends had once seen her without makeup and teased her about it for weeks after. The sort of face you put on a cereal box for kids—they had delighted in saying. Box-face—a face fit to sell cereal.

She unzipped her makeup bag and twenty minutes later, with her hair brushed back, her face covered by a layer of pale foundation and eyes sunken by a new film of black, she descended the stairs.

Her mother sat on a chair in the kitchen, tapping the face of her phone with petite fingers. Bailey offered a weak smile when their eyes met. 'Sorry, Mum,' she said, leaning against the door frame. 'I guess I got a bit cranky again.'

'It's all right, darling. These things take time.' Her mother stood. 'Did you sleep?'

Bailey shrugged. 'A little.'

'I made fish pie. Do you want to eat now or wait for Timmy?'

'I'll wait.'

'Would you like a Coke?'

Bailey walked across the room, wrapped her arms around her mother's slender frame and squeezed.

'Ooh.' Her mother squeezed back. 'What's that for?'

'Thank you,' Bailey said, feeling her chin quiver. 'I'm sorry for being so useless.'

'It's all right, Bailey Bee,' her mother said. 'We'll make it better. Just you see if we don't.'

Bailey sighed as the knot in her stomach loosened. Even before the split with Paul, depression and mood swings had afflicted her. Last year she had been a girl with ideas and aspirations, with passion and drive and determination to get things done. She'd left school wanting to work with animals, but Jacksons chicken factory wasn't what she had in mind. A vet would have been great, or a vet's assistant, or even helping out at the animal shelter on the edge of town. But her ambition faded when she fell in love and life had gone downhill from there.

She hated the fact that she could love and loathe the

same people in the time it took to swallow her medication. The doctor told her to expect days like that. His little yellow *comfort* tablets took the edge off, but she hated taking them and seldom did. One of Paul's friends had started his career in drugs that way—last she heard, the cops picked him up on the M3 walking naked to Portsmouth.

She sat with her mother in the lounge without speaking for almost an hour. A large room, it had a dining table on one side and a TV, sofa and two chairs on the other. Glass stretched the width of one wall from floor to ceiling, providing a clear view of the garden. Patio doors were open a few inches and a gentle breeze pinched through to cool the room. Bailey watched a neighbour's cat creep across the grass towards the willow tree where she guessed an unsuspecting bird waited.

Her mother broke the silence. 'Jenny called.'

Bailey blinked and wondered who Jenny was.

'They've lost their dog. The boys are distraught.'

Bailey turned her attention from the cat to her mother. 'What type of dog is it?'

'I don't know,' her mother said. 'Don't you remember? It dug a hole in the garden a couple of years ago. That blonde thing.'

Bailey nodded. 'Golden Retriever.'

'Probably. She's posted something online asking for help but nobody's come forward yet.'

'I haven't seen it,' Bailey said, peering through the window again and pleased to see the cat had made little progress. 'But I'll keep my eyes open.'

Keep my eyes open.

Something stirred in the vaults of her mind. The edge of an idea, too small to grasp but large enough to pick at.

As she concentrated, her thoughts were snatched away when the front door opened and footsteps pounded the stairs. 'Does he have to stomp around like that?' she asked.

'They do seem to be very noisy stairs,' her mother said as she got up. 'I'll get the pie. Can you set the table?'

It didn't take long for Bailey to arrange three settings on the dining table. She placed her mother at the head facing the garden and her brother against the far wall. Bailey sat opposite him with her back to the television.

At fifteen, Timothy was two years younger than Bailey, but at five foot eight he was just as tall. That's where the similarities ended. Timothy had a mop of curly blond hair, poor eyesight, bad skin and teeth as crooked as a halloween pumpkin. Bailey often teased—much to the annoyance of her mother—they found him in a field and were forced to adopt him because he was so ugly that nobody else would have him.

Steam billowed from the pie as her mother cut into it. Timothy gripped his knife and fork in anticipation and Bailey watched him start eating before she'd been served.

'Argh.' Timothy fanned his mouth as his glasses fogged.

Bailey sniggered.

'How was school?' her mother asked.

Timothy eventually swallowed. 'Okay. I've got a new partner for my project.'

'That's nice, dear.'

'He's coming round tomorrow night.'

'What for?' Bailey blurted.

'Gaming.'

She was about to tell him to get a life when a noise at the front door interrupted her thoughts. She leaned back on her chair and looked along the hallway to the frosted glass where she saw a shadowed figure get smaller as it walked away from the house. Caught in the flap of the letterbox was the evening newspaper. She turned back to the table and continued eating.

Mrs Jacobs leaned across and touched her arm. 'What are your plans for tomorrow night?'

Bailey shrugged. 'Nothing much.'

'Are you going out?'

'No.'

'Why not?' Timothy moaned. 'Isn't there a graveyard you want to visit?'

'Piss off.'

'Mum!'

'Language, Bailey.'

Timothy pushed up his glasses and pulled a face that reminded her of Mr Potato Head.

Her mother said, 'I'm going into town tomorrow night. With a friend.'

Bailey's interest was piqued by the way she said the word *friend*. 'Who's that then?'

'His name's Mike.' Timothy seemed rather pleased with himself. 'I've met him.'

'Oh,' Bailey said. She hadn't known her mother to have a proper boyfriend since her dad died. Not that she would mind in the least. They just never seemed to hang around for very long. 'Is this one serious?'

Her mother pulled a tissue from a sleeve and wiped it across her forehead. 'Don't be silly.'

Timothy held up four fingers. 'It's been almost *four* weeks.'

'We're just friends,' her mother said. 'Now, tell me, will you two be okay by yourselves tomorrow night?'

Bailey locked eyes with her brother. Probably not, she thought, because he's a nerdy-loser with bad breath and acne. 'Sure,' she said, 'we'll be fine.' She stood to gather the plates and took Timothy's with a sneer she was careful not to let her mother see. 'By the way …' She mouthed the word *wanker* at him before engaging her mother with a smile. 'Can I borrow some money?'

Chapter Three

The next morning Bailey woke feeling ravenous and irritable. Working at Jacksons had been mind-numbingly dull, the breaks were short and feathers got up her nose—but it was a paying job that got her out of the house, and she wondered what she was going to do without it. Watch an unhealthy amount of TV perhaps? Do some laborious housework for her mother? Or just mope around contemplating her inability to succeed at life? She desperately needed a distraction. But what?

She filled a bowl with corn flakes and stood at the kitchen window to eat them. The road in front of the house was quiet—at just before ten on a Friday morning, she guessed the kids were already at school and their mothers at home toasting the quiet with a much-needed gin and tonic. The sun beamed behind wispy clouds that scurried across a powder-blue sky. At least the fine weather was continuing, she thought. Maybe a walk to the river would provide the distraction she needed?

Bailey used to spend a lot of time by the river on the south side of town. She liked to sit in the meadow with a book and a drink, listening to the soothing sounds the water made as it splashed its way along. Paul had joined her there once but complained the whole time. He'd left after half an hour, grumbling dissatisfaction. She'd not gone back since and thought perhaps it was about time she did.

She showered and dressed then headed for the park

with one hand tucked into the side pocket of her leather jacket, feeling the reassuring presence of a ten pound note. Someone had cut their grass that morning—she could smell it.

It was going to be a good day.

A poster caught her eye at the edge of the park. Pinned to a tree it flapped in the wind and she held the corners down to read it. The words across the top were big, bold and unmistakeable: *Missing Dog*. A blurred picture of a poodle accompanied a paragraph of text that she didn't need to read in order to understand what it said—a dog was missing and the owners wanted it back.

Bailey remembered what happened to her dog all those years ago. She shuddered. Poor old Powder.

Unsurprisingly, the poster appeared elsewhere throughout the park—tied to trees and pinned to benches. She hadn't seen them yesterday and guessed somebody had put them up that morning.

She stopped beside a pond to study a rickety noticeboard. Among the notes and messages for garden fairs, handyman services and private tutoring, she saw the *Missing Dog* poster and a second poster of equal size entitled *Have You Seen Winnie?*

Apparently, Winnie, a three-year-old Pomeranian, had not been seen for the last two days. There was a picture of a young girl holding a dog with *Bring Winnie Home* printed underneath and although the amount wasn't mentioned, a reward was offered for the dog's safe return.

That's interesting, she thought, wondering how much they would pay for the safe return of their beloved Winnie.

The path veered around a large bush and she looked up in time to see a cyclist appear at speed with head down and legs pumping. He passed in a blur and she felt a sting as the zip of his jacket caught her hand. She swore, held up a finger and continued on her way.

Bailey followed the path through a row of trees to the field beyond. There she saw a group of people circling a man who barked orders as they pranced and jumped around. Bailey groaned at the sight of their sweaty bodies heaving in the sun. Exercise had no place in her world. Why run around and get out of breath for no good reason? If you want to lose weight, eat less. If you want to stay healthy, eat well. It wasn't difficult.

At the exit to the park, between the golf club and cricket ground, she noticed a different group of people. These were loud and boisterous and they bustled together as a handful of dogs skipped between them. Bailey approached at a safe distance and when a gap appeared between the bodies, she noticed a bright yellow jacket and saw a policeman standing in the middle of the throng. He didn't look happy.

Curious, she slowed her pace and edged closer. They were discussing dogs. Missing dogs. One lady had a finger raised to the policeman's face and even though she was a foot smaller than him, she commanded his attention. Bailey recognised her as the Chatterington woman she had met in the park the previous day. The stocky woman's voice rose above the others as she let the policeman know how upset and disappointed she was.

Careful not to get too close, Bailey sauntered by inconspicuously with hands tucked into her jacket pockets and eyes fixed to her boots. The people seemed agitated. One asked if the warden was to blame. Another suggested teenagers. They all wanted to know what the police were doing about it.

Apparently unable to control the situation, the policeman appeared flustered and Bailey felt sorry for him. He looked out of his depth and unable to swim. Her mother had a soft spot for the police and although Bailey was less inclined, she felt a sudden urge to step in and help. But the feeling quickly passed and so did she, heading out of the park and picking up the road towards Farnham town centre.

It didn't surprise her that so many people could be upset by the disappearance of a few dogs. She loved animals—especially dogs—and it troubled her to think of them lost and alone on the streets. The only dog she ever owned was a snow-white Terrier called Powder. It ended up as food for the foxes and she hoped these local dogs had better fortune.

Around the next corner, Farnham loomed—stately Georgian and Victorian buildings lined both sides of Castle Street, glaring disapproval as Bailey sauntered by. She weaved between pedestrians as she passed a handful of bay-fronted shops with white latticed-windows. A smartly dressed woman rushed out of one and tutted between tight lips as she narrowly avoided a collision. Bailey tutted back and continued on without breaking stride—she loved the town, but cared less for the people.

Making slow progress along Castle Street, traffic edged towards Farnham's congested one-way system like a river of metallic bugs all scrapping for position. Some of the vehicles had windows rolled down with arms and heads poking out. She heard one man swear and another shout, but didn't stop to see if either were directed at her.

Vehicles gridlocked the t-junction at the end of Castle Street and pedestrians walked between them. Bailey knew the roads around Farnham could be hazardous—narrow pavements and heavy traffic was a dangerous mix—but she stepped out anyway and crossed the road carefully, avoiding a car that nudged forward as she passed in front of it.

A bell tinged and a cyclist flashed by. He darted between vehicles and clipped the mirror of a black van as he went. There was a loud crack and the sprinkle of glass as half the van's wing-mirror fell to the ground. The cyclist corrected a wobble, waved an arm and continued on his way. Bailey waited for the van driver to react—the least she expected was for him to roll down the window and issue a barrage of abuse, perhaps a threat of violence —but nothing happened and that seemed strange to her. When she looked inside the cab, she saw a young Asian man tapping his fingers furiously against the steering wheel, seemingly oblivious to the fact he'd just lost a mirror.

She skipped onto the pavement and into a cobbled alley that ran between a bank and a shoe shop. Behind her, somebody shouted something she didn't understand and a car horn blared, followed by the sound of dogs barking.

Dogs? She hadn't seen any dogs.

When she turned to look, her view of the street was restricted by the surrounding buildings and all she saw was the shiny wheel of the black van as it rolled passed the neck of the alley.

Nestled in the corner of the shoe shop window, a pair of boots caught her eye. Tall and black with red stitching that wrapped the ankles in the shape of a rose, they looked amazing. She spent a few moments wondering how she might persuade her mother to buy them for her, before moving off in a state of pensive contemplation.

The alley led to a busy car park and the stink of fumes made her gag. Vehicles queued as far as she could see, feeding in from a single road at the far end. They filtered into both sides of the car park and circled slowly in search of a place to park. She hated congested places and covered her mouth as she snaked her way across. When the worst of it was behind her, she took a moment to catch her breath.

A black van joined the queue of incoming traffic. She spotted it straight away because it was bigger than the other vehicles, extremely shiny and sported a broken wing-mirror. As it approached at a sloth-like pace, she noticed the driver inside the cab didn't look too well. Lines in his face seemed etched by anxiety and sweat ran between them, dripping from his chin like tears.

He turned his head sharply and his pin-tight eyes burrowed into hers. She didn't know whether to run or raise a finger, but the moment quickly passed when the van rolled forward. And then concern replaced alarm when she heard the delicate, but unmistakeable tone of distressed whining coming from the back of the van.

Dogs?

A thought sparked inside her head and she fanned it with curiosity, but it smothered and died beneath the weight of trying. There was only one thing crystal clear to her at that moment: something was alive in the back of the van and it sounded like dogs. Multiple dogs. And apparently, they were in some distress.

The van turned left and she followed it to a corner of the car park where it pulled onto a grass verge. When the driver jumped out and slammed the door shut behind him, the dogs barked and Bailey's head ignited into a glorious blaze of realisation.

This man was the dog-thief.

'Excellent,' she said through a grin.

The Asian man was the dog-thief and he was probably taking them for a sacrificial ritual. Offering them to a god and grinding their bones to make medicine for a sick aunt. Or something equally as twisted.

A thrill crept from her stomach to her chest, making her shiver as it climbed.

It all made perfect sense … but she had to be sure.

Watching from behind a tree, Bailey saw the driver run into the back yard of a red-bricked building and disappear between some industrial waste bins. Gripping a branch, she leaned over far enough to catch sight of him pounding on a door with his fist. The door opened with a rusty groan and he stepped inside.

Bailey estimated the distance to the van to be no more than twenty paces. Aside from a fat woman extracting a pushchair from the boot of a car, there was nothing in her way and she could be there and back again in no time at all. Her chest heaved and fear had the better of her, but she gave it no mind as she pushed back her sleeves, lifted her dress and ran.

The shiny black metal was hot to touch and she wondered what the temperature was inside. The rear window was as black as the bodywork and impossible to see through, but she pushed her face against it anyway and cupped her hands around her eyes to shield them from the glare of the sun.

Something slammed against the glass, followed by a barrage of barks and scrabbling.

She pulled back, caught her foot in the grass and fell over, almost tangling with the pushchair as the fat woman scurried past with a tut.

The barks subsided and Bailey picked herself up. She was about to take another look when the back door of the building groaned open and the Asian man stepped out. He headed straight for the van, but didn't see her because his eyes were fixed to the object he held. Long and narrow but large enough to fill both hands, it was bound by a black cloth. She couldn't tell what it was, but it chinked as he unwrapped it and she saw the flash of metal.

She ducked around the side of the van and slipped away in the opposite direction, hiding behind the nearest tree. Above the rasp of her burning breath, she heard the chink of metal again and he muttered something strange as he climbed into the driver's seat. When the engine started, she watched him manoeuvre the van across the car park, down the lane beside the church and out of sight.

Adrenalin surged, her fingers tingled and her heart pounded so hard she thought it would burst. Not since rescuing her brother from an altercation with the school netball team two years ago, had she felt so charged.

She caught her breath and her cheeks dimpled with the stretch of an untamed smile.

She was desperate for a wee.

Chapter Four

Farnham police station was only a short walk from the tree Bailey stood beneath as she chewed her nails and considered her options.

She had visited that police station once before, when Paul was questioned about his role in an off-licence burglary the previous year. At the time, she never understood why they were so interested in Paul because he swore to her that he had nothing to do with it.

That visit hadn't ended well. She'd got excited, lost sight of the fact that it wasn't a debate, and ended up having a verbal altercation with a rotund desk sergeant who didn't appreciate being told that he was too fat for real police work. Eventually, after giving up trying to subdue her with logic, they gave her a choice: leave quietly or be arrested. So she'd left.

Determined not to repeat the experience, she recalled the policeman she'd seen in the park earlier that day. He seemed a tolerant, sympathetic sort and she decided to seek him out. But first there was something she had to do.

Making her way out of the car park through the main entrance, she turned right onto Downing Street and began counting shops. It wasn't easy to keep track because some buildings shared entrances and others had more than one door. When the ninth shop turned out to be a restaurant with a notice in the window saying *Under New Management*, she was confident she had found the right one.

Pushing the *closed* sign to one side, she peered through the pattern-frosted glass. She didn't know what she expected to see, but a half-empty room wasn't it. There were no dogs, no people, no activity of any kind. Just a few tables, chairs and a bar of some sort against the far wall. Feeling a little deflated, she turned and left, pondering the facts as she made her way across town towards the policeman in the park.

At least three dogs had gone missing recently: the Bernese Mountain Dog, the Poodle and the Pomeranian. Hadn't her mother said Jenny's boys were upset because their Golden Retriever had disappeared? That made four dogs she knew of. And from the crowd in the park that morning, there had to be others.

There was also the black van. She didn't know how many dogs were in the back, but it was definitely more than one. That van seemed very familiar and she tried to recall where she'd seen it before. She knew it had been recently. And perhaps more than once. But where?

Bailey massaged her temples in an attempt to ease the confusion inside her head. Plucking chickens at Jacksons had done nothing to prepare her for this. At school the teachers said she had a bright future. But she found it hard to concentrate, especially when there was so much to concentrate on.

Her pace slowed as the sun rose and the temperature increased. She removed her jacket and wrapped it over one shoulder. It was a long, slow climb back up the hill to the park and when she reached the spot where she'd seen the policeman two hours earlier, he had vanished.

Huh, she thought as she sat on a bench at the edge of the park, a pointless waste of time.

She stretched out her stockinged legs and the sun

warmed her from a cloudless sky. She yawned and looked around. The park was busy. There were walkers, joggers and a lone cyclist. Bird song, broken conversations and distant boyish laughter. Fumbling through her jacket, she found the money her mother had given her and balled a fist around it.

Perhaps, she thought, it wouldn't be too much of a problem to call in to the police station in town after all. Even if the obnoxious fat policeman was still there, chances are that he wouldn't remember her from last year. Then afterwards, she could make her way to the meadow and enjoy a cold drink by the water. She nodded. The idea of sipping Coke by the river was too good to resist. She tucked a wayward lock of hair behind her ear and stood, but before she could take a single step back towards town, something caught her eye. Something yellow. At the far end of the field.

She studied it for a moment to be sure, then lifted the hem of her dress and set off, running towards what could only be the yellow vest of the policeman.

The last time Bailey had run anywhere was at school. She hadn't enjoyed it then and didn't like it now. Her breathing increased rapidly and her stride quickly shortened. She wondered what she looked like, labouring across the muddy field in her army boots, one hand lifting her dress, the other trying to hold on to her jacket and the ten pound note.

A dog barked and a man shouted for it to stop, but it didn't and the barking grew louder as the dog closed in, snapping at her heels. She tried to speed up but her chest ached and there was no way to outrun the animal, so she settled into a stride and hoped for the best.

Sweat trickled down the small of her back as she

ploughed across the field, hair whipping her face and boots growing heavier with every step. Her lungs threatened to burst and she wheezed like a steam train struggling against a hill.

The policeman was over there, by the trees, she could see him. She wanted to call to him, but it was all she could do to suck in the next breath and keep ahead of the dog. And then everything stopped as the toe of her boot caught in the ground and she lunged forward, arms sprawling and jacket flying from her grasp. She hit the ground with a slap and braced herself, ready for the snap of the dog's jaws around her leg or the heat of its breath on her face. But as her panic ebbed and her lungs settled and the ringing in her ears waned, the only thing she heard was a throaty roar of laughter.

The mud pulled at her body. As she heaved a limb free, it sucked it back down. She twisted and struggled and when she eventually picked herself up, she saw a group of lads perched along a fallen tree. They could hardly keep their balance for laughing and her best sneer only heightened their enjoyment. Dickheads, she thought as she scraped mud from her face and limped on.

The policeman had disappeared, but Bailey knew the park well and was sure he'd taken the perimeter path along the east side. With laughter fading behind her, she passed through an avenue of tall oaks where the firmer ground quickened her pace and sure enough, over the next ridge, she spotted the policeman talking to a man. She ran to them, her arms pumping, face hot and breath bellowing like a shire on heat.

Concern skipped across the policeman's face and as she neared, he held up a hand for her to stop. 'Are you all right, Miss?'

She nodded as she wheezed and her cheeks puffed.

The other man—dressed in lycra bottoms and a rugby top—pushed a wave of untamed blond hair to one side and grinned at her. He said something to the policeman and then left, jogging back along the path she'd come. When he'd gone, the policeman stiffened, apprehension dripping from his suspicious face.

Finally, Bailey found the words. 'Dogs,' she said. 'Missing dogs.'

He frowned, folded his arms and leaned forward. 'Do you know something about the disappearance of the local dogs?'

'No,' Bailey said, shaking her head. 'I mean, yes. I think so.'

'Slow down, Miss. Take a moment and tell me what you know.'

Bailey shifted her jacket to the other arm and pushed back her hair, scraping the worst of the mud away. 'It's like this,' she said as she told him about the mysterious black van filled with dogs, and the Asian driver who had snuck into a restaurant and reappeared with an ominous-looking cloth roll containing something metallic.

As she spoke, the policeman's face changed. She guessed he was twice her age, but whatever curled his lip and pushed his brows into a frown, made him look a lot older—assuming it was concentration, she continued. Encouraged by his apparent absorption in her story, she found herself embellishing the bits she knew and making up the bits she didn't. She couldn't stop herself from suggesting the driver had stolen the dogs for some kind of voodoo ritual, and although she didn't know the connection with the restaurant, she urged the policeman to send someone to investigate straight away.

When she stepped back to catch her breath, signalling she had finished, he reached into a pocket and removed a notebook and pen. With the pen hovering in position he lowered his head, raised his eyes and asked, 'What's your name, Miss?'

Bailey was somewhat taken aback. She was so sure his first question would be to ask her where the restaurant was, so he could call the station and arrange for one of his colleagues to take a look. Even if it was the fat sergeant. Someone. Anyone. 'Why do you want my name? Shouldn't you go and investigate?'

'All in good time, Miss. Your name first, please.'

She huffed and said, 'Bailey, Bailey Jacobs.'

He wrote it down. 'Where do you live, Bailey?'

'What does that matter?'

'For the records.'

'Shit on the records, he's getting away.'

'Language, young lady. Now calm down and tell me where you live.'

She huffed again, this time louder. 'Number 10, Brampton Road. At the top of the park.' As she watched him write, she wondered how hot it must be in the back of the van and whether the dogs had access to water.

'How old are you, Bailey?'

'Why do you need to know that?'

'Did you get the number plate of the vehicle?'

'No.'

'How many dogs were in the van?'

'What?'

'How many did you see?'

She hesitated.

'You did actually see dogs in the back of the van, didn't you?'

'Um, no but—'

'Wait.' He wrote something down, and during the time it took him to finish, her unease grew. 'Describe the driver to me.'

'Asian. My height. Black trousers. Grey shirt.'

'How tall are you?'

'Five foot eight.'

He stepped back and looked her up and down. 'You look taller.'

'It's the boots,' she said, lifting her dress enough to show her mud-caked boots.

'Your laces have come undone.'

'I know.'

He waved the pen in front of her face. 'And how did you get to look like this?'

'What? The makeup or the mud?'

He tutted. 'The mud.'

Bailey wanted to start by saying *it's a funny story* but thought he might appreciate the short version. 'I fell.'

'I see.' He bit down on his lip as he wrote. 'What about the man's face and hair? Did he have any distinguishing features?'

She shrugged. 'Short black hair. Round face. You know, Asian looking.'

'Asian looking.'

'Yeah, he had piercing eyes that gave me the shivers. And he sweated a lot too.'

The policeman spoke as he wrote. 'Would you recognise him again?'

Bailey didn't know if she would. Perhaps if he was sitting in the same van wearing the same clothes then maybe, yes. But if he passed her in the street wearing something else? 'No,' she said. 'Probably not.'

He tucked the notebook into a pocket and when he lifted his head again, his eyes had narrowed and his lips tightened. He sucked in a breath and said, 'Now listen to me carefully, Jacobs.'

Something felt wrong.

'I'm the first to encourage the public to come forward with information about crime, any crime. But I don't appreciate having the piss taken by someone with questionable motives. Are you a racist, Jacobs?'

She gasped. 'What? No.'

'I hate racists.'

'I'm not.'

He sneered and leaned closer. 'I can't decide if you're a prejudiced ignoramus or a narrow-minded bigot.' He stabbed her shoulder with a finger. 'And there's no room for either on my beat, Jacobs. Do you understand?'

Bailey did understand, she understood all too well. She nodded vigorously and felt a tear escape. It rolled down her cheek but she didn't wipe it away because the last thing she wanted was for him to see her hands trembling.

'Good,' he said. 'Now piss off.'

* * *

Cold and weak, Bailey woke in her bedroom a couple of hours later. The house was quiet but for the muffled chink and scrape of activity in the kitchen. She ran a bath, slipped into it slowly and covered herself with bubbles.

Racist?

She couldn't get the policeman out of her head—he'd spattered her cheeks as he spoke and his foul breath repulsed her.

Why had he been so vile when all she wanted to do

was help? She realised how odd she must have looked covered in mud, but that was no reason for him to be so nasty. Paul had hardened her to ridicule, but this was something new—it really upset her.

She had been brought up to respect the police. Her mother always made time for them. According to her, Bailey and her brother wouldn't be where they were if not for the support of the police. She never knew what her mother meant by that and guessed it was something to do with her father not being around.

Respect had to be a two-way-street, didn't it? But what hope was there if *that's* the way people in authority acted. So patronising. What right did he have to treat her like that?

Her thoughts were snatched away by the sound of the front door slamming shut and feet thudding the stairs. Seconds later, the bathroom door burst open and her brother rushed in.

She shrieked. 'Get out.'

He looked as shocked as she was. 'Why don't you lock it then?'

Bailey swore beneath the bubbles as he exited and closed the door.

'How long you gonna be?' His muffled voice came from the landing.

'Ages.'

'Mum! She's hogging the bathroom again.'

Bailey reached for the shampoo and ran the hot tap. It was almost twenty minutes before she climbed out and wrapped herself in towels. When she eventually opened the bathroom door, Timothy forced himself through. 'Don't touch me,' she said as the point of her elbow found the flesh on his arm.

He grunted and locked the door behind her.

In her bedroom, she sifted through a chest of drawers for clothes. She pulled on a pair of blue jeans and a loose fitting black t-shirt with *Megadeth* emblazoned above a fluorescent skull. Standing in front of a full-length mirror fixed to the wall beneath a Guns 'n' Roses poster, she ran a brush through her hair and pulled her fringe forward to cover her brows. Her nails needed repainting but that, along with a fresh layer of makeup, could wait until tomorrow. She ambled downstairs feeling hungry and depressed.

Her mother greeted her with a smile and pointed to a dish topped with steaming cheese. 'Moussaka,' she said. 'Your favourite.'

Bailey slumped against the door, her shoulders sagging with defeat. 'What am I going to do?'

'About what, darling?'

She wanted to tell her mother everything that had happened to her that day—about the policeman, the dogs and the Asian man—but what was the point? Her mother didn't see things the way she did and bad-mouthing the police always got her into trouble. Bailey wouldn't win, she couldn't. So why bother trying? 'Nothing,' she said.

'I bumped into Fiona's mum today. Do you remember Fiona?'

Bailey sniffed. 'From the riding club?'

'Yes, she asked about you.'

'Who? Fiona or her mum?'

'Her mum. Fiona's riding dressage now. Apparently, she's doing very well.'

'Huh, s'not my thing anymore.'

'No,' her mother said, wiping her hands on her apron. 'But she's a lovely girl. Just like you—'

'What?' Bailey stood tall, stealing two inches over her mother. 'Just like I *used to be*? Is that what you were going to say?'

'No, my sweet. That's not what I—'

'Yeah, right. Whatever.'

'I just thought it might be good for you if—'

'Don't.' Bailey held up a hand between them. 'Just don't.'

Her mother turned to the sink, filled a glass with water and drank. Without looking at Bailey, she said, 'Why don't you start drawing again?'

'What?'

'Or bird watching. We've still got your binoculars and books in the attic and I could ask Timmy to get them down.'

'Don't want them.'

Her mother turned from the sink, reached for Bailey's shoulders and began massaging them. 'Why are you always so angry these days? You know, I haven't seen your dimples for far too long now.'

Bailey tried not to smile but couldn't help it.

'There they are,' she said as she touched Bailey's cheek and teased her fringe into a parting. 'My beautiful Bailey Bee.'

Upstairs the toilet flushed and the bathroom door slammed, followed by a cacophony of thuds as her brother thundered down and eventually poked his head into the kitchen. 'What's for tea?'

Fifteen minutes later as Timothy scraped an empty serving dish clean of crusted cheese, Mrs Jacobs said to nobody in particular, 'Mike's coming to pick me up at seven.'

Bailey hid her interest behind a monotone reply,

'Where are you going?'

'Into town. I'm meeting his mum tonight.'

Oh, Bailey thought, it must be getting serious.

'I shan't be home too late,' her mother added.

'Whatever.'

'Are you two going to be okay? What have you got planned?'

Timothy smacked his lips as he slapped the dish down. 'Martin's coming over.'

'Oh yeah, I forgot about him,' Bailey said. 'Your new bestie.'

'Shut up,' her brother protested. 'It's not my idea. Mr Philips put us together, he made us project buddies.'

Bailey laughed.

'Don't mind her,' her mother said. 'What's this boy like, darling?'

Timothy pushed up his glasses. 'Dunno. A bit like me, I suppose.'

'What?' Bailey said. 'Another clammy kid who plays with toys?'

'Tell her, Mum.'

'Bailey.'

'Anyway,' Timothy said. 'They're not *toys*. They're *computer games*. We code them and that's pretty trendy.'

Bailey scoffed. 'You *code* them … is that what the boys call it now? Locked in your bedroom for hours on end *coding*. Does all that coding make your hands ache?'

Timothy blushed and his mother reached across and squeezed his fingers. 'She doesn't mean it,' she said.

Bailey mouthed *yes I do.*

'Don't worry, darling. She won't get in your way tonight,' her mother said as she carried the plates away. 'One of her programmes is on the telly.'

'The Walking Dead?' Timothy said. 'Good, I hope she joins them.'

Bailey chuckled conspiratorially. 'Watch it, half-brother. Do you really want to wake up in the morning with one less eye-brow? Because you're going the right way about it.' She tried not to smile as an uneasy grimace creased his face. 'And trust me, it's not a trendy look to have.'

Mrs Jacobs returned with two bowls of ice-cream and set them down. Timothy attacked his without mercy, the clatter of his spoon punctuated by vulgar slurps. After his last mouthful, he dropped the spoon into the bowl, rubbed his stomach and belched. 'Sorry,' he said, looking sheepishly around.

Bailey was about to share her disgust when the letterbox squeaked. She leaned back on her chair and sure enough, there was the evening paper hanging from the door. She afforded her brother a quick glare before collecting the bowls and taking them to the kitchen where she dropped them in the sink.

Outside, children chased a ball around, screeching and yelling for no apparent reason. She didn't like kids. They were noisy and smelled bad, and far too quick to take the piss. She was never fast enough to catch them and, according to her mother who seemed rather worried that Bailey raised the subject at all, she wasn't allowed to hit them.

A young man crossing the road took Bailey's eye. She didn't recall having seen him before, but his lean figure appealed to her instantly. He looked about her age, perhaps a little older. She liked the way his rucksack swung in time to the sway of his broad shoulders. When he stopped outside her house and glanced up, Bailey pulled away from the window and immediately wished she hadn't. A few seconds later when she chanced another look, he was half-way up the drive and heading for the front door, a handsome smile making his tanned face beam.

Something stirred inside and she remembered the first time she saw Paul at the chicken factory. She opened the front door before he had time to knock. 'Hi,' she said, trying to remain poised. He had neat brown hair and bright eyes that pierced his olive skin. 'Can I help?'

'Bailey?'

His voice was deep and powerful and his eyes never left hers. She ran a hand through her hair, wishing that she'd taken the time to retouch her nails and put on some makeup. 'Yeah.'

'Is Timothy in?'

'What?' She felt a shove from behind and stumbled against the door.

'Don't mind her,' Timothy said as he pulled the young man into the house and pushed him up the stairs. 'She's always been kinda *special needs.*'

She righted herself in time to see them disappear into her brother's bedroom.

'That's Martin.' Bailey hadn't noticed her mother approach so it was a surprise to see her standing beside her now. 'His project buddy.'

'Oh,' Bailey said, gazing up the stairs in his wake. 'The clammy kid who plays with toys?'

'Apparently so,' her mother said before she turned on her heels and slipped into the kitchen, a playful tune humming from her lips.

Bailey retrieved the *Farnham Echo* from the letterbox and headed into the lounge where she dropped into her favourite armchair facing the garden. Her lighter, brighter mood lasted for the length of time it took to read the headline on the front page. It was big and bold and very clear: *Disappearing Dogs.*

She sat up and read on.

The article was written by Lawrence Williams, it said seven dogs had been reported missing in the last fortnight. *Seven.* Only one had been found safe and well—a greyhound named Duke whose owner was delighted at his return. The others remained unaccounted for and the distraught owners feared the worst.

The paper had a double spread across pages four and five with photos of the missing dogs and detail of various rewards offered by the owners for their safe return. It wasn't known if the disappearances were connected, but speculation provided various theories that included: a personal vendetta against the owners, who all lived within half a mile of Farnham; being stolen for an underground dog fighting syndicate; and being used to breed on puppy farms. The fact that all the dogs were healthy young females, strengthened the breeding theory.

A large photo at the foot of the page showed some people holding up empty leads. In the middle were two police officers wearing yellow jackets. She recognised the policeman who had reprimanded her in the park earlier that day. Beside him was a policewoman she had never seen before. The caption beneath the photo read: *PC Steven Tierney and PC Wendy Mundy with local dog owners unhappy about the spate of disappearances.*

Anger made her head throb as she remembered the vitriol that had spewed from his hateful face. She burned his features into her memory and added a note to avoid him and his kind in future. But a restless ache in the pit of her stomach told her that she hadn't seen the last of Constable Tierney.

Towards the end of the article was a telephone number of the local police station for people to call with information. It mentioned that all calls would be treated in strict confidence with anonymous callers welcomed.

Anonymous callers welcomed.

Bailey read the words again as an idea seeded. She closed the paper, sat back and let it grow.

Later that evening, when her mother had gone out and her brother was tucked away playing games with his interesting—and not in the least bit *clammy*—friend, Bailey closed the front door quietly behind her and headed to a nearby telephone box with a pocket full of change.

She muttered to herself as she went, practising a cackling voice that sounded older than her years, like the swing of a rusty hinge.

Anonymous callers welcomed.

Chapter Five

Bailey grinned so much that her face felt like a stretched balloon. Whilst she applied her makeup, brushed her hair and topped her nails with a new layer of blue, all she could think about was that phone call and her role in solving the mystery of the disappearing dogs. She skipped breakfast and kissed her mother for the first time in months as she left the house and headed into town.

Saturday morning in the park was hectic with the usual mass of dog walkers, joggers and cyclists to avoid. And so many pedestrians who all seemed happy enough to amble around without care or concern for anybody else. But none of them bothered Bailey that morning and she passed them all with a smile.

How had the police acted on the information she'd given them last night? She was impatient to find out. A sweet old lady calling to report strange goings on at a local restaurant; surely they were bound to follow up on information like that.

She imagined the building surrounded by police cars and uniformed officers, with hordes of people gathered to watch the proceedings. There would probably be TV crews and reporters as well. She quickened her pace.

Beneath the weight of congested traffic and an army of eager Saturday shoppers, Castle Street bustled and Bailey groaned at the sight of it. With head lowered and elbows raised, she battled through the crowds, her mood deteriorating with every side-step and *excuse me*. Central car park was a third full when she reached it, with more cars queuing to get in. She selected a spot beneath a tree with good view of the back door of the restaurant. As she settled, she was surprised to see a man dressed in denim exit the restaurant with something large and thin tucked under his arm. He stopped and looked around furtively, then dashed across the car park and disappeared into the press of pedestrians. Who he was and what connection he had with the restaurant, could wait. She currently had more important things to occupy her mind.

There was no sign of a police presence or evidence they had already been. This suggested to Bailey that they were preparing a mid-morning raid, probably to catch all the perpetrators together at the same time. That made perfect sense. She fizzed open a can of Coke and waited for things to unfold.

Half an hour later, with a stubborn branch troubling her spine and nothing more notable happening than a collection of curious stares from passers-by, she decided to leave her vantage point and take a closer look.

She crossed the car park and followed a lane to the shops on Downing Street where she turned left and joined the flow of pedestrians. The pavement heaved with busy people and two fat women growled when she elbowed her way between them. Eager to get where she was going, Bailey ignored them but readied a retort in case they wanted to discuss the matter—they didn't. When she reached the restaurant a little further along, she held her breath and pressed her face to the glass.

If the police were still inside, she was bound to see activity of some kind. Of course, if they had already been and gone, they would have taken the suspects away for questioning. Which is probably what happened, she thought, because the place looked lifeless. But looks could be deceiving and she had to be sure, so when she tried the handle and the front door opened, she stepped inside and let it rattle shut behind her.

Despite the heat of the morning, it was cold inside. The room smelled of curry and alcohol with a tang of bleach and a hint of cinnamon. A dozen tables filled the area to her right. A bar covered the far wall and a fish tank bubbled beneath its counter. She heard the muffled hum of cars and pedestrians as they passed by outside.

But there was another sound. A faint sound. She held her breath and listened.

Tap. Tap. Tap.

It came from behind the blood-red door at the far end of the room. She couldn't stop herself heading towards it and her boots squeaked on the tiled floor as she went.

The fish tank wasn't lit but there was light enough for her to see something swimming around inside. And at the bottom of the tank, where shapes were distorted by shadows, something wriggled.

The red door had no handle but it eased opened when she pushed it. She let it swing silently back into place and paused to listen again. The only sound she heard above the bubbling fish tank, was her quickened breath and the rhythmic *tap, tap, tap* from behind the door.

She stepped through in a single bound and found herself in a kitchen. It looked old and well-used and in need of a clean. A steel worktop ran the length of one wall. Upon it lay a pile of plastic cartons, a set of knives and a stained butcher's block. On the other side of the room, she recognised a large stove but not the equipment that flanked it. From the ceiling, a series of chains and hooks supported a variety of pots and pans.

A shabby white door sat in the far wall, alongside a window with brown frosted glass that added gloom to the light passing through it. Beneath the window, a water tap dripped into a steel sink, each drop releasing a beat that reverberated around the room. *Tap. Tap. Tap.*

She was drawn to a pot on the stove. Larger than any pot she'd seen before, it was big enough for a small child to climb into. She reached over, took hold of the lid with both hands and peered inside. Empty.

The front door of the restaurant rattled open and she froze. 'Mr Cheung,' a male voice called.

Bailey held her breath and started shaking as she fought the instinct to flee. She lowered the lid of the pot back into place with a clunk that seemed loud enough to wake the dead.

'This is the police.'

She turned slowly towards the back door, the squeak of her boots threatening to give her away.

'Is anybody there?'

She tiptoed across the kitchen and caught the zip of her jacket on the edge of the worktop. It scraped along the metal surface and she stopped.

'Mr Cheung. It's Constable Tierney from Farnham Police.'

Hairs stiffened along Bailey's spine. Her chest heaved and her temples pounded so hard they might explode. She took slow, careful steps, letting her boots caress the tiles like soft kisses.

Footsteps squelched in the next room as Tierney moved around.

How close was he? And how long before he walked into the kitchen and found her? When she eventually reached the back door, she grabbed the handle and turned it with a trembling hand. But the door didn't open.

'Mr Cheung?'

Having considered the window above the sink as her next possible hope of escape, she leaned across to try it and her arm brushed a leather strap dangling from a rusty hook on the door frame. At the end of the strap hung a single key. She fumbled it free and almost dropped it in her haste to push it into the door. When she twisted it, the lock clicked open.

Bailey launched through the door and ran blindly into the back yard where she collided with something soft. Dazed and unsettled, she saw a grey-haired woman lying on the ground covered in lemons and lettuce. The woman pointed up at her and screamed.

Bailey turned to flee, but her stomach fell when she saw a black van preventing her escape. It had reversed into the yard and with its doors open wide, there was no way around it. In the back of the van a man crouched between a pile of bags and boxes. She recognised him instantly as the creepy Asian driver—the dog-snatcher.

Someone grabbed her arm and she looked down to see the old woman clawing at her jacket as she tried to get up. Bailey prised the woman's fingers off and pushed her back down. Meanwhile, the dog-snatcher had climbed from the back of the van but caught his leg between two boxes and now struggled to get free.

She saw her chance and took it.

Running to the vehicle, she threw herself to the ground and crawled beneath the van door. Before she could scramble clear, a hand grabbed her foot and she kicked out instinctively, hearing someone moan as her heel connected. The hand released its grip, she struggled to her feet and fled across the car park, the shouts and screams behind her growing more distant the further she ran. Only when they faded completely did she stop, buckle over and gasp for air.

It took a while before she found the strength to lift her head to see if anyone had followed, but aside from a few faces turned her way, nobody showed any interest.

Bailey cursed herself for being so stupid. She knew why she'd run but she was upset that she had. Any other policeman and she'd have stuck around to explain why she was there, and then maybe together they could have searched the place and found the evidence they needed to close the case.

Sweat pulled her shirt tight in patches as she stood up and looked around. She had come to rest in a quiet corner of the car park where many of the spaces were empty. The neck of an alley ran between two buildings and she headed towards it.

'Hey.'

She jumped at the voice and span around quickly.

'Are you all right?'

Dressed in clothes the colour of mud, a bearded man sat on the ground with his back against a wall and a patchwork dog alongside him. He looked like a dusty musician. 'What?' she said with a scowl.

'Are you fleeing for your life or just playing hard to get?'

'What?'

'You look like you need some help. Do you?'

The man hadn't got up. He seemed quite comfortable sitting on the ground and happy enough to stay there. 'No,' she said.

'What's your name?'

She was going to ask *why* but instead she pulled a face,

scoffed then turned and hurried down the alley without another word. A short way along, it opened into a courtyard with craft shops and a coffee house. A handful of tables outside the coffee house lay empty so she selected one with a view along the alley and sat. She didn't know what she would do if she saw the policeman appear, but at least she had bought herself some time to come up with a plan.

A skinny girl dressed in black and white approached her table. Her legs were so thin they looked ready to snap. The girl tapped her pen impatiently against a notepad and pulled a face that didn't come across as friendly. 'What'll it be then?'

Bailey forced a smile and pushed her hair back. 'Coke, please.'

The skinny girl wrote it down and turned to leave.

'And a couple of napkins,' Bailey added.

The girl grunted.

Bailey settled back in the chair and stretched out, feeling her heart slow with every moment that passed.

A short while later, the waitress returned with a glass and a can and slapped them on the table before handing across a couple of napkins and the bill. Bailey fought back the urge to thank her as she took the napkins and drew one across her forehead. She snatched the piece of paper from the girl's bony fingers and checked the amount. 'Fuck.' The word escaped before she could tie it down. 'Sorry,' she said as she probed her jacket for the money her mother had given her. 'But that's a lot for a Coke, isn't it?'

The waitress clicked her ballpoint and smiled.

Bailey continued checking pockets.

'Is everything okay?'

49

'Uhuh.' Bailey nodded. 'I think so.'

'You haven't got it, have you?'

Where the hell had it gone? It was there yesterday. She had it in her hand in the park, moments before … before being chased by that bloody dog. Shit. She must have dropped it when she fell. She looked up and frowned. 'Sorry.'

The waitress sighed. 'Wait here.' She turned and marched away.

Bailey had only once left a place without paying—just before Christmas when Paul needed money for cigarettes —and although the thought crossed her mind as she waited for the waitress to return, she decided she'd done enough running recently and would stay put and face the consequences. After all, what's the worst that could happen? She poured from the can and drank.

When the girl returned, Bailey was surprised by her improved attitude. 'Sorry for being so snappy earlier,' the waitress said as she held out a small black book and pen. 'If you can write your contact details in here—name, address, number—we'll make a note of what you owe and you can finish your drink in peace. Of course, as long as you promise to call back and settle up another time.' She checked her watch and smiled. 'How does that sound?'

Bailey thought it sounded fine and took the notebook. 'Thanks.' She hesitated for a second as she considered giving false details before deciding not to.

'And your address.'

'Sure,' Bailey said.

'Is that your current address?'

Bailey looked up as she returned the notebook and pen. The girl still held a smile although it had waned a little. 'Yep. That's the one.' She smiled back, hoping it was received with the pinch of condescension intended.

The waitress checked her watch again, looked around and then pulled up a chair and sat. 'This job is exhausting,' she said as the full stretch of her smile returned.

Bailey wasn't sure what just happened. She hadn't invited the girl to sit and felt a little awkward with her being there. Although, her improved attitude was welcomed and if that continued then she was happy for the girl to stay. And who knows? She might even wangle a slice of cake.

A badge pinned to the girl's blouse said: *Ask for Linda*.

'I'm on my feet all day, serving drinks and food and taking care of everyone's needs. You wouldn't believe how much walking I do. Okay, so the tips are good,' Linda said, hardly pausing for breath. 'And you get to meet some great people.' She smiled again. 'But by the time I get home I'm just about finished for the day. D'you know what I mean?'

Bailey listened as Linda prattled on about the pros and cons of being a waitress. Being on her feet all day was probably the reason she was so thin. Bailey let her hands fall to her own tummy and felt the loathsome layer of fat that had built up over recent weeks. Waitressing might do her some good. Chances are though, she wouldn't find a boss as accommodating as Linda's—someone who'd let her sit with customers and engage in idle chitchat.

As Linda spoke, Bailey's thoughts drifted to Martin. Tall and lean, dark-skinned and a smile to melt chocolate —he had a lot going for him. But when she thought about actually dating one of her brother's friends and what the repercussions might be … urgh, she shuddered, that would never happen.

She became aware that Linda had stopped talking. Had she asked a question? Was she waiting for her to say something? She didn't understand why the girl's smile had disappeared and her eyes drawn as tight as her lips. Linda raised an arm and waved to someone. Bailey didn't know who, but it became clear when she heard movement behind her and turned to see the fluorescent yellow of a policeman's vest.

'Bailey Jacobs. I'm arresting you on suspicion of breaking and entering into number 48 Downing Street, also known as The Dragon's Palace. You do not have to say anything but it may harm your defence if ...'

Bailey's head spun as she looked up into the dour face of Police Constable Tierney.

Chapter Six

Leaving the police station and her mother behind, Bailey lumbered towards the park—a hunched figure of failure muttering to herself as she went. With every listless step, her boot-laces dragged like the tail of a smacked dog, and her face suggested the same.

In had taken almost three hours for her mother to turn up and in that time, Tierney had prowled around like a hungry cat, claws bared and ready to pounce. She'd seen delight in his face as he led her to the cell, hand-cuffed like a common criminal. Sure he'd been professional and reserved in front of his colleagues as they processed her, but his mouth twitched repeatedly and she could tell he loved every minute of it.

He'd made her wait in a room that was cold and bare and uncomfortable. Light from a tiny window did nothing to brighten her mood. Her only distraction was guessing whose ugly face she'd see when the hatch opened every few minutes: Tierney's or the fat sergeant's. Her anxiety had heightened when she first saw the fat sergeant smiling at her from behind the glass, but the fact he didn't seem to recognise her felt like a minor victory.

She hadn't wanted to name her mother as suitable guardian, but she didn't have a choice—with her dad dead and no adult friends to rely on since she'd split with Paul, her mother was the only option. She could imagine the glee in Tierney's voice as he broke the news to her.

Unsurprisingly, Tierney's attitude improved as soon as

her mother arrived. He was smooth, attentive and accommodating. He even produced drinks for the formal interview: a Coke for her and a coffee for her mother. But Bailey knew he was a sneaky shit and didn't let her guard down.

It was obvious from the start that he had no intention of believing her. Sitting across the desk from them— shoulders arched and chest puffed out—Tierney leafed through a folder, shaking his head and drawing a discernible breath at every page. Throughout the interview he patronised her, belittled everything she said, even tried to twist her motives for being there. All she'd wanted to do was save the lives of innocent dogs, but Tierney suggested she had racist tendencies and intent to rob.

Racist tendencies? She swore beneath her breath and kicked away an empty crisp packet that floated into her path. A passing person tutted disapproval and Bailey glared back.

'Have you ever been involved in anything similar?' Tierney had let the question hang between them before continuing unprompted. 'Ah yes, Sergeant Bellows told me you were connected with the robbery of an off-licence last year. Together with one Mr Paul Thacker. Is that correct?'

Bailey had felt her face blister and the heat from her mother's stare warmed her further. Even though she had nothing to do with the break-in and had never been officially named, she didn't mentioned what happened because she didn't know how her mother would react. Well, she thought, pretty soon she was going to find out.

'So please tell me …' Tierney squeezed his fingers so hard they cracked. 'Because we're all very curious. What did you do with the painting?'

She had stared at him, open-mouthed, trying to decide if he was genuinely stupid or just pretending.

'That's right,' he'd continued in a condescending tone. 'We know about the painting. Perhaps, in the commotion, you thought it would be overlooked, even forgotten. Was that your plan?'

'What plan?'

'Your plan to rob the place. Did you think it was expensive? Worth the risk?'

'What?'

'The painting you stole from the restaurant. Where did you hide it? Sergeant Bellows believes you had an accomplice, but I don't think you're that smart. So tell me, where did you put it?'

She'd repeatedly denied taking the painting and although it was clear he refused to believe her, he eventually let it drop. Then she reminded him about the van and the dogs and he almost spat his contempt in reply. He cared about evidence, not assumptions. He wanted the number plate of the vehicle and preferably a photo of it at the scene.

Did she have a camera-phone?

No.

Could she have written the number down?

No.

Or simply remembered it?

Er ...

Tierney had shaken his head at that point and the room fell silent.

She'd only wanted to help. When she made the anonymous call in the voice of an old lady the night before, she figured the police would go in, turn the place over and pull the staff in for questioning. But no, the only reason Tierney had been at the restaurant was because a member of the public had spotted her entering and thought it looked suspicious. Probably those two bitchy fat women who'd growled at her on the pavement.

Her mother had been no help at all, sitting like a lemon as Tierney twisted the truth. She'd expected more support from her, especially when Tierney accused her of being a racist. But no, her mother had sat quietly sipping coffee, watching her daughter get verbally torn apart by a uniformed-bigot.

Unknown to Bailey at the time, Mr Cheung—the restaurant owner—had called in to the station to help the police with their enquiries. According to Tierney, Mr Cheung was shocked by the altercation which had left them all traumatised. His wife needed comforting at the scene and his son required medical attention for a black eye delivered by the heel of Bailey's boot.

'So,' the policeman summarised as he tried to suppress a grin that gave his face a maniacal twitch. 'Breaking and entering, the theft of a painting and two counts of assault. None of it makes good reading, young lady.'

Bailey remembered fighting back the urge to scream as any chance of a promising future dissolved around her. *Fuck*—the word had flashed in big red letters as she stared into Tierney's twisted face. What hope was there if she got saddled with a criminal record at seventeen? Would she go to prison and become someone's plaything, only to be released a few years later with more bent tendencies than she'd started with? How would she handle being locked up in a cell all day when she couldn't even stand locking the bathroom door?

She sighed and wished for it to end.

'Fortunately for you,' Tierney had continued. 'Being the nice the man he is, Mr Cheung doesn't wish to press charges.'

She couldn't believe it.

'Yes,' Tierney said. 'He's been very lenient. And you've been very lucky. I doubt most people would be quite as forgiving as Mr Cheung.'

And that was that. She escaped with an informal caution from Tierney, which her mother—having finally found her voice—thanked him for. Ten minutes later, Bailey was on the police station steps pulling on her jacket as her mother told her off through clenched teeth. Before she had time to finish, Bailey had turned and walked away.

That had been half an hour ago and she'd spent every minute since, cursing Tierney and running through the facts of the case.

What was his problem anyway? And why take it out on her? The police were supposed to solve crimes and keep people safe, not try and fit them up for things they didn't do. Dickhead.

But why had Mr Cheung not pressed charges? Was it possible she had misjudged the situation and he was actually the nice person Tierney made him out to be? Or had he done it to stop the police poking around and asking too many questions? She couldn't be sure, but one thing she did know was that his son, Cheung Junior, was as sneaky as an assassin in slippers.

Bloody Tierney. He kept going on about collecting evidence, getting the number plate, making notes, taking a photo. He made her feel so stupid. Leave it to the professionals, he'd said. Don't get involved. Stay out of our way.

She felt certain she could oblige because in future, she would do all she could to avoid that dickhead.

A rush of wind tickled her face and she looked up, not immediately realising where she was. The building in front of her looked unfamiliar and four oddly-dressed men straddled the path with bags and trolleys. She felt their eyes on her back as she passed between them.

Bloody golfers.

Would her mother throw her out of the house? She'd been remarkably reserved at the station and her eye had hardly twitched at all. But that was her mother: silent and deep and capable of bursting like a torrent when the pressure got too much. She'd threatened to take Bailey to a children's home once. Bailey had been a lot younger and couldn't remember the details, but the image of a creepy grey building looming large into the night sky, stayed with her.

She turned with the path and crossed a stream flanked by forest. As the sound of water tumbling over rocks distracted her, someone wrapped an arm around her throat and dragged her into the woods. He was quick and strong and forced her to the ground.

'Whadya wan?'

Something warm spat across her face and she smelled bacon.

'You sniffin' around? Maybe see summin' and go tell copper?'

She looked up to see a man with fierce eyes, one of them bruised and swollen. Mr Cheung's son. The dog-thief. He loomed over her with mouth open and saliva dripping from blackened teeth.

'Freaky girl.'

Bailey tried to push him off but he was too heavy. She

dug her heels in the ground, but they slipped. He covered her face with his hand and she desperately wanted to scream, but it was all she could do to fill her lungs for the next breath. Lashing out with both fists she caught a part of him she couldn't see. He grabbed her right arm and lodged it beneath his knee, then caught her left arm and twisted it until she thought it would snap. He lowered himself onto her, his face close enough to taste. 'Not so clever now, freak.'

His hand muffled her cries, she could hardly breath and her lungs ached. She dug her heels into the ground again and this time they caught. She pushed, launching her hips high as she tried to buck him off. His sweaty hand slipped from her face and she opened her mouth to draw a breath. He slapped her ear and covered her face again, but this time she was ready and sunk her teeth into his hand, grinding them to the bone.

He squealed and punched her in the side of the head, ripping his hand from her mouth as he stood. 'Fuck.' His arm shook as he pointed at her. 'You got big trouble now, freak. Big fuckin' trouble.'

Bailey rolled away as he directed a kick at her head. He missed, lost balance and fell. She scrambled to her feet and ran blindly through the forest, leaping ferns, dodging trees and parrying branches as she fled. She could hear him behind her, shouting and swearing and getting closer with every step. Something whipped her face and she cried out but didn't slow and finally, as the trees thinned, she pushed through the last of them and found herself at the edge of an empty field.

It only took a second to get her bearings before she set off towards a distant row of cars. He was right behind her and she ran as fast as she could across the muddy field.

But as fear drove her, exhaustion held her back. She wanted to stop, to breathe, to vomit.

Her foot slipped, she hit the ground and he was on top of her, pinning her down with his weight, pushing her face into the mud. He grabbed her hair and pummelled her head again and again. Pain exploded between her nose and lips and her eyes filled with tears. The assault was too fast, too strong and she could do nothing to stop it.

Above the chaos of his rage and her struggles, she heard something. Distant at first, but growing louder. The sound of someone calling her name.

She felt the blast of the attacker's breath as he spat words into her ear. Then his weight lifted and the smothering ended. She raised her head and gasped her next breath, and through mud-matted hair she saw him escaping towards the cars.

'Are you okay?'

She forced herself onto her hands and knees.

'Are you hurt?'

Someone hoisted her up and turned her around.

'Jeeze,' a man said.

'What?'

'You look awful.'

She found herself facing the athletic blond man she had seen talking to Constable Tierney the day before. His pleasing features were distorted by a grimace as he examined her. Ignoring him completely, she turned away in time to see her assailant climb into a van, throttle the engine and reverse out of a parking spot. She ran towards the van, fell, scrambled to her feet and stumbled on.

'Hey, where are you—'

There was a moment of clarity when Bailey saw the back of the van and everything around her disappeared into a misty haze of insignificance. She made sure she did things right this time. She closed her eyes, took a mental snapshot and saved it to memory. 'A. R. 6. 4. F. H. T.'

'What are you—'

'A. R. 6. 4. F. H. T.' She wiped dirt from her forehead and blood from her nose and pushed muddied hair back into place. The blond man stood in front of her again and beneath his worried expression, he seemed pretty cute. She tried to smile. 'Ever so sorry,' she said. 'But I've really got to go.' And then she was off, pounding the ground with mud-laden boots as she headed home across the field, her face dirty, her hair a mess and her lips moving to the sound of *AR64FHT.*

* * *

The origins of graffiti occupied Bailey's thoughts as she waited for the line to connect. Etched and inked on small glass panes, it served as a curious insight into local opportunities and opinions. Apparently, Amber wanted company, Pete was less than complimentary about politicians, and Baz thought life sucked big time.

Welcome to my world.

She had gone home, grabbed a pen, and without washing or cleaning or even checking herself in the mirror, headed straight back out again. Now she stood in the telephone box, picking dried mud from her face while reading messages from previous occupants.

Her whole body ached, but while her bones and muscles demanded attention, her nose protested the most as it struggled to cope with the smell. She was certain someone had pissed in the box since yesterday evening.

Where was the decency?

Although bruised and shaken with one ear ringing like a church bell on Sunday, she wasn't upset that Mr Cheung's son had attacked her. Quite the opposite, it galvanised her determination to put things right. And that's precisely what she was going to do.

A small boy on a bicycle pedalled in front of the Lazy Fox pub where a handful of patrons stood outside smoking. She'd never tried that pub before. Although just around the corner from her house, under-age drinking was tricky to pull off at the best of times, without the added complication of the landlord having once dated your mother.

Her breath was loud and every shift and fidget intensified inside the small box. She tried to remain still, to clear her head and focus on the job in hand.

Keep it together. Keep it together. Keep it together.

When the line connected, Bailey hunched her shoulders and crumpled her face to get into character. 'Hello, my dear,' she said with a slow, tired voice that cracked like melting ice. 'Would this be the local police station?'

'Yes, ma'am, this is Farnham Police Station. How can I help you?'

'I would like to report some suspicious behaviour.'

The lady at the other end paused briefly before, 'Can I take your name, please?'

'My name? No thank you. I'd rather this call be made anonymously if that's all right with you, my love.'

'Yes, of course. What would you like to report?'

Bailey took a breath. This was going well, she thought. 'It's very peculiar, love. You see, today in the park, I saw a creepy-looking Asian man wrestling a dog into a black van.' She heard noises at the other end, a muffled conversation and then the line went silent. Too many uncomfortable moments passed before she heard a click and the policewoman replied.

'Did you report this to the station yesterday?'

Bailey heard a thud and looked down to see the bicycle-boy resting against the telephone box, his face split with a grin. She turned her back on him, keeping her shoulders hunched and face crumpled as she tried to stay in character. 'Er, no, lovey,' she said into the mouthpiece.

'Are you sure, ma'am?'

Bailey hesitated as the boy appeared in front of her again and started pulling faces. 'My friend was with me at the time it happened.' Her voice lost some of its crack and she worked to regain it. 'She might have been the person who previously reported the incident.'

'Okay,' the policewoman said rather too hesitantly for Bailey's liking. 'But the previous report was made yesterday and the incident you saw was today, wasn't it?'

'Oh, silly me. I must be getting my days mixed up. Happens to us all at my age.'

'I see. Very well, can you describe the man or the vehicle?'

'Just a moment, love.' Bailey held the mouthpiece tight to her thigh as she pushed the door open, leaned out and shook the boy by the collar. 'Fuck off.'

'Ma'am, is everything okay?'

'Yes, love. Everything's fine,' Bailey said as the boy pedalled away at speed.

'Can you describe the man or the vehicle to me?'

'I can do a bit better than that. You see, I had the presence of mind to write down the number plate of the vehicle in question.' Bailey recited the registration scribbled on her hand.

'That's very helpful, thank you. Is there anything you'd like to add? Can you describe the man perhaps?'

Bailey considered explaining that he had a black eye and a bite mark on one hand, but decided not to. 'He was creepy-looking,' she said. 'Things just didn't look right, him bundling a dog into a van like that. They didn't look right at all.'

'Okay, thank you. We'll create an incident report but because we don't have your details we can't—'

Bailey put the phone down and headed home, feeling rather pleased with herself and confident that this time the police would surely take action.

The house was empty when she arrived. Something simmered in the kitchen but her mother was nowhere around. She went upstairs, kicked off her boots in the bathroom, undressed and climbed into the shower.

Bruises blotched her arms and the tops of her thighs. Her nose smarted when she touched it and scratches marred one cheek. But the flow of hot water helped. As the shower massaged her body to a glow, the worst of the pain washed away with the soiled brown water.

A quarter bottle of shampoo later, she got out and wrapped in a soft towel that covered everything from her chest to her thighs. She put another around her head, then wiped condensation from the mirror.

Not too bad, she thought, considering. She had a bruised temple and a swollen lip, but her nose didn't look as sore as it felt and the cuts on her cheek were shallow.

Leaving her dirty clothes in a pile on the floor, she reached for the bathroom door and was surprised to find it open. She tried to think whether or not she'd closed it properly in the first place. Perhaps she hadn't? With an aversion to confined spaces and locked rooms, it was common for her to leave doors ajar, but never usually the bathroom door.

On the landing she heard voices coming from her brother's bedroom. She edged closer, held her breath and pressed an ear against the door.

In the time it took her to realise there were two voices coming from the room and one of them was Martin's, the door opened and Martin stepped out.

'Oh,' she said, a charged quiver exciting the hairs on her arms. 'It's you.' He was a few inches taller than her and even in the dim landing light, his eyes and teeth flashed.

He pointed to her face. 'What happened to your face?'

'It's a long story.'

Timothy coughed theatrically from his room. 'Get out the way, vamp. The boy wants to pee.'

'It's in there,' said Bailey, pointing to the bathroom.

'I know.'

As he passed, she tingled and let out a muted sigh.

'Oi, leave him alone. He doesn't want to be contaminated by your filth.'

She turned to her brother and mouthed the words *fuck off*, then ducked into her bedroom where she took time to dress and make up her face before heading downstairs.

The pot on the stove was three-quarters full and simmering away. She turned down the gas and gave the contents a stir. Dirty items filled the sink and flour covered part of the worktop. She began to tidy up, thinking how strange for her mother to leave the place in such a mess. As she worked, boisterous noises leaked from Timothy's bedroom: the sound of gun fire and grenades accompanied by juvenile cheers. Little boys with their little toys. She promised herself never to fall for anyone who got so much pleasure from a computer.

The children were back, kicking a ball outside amidst a chorus of screams. One child stood astride a bicycle and faced the house. She couldn't be sure if it was the kid from the phone box because they all looked the same. They scattered when a sleek black saloon rolled by. She watched it go until out of sight, then a moment later it returned and pulled to a stop in front of the house.

She dried her hands and watched. The car windows were too dark to see inside and it felt an age before the passenger door opened. When finally it did, the first thing to appear was a curvy leg, followed by the rest of a woman extracting herself from the vehicle. The woman shut the car door and strode towards the house with purpose.

Mum.

The black saloon had disappeared by the time Bailey opened the front door. Her mother looked upset: her knotted brows and twitching eye foretelling her mood.

'Hi,' Bailey said cheerfully as she stood aside to let her in. 'What took you so long?'

'Hmph,' her mother said, removing her coat. 'You, me and Lippy. In the lounge. Bring biscuits.'

Bailey knew it had to be bad. She hadn't seen Lippy since they discussed the options surrounding her pregnancy. 'Yes, ma'am.' She folded into a curtsy and finished with a salute, but it didn't have the effect she was hoping for. Shit, she thought, tough crowd.

They sat opposite each other at the dining table, a plate of digestives and a four-inch plastic leprechaun between them. The leprechaun had its head twisted backwards.

Her mother snapped a biscuit in two, pushed one half into her mouth and chewed without breaking eye contact.

When she'd finished both halves, she took another, snapped it and chewed.

Disturbed by the erratic twitch of her mother's eye, Bailey managed two and a half biscuits before she could endure it no longer. 'Come on then, what?'

Snap.

Bailey inhaled. Waited. Blinked. 'What do you want me to say?'

'Start with the truth.'

'Well *he* didn't believe me so why should *you*?'

'Because I'm your mother.'

'Huh.'

'What does that mean?'

'Nothing.' Bailey folded her arms, then unfolded them and took a biscuit. 'You didn't stand up for me. You said you'd always be there for us, but you didn't stand up for me today.'

'Don't be so dramatic.'

'I waited for three hours in that cell. You didn't see it. I was there for three fucking hours.'

Her mother flinched and her eye twitched faster. 'I came as soon as I could.'

'What were you doing for three hours that was more important than rescuing your daughter from a prison cell?'

'I came as soon as I could,' her mother said again. 'When the constable told me what happened I was shaken, I had to rest.' She hesitated. 'I made a cup of tea.'

'You did what?'

'But I phoned a taxi soon after and was on my way within half an hour, I promise.'

'Three hours, Mum.' Bailey pushed back a tear. 'I was alone and I had no idea what they were going to do to me.

For three whole hours.'

Neither of them spoke for the length of a biscuit until her mother said, 'What on earth were you thinking?'

Bailey shrugged.

'Breaking and entering, theft, *assault* for heaven's sake. You evaded the police and lied as well. And you tried to obtain goods without paying for them at a coffee shop?'

'That's not true.'

'Which part?'

Bailey hesitated.

'Okay,' her mother said, poised to take another bite. 'So tell me your side.'

'What's the point?'

'Really? One opportunity to say your piece without judgement and you choose not to take it?' Her voice pitched higher. 'You're seventeen years old. Almost an adult. When are you going to start acting like one?'

Bailey flashed. 'I didn't steal and I didn't lie. And I didn't intentionally assault anyone.' She dropped the biscuit and crumbs scattered across the table. 'And the front door to the restaurant was already unlocked when I tried it.'

'That doesn't give you the right to go in.'

'I wanted to *help*. You know, do some good. Someone's driving around snatching dogs for God knows what reason and nobody's doing anything about it. Police Constable Tierney is a jerk by the way,' Bailey added. 'I mean, *me* a racist?'

'Don't.' Her mother raised a finger between them. 'I'll not have you speak like that about the police.'

'But he clearly has it in for me. Come on, you saw that.'

'He dropped the charges.'

'*Mr Cheung* dropped the charges,' Bailey said, massaging her ear. 'And that's strange, don't you think? Why did he do that?'

Her mother snapped another biscuit. 'Because he's a nice man.'

'Huh, you think? Listen, I'm sorry about his wife,' Bailey said. 'I didn't mean to hurt her. But I couldn't get away and I panicked.'

'You're a strong girl, Bailey. Stronger than you think.'

Bailey's lip throbbed and she massaged it.

'But you've got to show people more respect. Especially the police.'

There was little point arguing when it came to the police. Even if she had a free pass to say anything she wanted while Lippy looked the other way, some subjects were beyond approach and that was one of them.

'Why didn't you tell me about the off-licence robbery?'

Bailey didn't answer.

'Were you involved?'

She shook her head.

'Then why didn't you tell me?'

'Because it was just before Christmas and you'd been going through a rough time.'

Her mother looked at her inquisitively.

'Remember? The weekend before Tim's birthday? You'd split with your latest *boyfriend*,' she said the word carefully, 'and devoured a packet of Hobnobs.'

'But still ... you should have told me.' Snap.

'Maybe.'

'Was he always like that?'

'Who?'

'Paul.'

'Like what?'

'You know … dishonest.'

Bailey picked a hair from her biscuit. 'Not really.'

'He seemed so nice whenever I met him. I thought you made a lovely couple. Everyone said so. He never struck me as the sort to do something like that.'

'Who was in the car?' Bailey interjected.

'Sorry?'

'In the big black car. Was that Mike?'

'No.'

She didn't care if it was Mike or another fancy-man. All she wanted to do was deflect the conversation to something less awkward. 'Are we done?'

'Almost,' her mother pointed to Bailey's face. 'Tell me about that?'

Bailey felt the scratches on her cheek. 'I fell.'

'You fell?'

Their eyes locked. 'Yes.'

'Was it Paul?'

'No.'

'Or somebody else?'

Bailey looked away.

'Was it somebody else?' Her mother asked again.

Bailey wondered what good reason there could be for explaining that Cheung Junior had beaten her up and probably tried to kill her. Would they end up back at the police station raising charges against the son of the man who'd recently dropped charges against her? Or would her mother sit on idle hands with a vacant expression and say something profound but useless? Either way, she could see no benefit in telling her the truth. 'No,' she said. 'I just fell.'

'If that's the way you want it.' Her mother took the leprechaun and twisted its head forward, then slapped it back down on the table. 'Okay,' she said. 'Now we're done.'

Chapter Seven

The sweet scent of zesty roses permeated the lounge as her mothered entered. 'That looks interesting,' she said.

Bailey rolled her eyes and changed the channel. She'd been curled up in the armchair for the last two hours, drinking Coke and watching TV. Her surprisingly happy, but nonetheless annoying mother had spent most of that time trying on dresses. Bailey flicked through the channels before settling on the original programme she'd been watching.

Ever since Timothy and Martin had left the house earlier that evening, her mother had been busy getting ready for a night out with Mike. She'd clattered up and down the stairs presenting dress after dress after dress, each one a little sluttier than the last. Now she stood with her hands on the back of Bailey's chair, invading her space and breathing down her neck like a bison on heat.

'Here,' her mother said. 'Get something nice from the shop.'

A ten pound note dropped onto her lap and Bailey grabbed it.

'I shan't be home too late tonight. Mike's got an early start tomorrow.' She leaned forward and folded her arms around Bailey's neck, squeezing tightly as she planted a kiss on her cheek.

'Off me,' Bailey said, trying to untangle her limbs.

'Come on, Bailey Bee. Let mummy kiss it better.'

'No. Just go.'

Mrs Jacobs laughed and ruffled her hair, then laughed some more when Bailey waved her away in protest.

The front door opened and closed, followed by footsteps on the stairs.

'That'll be your brother. Shall I send him to the shop for you?'

'Yeah. Would you?'

'Of course. Anything for my favourite child.' Her mother called upstairs and her brother ran down moments later. There were muffled voices in the hall, a raised objection and predictable stomping as he thundered into the lounge.

'What d'you want, zombie?'

Bailey gave him a look and held it for a second longer than comfortable. 'Four Carlsbergs and a bar of Galaxy.'

'I can't buy alcohol.'

'Dickhead.'

'And you can't drink it.'

'Whatever. Just get me the chocolate then. But make sure it's a big bar.'

She heard the front door slam as Timothy left and the house fell quiet. The local store was a couple of streets away and Bailey knew that if he didn't stop to read the magazines, Timothy could be there and back again in less than fifteen minutes. As it turned out, it took him ten but he was out of breath when he returned.

'Two quid will cover it,' he said, dropping the chocolate onto her lap and presenting his palm for payment.

Bailey slapped his hand away. 'Get it from Mum.'

'Again? When you going to get a job?'

'I'll get a job when you get a life.'

'You don't know anything about my life.'

Bailey dismissed him with a flick of her hand and turned her attention to the chocolate bar. She was enjoying her second piece when her mother skipped into the room and hid the TV behind a tight red dress.

'Final one, what do you think?' She twirled.

Bailey hoped she looked as good as her mother when she was her age. Hell, she would be happy looking that good at any age. Shorter and slimmer, her mother had a curvy figure that Bailey envied. 'I suppose it's all right,' she said, licking chocolate from her lips.

'I think this one would look great on you. Try it on. A bit of colour, you'd look stunning.'

'Er, no.'

'Well, how about you and I go into town next week and see if we can pick you up something nice? Would you like that?'

'Great,' Bailey said. 'I saw some amazing boots.'

'You and your boots.'

'But these were beautiful, you'd love them.'

Timothy reappeared and dropped onto the sofa. 'What would she love?'

'Nothing butt-head. Why don't you go back upstairs and have a *code*? Or have you done that already today?'

'Nice,' Timothy said, playing with his phone.

Mrs Jacobs ruffled his hair and laughed. 'My little Timmy.'

Surrounded by idiots, Bailey thought. A lonely mother desperate for love and a nerdy brother consumed by computers. There's no way they could ever understand what she'd been through the last few days. But that was fine. She wasn't looking for sympathy, just answers. And maybe someone with half a brain to discuss things with.

Timothy sat up and pointed at his phone. 'Have you

74

seen this?'

Bailey licked her fingers and feigned disinterest.

'What's that, dear?' Mrs Jacobs asked as she flattened the material across her stomach.

'The missing dogs.'

Bailey looked up.

'Ugh, that's gross.' Timothy squirmed. 'Says here, they've been found in a warehouse near Alton. Well, some of them at least.' He read on. 'They think there could be as many as ten of them.'

Bailey wondered why they couldn't be sure exactly how many dogs had been found.

'According to this, they found a bag of skins and a box of feet.'

She was about to ask what he meant when his next sentence stopped her dead.

'An anonymous tip-off received earlier today was acted upon by Constable Wendy Mundy who arrested two men at the scene.' Timothy laughed. 'Wendy Mundy. What sort of stupid name is that?'

'Not as stupid as Timmy Jacobs?' Bailey struggled to contain her frustration and urged him to read on.

'Here, Mum. Where are you going tonight?' Timothy asked in a quizzical tone.

'Out for a meal and then—'

'Are you going to the Dragon's Palace?'

'No.' Her mother's expression changed, but Bailey couldn't be sure what to. 'Why do you ask?'

'Did you know they serve dog there?' He laughed. 'Yeah, apparently they've been nicking dogs and deep-frying them to order. Some sort of delicacy. Blimey, how is that ever better than chicken?'

Her mother sat in the chair opposite and covered her

face with her hands. 'Mum, are you okay?' Bailey saw her shoulders begin to shake. 'Is that the restaurant you're going to this evening?' she asked.

'No.' Her mother peered between fingers and Bailey saw her eyes glistening with wet. 'That's the one we went to last night.'

'Gross.' Timothy edged away from her. 'Did you eat dog? What's it like?'

Bailey got up and snatched the phone from him. As she flicked to the top of the page and started reading the article, her emotions tangled like string in a blender.

Anonymous tip-off. Constable Wendy Mundy. Two arrests.

There was no mention of her by name or any more about the anonymous informer, but she knew exactly what they meant. It was her phone call that did it.

Her shoulders tingled as the touch of a warm thrill caressed them. Something was happening that she struggled to understand. But it felt good. And she welcomed it. Excitement had stepped from the shadow of dismay and raised its hat to say *hello*.

'I don't feel so well,' her mother said, staggering out of the room. 'I'd better phone Mike.'

'She ate dog.' Timothy laughed, holding his stomach as he rolled on the sofa. 'Wait until I tell my mates.'

'Don't,' Bailey snapped. 'If you tell anyone, I swear I will come into your room and glue your lips together.' She glared until he stopped laughing and sat up straight. 'Dickhead.'

Upstairs, she found her mother sitting on the edge of her bed, hands covering her face as she cried. Bailey sat next to her, placed an arm around her shoulders and whispered, 'It's all right, Honey Bee. We'll make it better. Just you see if we don't.'

They rocked gently together and when Bailey closed her eyes, she drifted.

She'd lost her job, split up with her boyfriend, been bullied, humiliated and almost killed. But despite all of that, despite her mood swings, her anger and frustration with life, and despite her mother's present suffering, she felt an unexpected sense of serenity.

The taste of adventure excited her.

And she wanted more.

Episode Two

Bailey Jacobs
and the
Flying Thief

Prologue

He pulled on a new face and climbed through the broken window.

Inside the shop, the painting hadn't moved. He lifted it and retreated.

On the way out, a tray of jewellery caught his eye. If things went to plan he could buy his wife all the bling she wanted, but he filled his pockets anyway.

He adjusted his face before leaving through the back door and disappearing into the night.

Chapter One

Bailey took a deep breath and channelled it into a single word, 'Muuum.'

She had folded into her favourite armchair an hour ago, drunk a copious amount of Coke and recently run out of fingers to chew. Outside, the willow tree danced in the wind, its spindly branches rolling like seaweed in a turning tide. Grey clouds cloaked the garden with gloom and the first spots of rain drove her mood even lower.

A dreary Wednesday afternoon in May. Could there be anything as boring?

Floor-to-ceiling windows stretched the width of the lounge and the wind besieged every inch of them, searching for places to penetrate, making its presence known at every opportunity.

An empty glass and a copy of the *Farnham Echo* lay on the floor beside her—a collection of fingernail fragments heaped in the middle of the newspaper. She lifted the glass and shook the last drops onto her outstretched tongue, then took another breath. 'Muuum.'

Bailey had been on such a high after solving the mystery of the disappearing dogs. Having put her neck on the line to identify the dog-nappers, she'd disguised her voice as an old lady and made an anonymous call to the police. Her information led the arrest of the criminals, saving the lives of countless dogs.

In the days that followed, her mood brightened, her head cleared and sleep came more easily—even without the chemical boost of the little yellow *comfort* pills her mother encouraged her to take. For the first time in a long time, the future excited her.

But that had been ten days ago, and as the days passed and the weather dampened, her excitement waned and she succumbed to the pull of depression.

And the people around her made things worse.

Paul, her cheating, thieving shit of an ex-boyfriend, refused to accept the relationship was over. She didn't take his calls, but that didn't stop him phoning. She knew that she would have to talk to him someday, if only to make him realise how much she hated him. But not now. Not today.

Timothy was being a tosser as usual. After she'd told him—in the strictest confidence—of her involvement in solving the case of the disappearing dogs, he delighted in spreading stories about her at school, saying that she dressed up as a witch and hunted men in the park. He also told Martin, his new best friend, that she fancied him. But that wasn't exactly untrue. Martin was a good-looking lad and she'd often caught herself thinking about his … suitability. However, she had one hard and fast rule when it came to dating her brother's friends: don't.

No policemen, sporty types or computer nerds. She scoffed. The list was getting longer.

Her mother had been feeling depressed as well. The fact her latest love interest hadn't been in touch for two weeks was the least of her worries. She was trying to forget she'd eaten dog at a restaurant in town, a task made more difficult by the *Farnham Echo* who thought the topic too good to drop.

Lawrence Williams, the *Echo's* pain-in-the-arse reporter, had written something about it every day since the story broke. He'd tracked down and interviewed several customers from the restaurant, but so far none had admitted actually eating dog. When he showed up on the Jacobs' doorstep asking to speak to someone about the alleged incident, Bailey had flown into a rage and verbally attacked the man, chasing him off their property. During the attack, she let slip that her mother had no idea someone had put a piece of dog-meat on her plate. She was the victim in all of this, it wasn't her fault it happened and anyway, she couldn't even tell the difference.

The next day the paper carried the headline *I Thought It Was Chicken*. A short article with a made-up account of her mother's time in the restaurant—including a long list of drinks they were supposed to have consumed at the table that evening—accompanied a photo of her mother peering through the kitchen window of their house, looking confused.

Understandably, her mother was distraught and even though she and Bailey—and anyone who would listen—knew the story was almost completely made up, she didn't leave the house for five days afterwards. When she did eventually go out, it ended badly. An hour into her first shopping expedition since becoming a reluctant local celebrity, her mother arrived home in a flood of tears and went straight to her room. When Bailey took her a cup of tea and a plate of biscuits ten minutes later, she was on the bed with her face in the pillow crying. That had been five days ago and although her mother refused to talk about what happened, Bailey guessed it had something to do with the dog biscuit she found on the bedside table.

Dislike of the newspaper didn't stop them having it delivered every evening. Aside from the growing amount of fake-news online and various social media outlets that

Bailey hated because nobody appreciated the comments she left, the only local daily news option was the *Farnham Echo*. She might hate the deceitful, lying, two-faced reporter Lawrence Williams, but Bailey still needed to know what was going on around town.

Climbing out of the armchair, she broke into a yawn and stretched. Her thick, black dress swished like a stage curtain as she walked to the kitchen, her bare feet slapping their applause on the tiles. A small cupboard above the fridge squeaked as she opened it. Inside, a tub of yellow pills seemed pleased to see her. Tempted, but not seduced, she nudged it aside and searched for paracetamol. She filled her glass from a bottle of Coke and swallowed a couple of headache tablets. Then she stood at the kitchen sink and peered through the net-covered window as she drank.

No children outside. Not a single one. The no-through road they lived on often swarmed with the brats. But not today. Not in the rain.

Part of her missed spending time at Paul's flat in Aldershot. Situated on the third floor in the centre of town, he had satellite TV and access to the best take-aways. The evenings got a little noisy sometimes, but when a passing person shared their drunkenness with the rest of the street, Paul never seemed to mind if she threw something at them.

She emptied the glass, filled it with water and stood it in the bowl.

It wasn't until she had good news to share that Bailey realised she had nobody to share it with. She desperately wanted to talk to someone about her role in solving the dog mystery. She wanted to share her excitement and explain her plans. Talking to her mother wasn't the same as talking to friends, but she'd dropped her friends since meeting Paul and done nothing to get them back. She felt frustrated. And lonely.

Outside, the rain gathered and puddled.

Resting her elbows on the lip of the sink, she played with the taps. A blackbird picked its way through the front lawn, nosing the grass between hops. It flew off when a car drove by. The car was big and black and shone in the wet—similar to one she'd seen dropping her mother off a few weeks ago.

She waited expectantly and, sure enough, it came back the other way a few moments later and stopped outside the house. There was a long pause before the passenger door opened and her mother climbed out. She dashed up the drive with her handbag protecting her head from the rain. Bailey heard a key turn in the front door, followed by her mother's voice.

'I'm home.'

She sounded annoyingly cheerful.

'Bailey?'

'Kitchen,' Bailey grumbled.

Her mother's smile entered the room before she did.

'Why are you so happy?'

Her mother removed her coat and hung it on a hook near the back door. 'Tea?' she asked, reaching for the kettle.

Bailey shook her head. 'So?'

'What, darling?'

'Why are you so happy?'

Her mother elbowed her way to the sink and filled the kettle. 'Oh, it's nothing. I've had a bit of good news, that's all.'

'Stop smiling like that. It's creepy.'

'Can't your mother be happy for once?' She replaced the kettle, flicked it on and reached up to kiss Bailey's forehead.

'Off me.' Bailey pushed her away.

'Anything in the paper?'

Bailey sighed. 'The garage break-in at the weekend, the one with all the car-boot stuff. Nothing else.'

'No, I meant, never mind. Actually, regarding that, I might have something for you.' Mrs Jacobs started humming as the kettle boiled. She poured the water, stirred the cup and spooned out the bag.

Bailey waited until she could bear it no longer. 'What?' she snapped.

Her mother put the cup to her lips and blew. 'Apparently,' she said, blowing again. 'There's been another robbery.'

'Oh, where?'

'The antique shop at the top of Pine Hill.'

'Someone broke into an antique shop? What did they take?'

'I don't know, but there's something else you should know ...'

Bailey watched as her mother blew and sipped and blew again. Unable to take it any longer, she flashed her arms in the space between them. 'What?'

'Learn some patience, Bailey.'

'Well c'mon.'

'You know the big house at the top of Castle Street? The one that's recently been sold. Well, three of their packing boxes have gone missing.'

'Someone broke into the house?'

'No,' her mother said. 'Someone broke into the warehouse where everything's being stored. Either that or they got the inventory completely wrong.'

Bailey wasn't sure whether it was exciting news or not. Since solving the mystery of the disappearing dogs, she'd been searching for a new crime to occupy her time. Nothing worthy of her attention had presented itself so far, and she wasn't sure about this one either. 'So what?' she said.

'Well, get this …' Her mother drank. 'The police think they're all connected.'

That sounded a bit more interesting. 'How come?'

'They think the garage, the antique store and the warehouse are the work of the same person.'

'What was in the boxes taken from the warehouse?'

'Are you sure you don't want a drink?'

'No. What was in the boxes?'

'Can we go and sit in the lounge? My legs—'

'Mum, tell me.'

'Mr Jenkins' old paintings.'

'Valuable?'

'No. That's the funny thing about it. They were just prints. The removal company logged them as copies, with only a nominal value in the frames. Now, had they taken the two boxes on the shelf at the front, they would have got away with his collection of silver. About three thousand pounds worth. Instead, they ended up with a dozen worthless paintings. It just goes to show …'

Bailey tethered her patience for as long as she could, then said, 'Goes to show what?'

'What?'

'You said, *it just goes to show.*'

'Did I?'

'Oh, Mum, you're impossible.' Bailey grunted. 'How do you know all this?'

'What?'

'How do you know about the antique store and the warehouse?'

'From a friend. I do have them.'

Bailey folded her arms to think. Three related robberies: a garage of car-boot crap, an antique store with secondhand tat, and a warehouse full of old man's stuff. She felt her stomach move, but wasn't sure if it was the paracetamols settling. 'Maybe I will have that drink.' She reached for the bottle of Coke, filled a glass and followed her mother into the lounge to consider the facts.

The newspaper said nothing had actually been taken from the garage at the weekend—there had been a break-in, but nothing had been reported stolen. But was that really surprising? Why would someone break in to steal car-boot stuff anyway? It must have been a mistake. Maybe kids messing around, looking for a place to party.

The only thing the car-boot lockup and the antique shop have in common is they both sell junk. But what about the warehouse? The warehouse doesn't *sell* junk, she thought, but it does *store* it. So, is *junk* the common theme?

'Did anyone call?'

Bailey lifted her head. Her mother lay on the sofa, showing off her shiny legs as she played with her phone. She was so curvy. So petite and perfect. 'What?'

'Did anyone call?'

'Like who?'

'Oh, I don't know, just anyone?'

'Do you mean, Paul? I thought you didn't like him anymore.'

'Whatever gave you that idea?' Her mother hummed a few bars of a nondescript tune as she tapped her phone. It was a while before she spoke again. 'Will you kids get back together?'

'Us *kids*?' Bailey pushed the nail remnants onto the carpet and picked up yesterday's paper. She flicked through noisily and paused at pages four and five. 'No,' she said. 'I don't think us *kids* will get back together. Can you drop it?'

'Of course, darling. Consider it dropped. Any jobs?'

Bailey peered over the top of the paper. 'What?'

'Are there any good jobs advertised?'

'Bloody hell, Mum, you're always at me.'

'No, sweetie, I'm just—'

'Interfering.'

'I'm just asking if there are any jobs suitable for my favourite child.'

'*Suitable?*'

'Worthy.'

Bailey delivered an intense stare before flicking to the section marked *Careers*. 'Nothing. Just half a page of shitty adverts for crappy ...' A small box in the corner caught her eye and she looked closer.

Waitress Wanted
Busy cafe in Farnham town centre. Good rate of pay. Experienced applicants only. References required. Cafe Luga, Lamb Yard.

She read it again.

Bailey fancied herself as a waitress. With tips, she heard there was decent money to be made. And she would surely get a lot of tips. Especially if she wore her baggy Guns'n'Roses t-shirt. Or that one by the Disturbed.

'Can I get you another cup of tea?' Bailey reached for

her mother's cup and saucer on the side-table. 'Don't look so surprised. Do you want one or not?'

'Thanks, do you know how I like it?'

'Yes, just black. Do you want biscuits as well?' Bailey smiled the smile she planned to use to get more tips, even though it was a struggle to hold it.

'Are you in pain?' her mother asked.

'Biscuits. Yes or no?'

'No, thank you. Let's start with the tea and see how it goes.'

Bailey returned a few minutes later, handed over the drink and scrutinised her mother as she inspected it, smelled it, and sipped.

'It's not very hot.'

'Huh?'

'I mean, thank you.' She took another sip. 'Now tell me, what is it you're after?'

Bailey picked up the newspaper and poked at the job advert. 'I'm going to be a waitress,' she said.

'That's nice.'

'I know, right? A cafe in town needs someone. I'm not that busy right now so I might as well take it. It could be a laugh.' She beamed. 'What do you reckon? Can you write me a reference?'

Bailey didn't know what caused her mother to splutter so much that she spilled her tea, but she found a cloth in the kitchen and helped her mop it up.

A job waitressing in a local coffee shop would be great, she thought. As long as it wasn't *Cafe Bitch* where that streak-of-piss waitress worked, the one who called the cops because she didn't have the money to pay for a drink.

'I'll check it out tomorrow,' Bailey said, pleased that

her day had just got a little brighter. And while she was in town securing her new job, she might be inclined to visit the antique shop at the top of Pine Hill to find out more about their break-in.

Chapter Two

Leaning against the corner of a shop displaying tweed jackets and waistcoats, Bailey watched a tall man tend tables in front of a cosy-looking coffee house. The uneven cobbles of the narrow lane made her feet ache and she hopped from foot to foot, wishing that she'd worn her boots instead of the flat-soled shoes her mother had insisted would make a better first impression. A nearby bench looked inviting, but three old crows with shopping bags had occupied it for the last ten minutes and didn't look ready to give up their perch any time soon.

Hello, I'm Miss Jacobs. Nice to meet you. I'd like to accept the waitress position you have advertised.

The rain had edged away overnight and the clouds thinned. Touches of blue teased the sky and the sun took advantage, pushing through to brighten the day. Bailey's walk into town that morning would have been uneventful, but for an errant cyclist who almost splashed her as he sped through a puddle. Imagine, she thought, arriving wet through and dirty because some dickhead cyclist didn't bother to look where he was going.

Hi. My name's Bailey. I know I look like shit, but don't let that put you off giving me the job.

Between the flow of chatty shoppers traipsing up and down the lane, Bailey watched the waiter serve a selection of cakes and drinks from a shiny tray. He seemed awkward, ungainly, like a nervous chicken—his thin head bobbing from a long neck, his unruly elbows twitching as he shuffled between tables.

Will I have to work with him*? He doesn't seem capable. Let me show you how it should be done.*

On her way through the park she'd stopped at the makeshift memorial to regard the flowers. The first bouquet had been left more than a week ago in memory of the dogs that had been killed. During the days that followed, many flowers, candles and collars were added, resulting in a shrine spanning two car parking spaces. Bailey figured the local florists were loving it. When she passed, a man dressed in yellow shook a bucket in her direction and she dug deep into her jeans to donate the last of her coins.

References? Of course, my Mum told me to give you this.

Her legs ached. According to the clock above the art gallery at the top of the lane, it was half-past ten. She didn't have an appointment at the coffee house, her plan was simple: ask for the manager, explain she was available, negotiate a salary and start work. She'd told her mother not to worry about lunch because they were sure to feed her. A fat piece of carrot cake and a Coke should see her through her first shift.

How much will I be paid? How many days holiday do I get? Will I have to share my tips?

She adjusted her footing on the cobbles.

'Careful, lady.'

Bailey turned to see a bearded man standing next to her. He wore a brown cowboy hat and was shabby in appearance, but somewhat familiar. It wasn't until she noticed a scruffy patchwork dog at his feet, that she realised where she had seen him before.

He smiled. 'Hello again.'

Ten days ago, when Bailey evaded capture at a restaurant she was investigating in relation to the missing dogs, a tramp had confronted her. She hadn't been receptive to him at the time and didn't feel any different now.

'Remember me?' he said.

She nodded curtly and turned back to the coffee shop, but she felt him alongside her, hovering.

'What are you doing?' he asked.

The old women vacated the bench and she hurried over and sat. Out of the corner of her eye, she saw him follow.

'Mind if we join you?'

She waved a hand. 'Whatever.'

'Looks like it's going to be a nice day.'

She grunted.

'Who are you spying on?'

She spun around. 'What?'

'You've someone under surveillance, right?'

Surveillance—the word excited her, but why would he think that? She was just a girl, in a crowd, with a particular interest in one of the shops. 'You make it sound like I'm a copper?'

'Aren't you?'

'No.'

'After the last time we met—'

'We didn't *meet*.'

'Okay. After the last time we *spoke*, I saw you get into a police car.'

She turned to him again. 'You saw that?'

'Yeah.'

'Well, I'm not.'

The dog settled on her shoe.

'He likes you.'

She resisted the urge to say something nice in return. Why was this guy bugging her?

'He doesn't like most people.'

'Why are you bugging me?'

'Is that what we're doing?'

'The dog's not, but you are.'

'I thought we were just chatting.'

Bailey eased the dog off her foot and stood. She felt a flash of anger and fought to subdue it. She needed to remain calm and level-headed. She had to focus on the task in hand. The last thing she wanted was to be upset by a dubious looking character such as him. She took a breath and exhaled. 'Please. Leave me alone.'

As she walked away she felt his gaze upon her back and anger flashed again, fogging her thoughts.

Hello, I'm Bailey. Why was he so interested in her? *I'm here about the job.* The dog seemed nice though.

Distraction turned to confusion, and as her concentration faded beneath a mist of uncertainty, she faltered. Sounds merged to a gentle hum, her hands tightened and tingled, and as the coffee shop loomed closer, her tongue dried and swelled inside her mouth. She felt hot and cold at the same time.

Keep it together. Keep it together. Keep it together.

Ahead, she saw the waiter.

His long face turned in her direction and his eyes narrowed as she stood before him open-mouthed.

'Can I help you?' He had coffee-breath and spoke through his nose. 'Miss?'

She counted the beads of sweat on his forehead. One. Two. 'I, um …' They gathered and rolled the length of his face.

'Would you like a table?' A globule of sweat caught

on his lip and his tongue flicked sideways to lick it away. 'If there is something you want, please take a seat and I will be with you shortly.' He pointed to a vacant table and Bailey sat without thinking.

The pleasing smell of warm cake seeped through the open front door. She inhaled and held it.

It was the tramp's fault. She'd known what to say because she'd been practising all morning, but the words had escaped her when she needed them most. The bloody tramp had stolen her thoughts.

The waiter returned a few minutes later and stood with pad in hand. A woman on the next table drank coffee from a mug and, under pressure from his penetrating stare, Bailey could think of nothing else … so she barked the word *coffee*.

'You would like a coffee?'

She didn't, but she couldn't stop herself nodding.

'Cappuccino perhaps?'

She nodded again.

'Very well. We're short-staffed but I'll be with you as soon as I can.'

She watched him go.

The lane looked different from her new position. Shoppers drifted by to the sound of snappy chat and clipping shoes. Their collective shadow darkened her table and encroached on her space, but even at the narrowest point in the lane where numbers concentrated, people avoided each other with polite comments and respectful nods.

Behind her, a large window spanned the front of the shop with *Cafe Luga* etched in the glass in fancy letters. She couldn't see through the shaded glass but it sounded as busy inside as it was out.

Fortunately for you, I can start straight away. Getting this job was going to be a breeze. *Give me an apron and a tray and leave the rest to me.*

She noticed the tramp had left the bench and now sat on a low wall with the dog at his feet and a sign alongside that read *Mouth and Muzzle to Feed.* He seemed to be watching her from beneath the brim of his hat.

When the waiter returned, he placed a cup and saucer on the table. Bailey took a deep breath and was ready to offer her services when he handed her the bill. She reached to her pockets and began probing for money, and felt her face blister as she remembered giving the last of her change to the man in the park.

The waiter drummed bony fingers against the tray as he waited.

Having been caught recently without the money to pay for a drink, she didn't want it to happen again, but the lane was too busy to make a run for it and the other customers had started to look her way. 'Er,' she said.

'Do you have the ability to pay, or not?'

'I think not,' Bailey said.

The waiter rolled his head and his neck creaked. 'In that case—'

'Here, let me get that.'

Somebody snatched the bill from her hand and she turned to see the tramp. He released a fistful of change onto the waiter's tray and the coins clashed noisily before settling—causing more people to turn and watch. Poking the coins with his pen, the waiter squinted over the bridge of his nose as he counted. Apparently satisfied, he returned some and then nodded and left.

The tramp joined her at the table. 'Thank you,' she said.

'That's all—'

'I'm so sorry I was such a bitch.' She wiped her forehead. 'I was hoping to get a job here and … well, I guess I was nervous.'

'That's all right. No harm—'

'The funny thing is, I don't even like coffee.' She pushed the cup towards him. 'D'you want it?'

'Is it any good?'

'Shit.' She slapped the table and groaned. 'Sorry. I mean, what a divvy. I really messed up, didn't I? That couldn't have gone any worse. Did you see the look on his face? He must think I'm stupid.'

'What's your name?'

Bailey hesitated. 'Bailey.'

'Isn't that a dog's name?'

She frowned.

'I'm Jack.'

She nodded.

'Do you want something instead of coffee?'

'No. I'm going to get off.'

'Just a minute. The way I see it, you owe me.'

'Because?'

'I bought you coffee.'

She scoffed. 'The one I just gave to you?'

'Well, I got you out of a fix anyway.'

'I guess you did.'

'And I'm only trying to be friendly.'

She had always liked the name *Jack*. It made her feel secure. 'How old are you?' she asked.

'You'd be surprised. Don't let the disguise put you off. I used to be just like you. Well, not *exactly* like you. What are you? A goth?'

'What? No. Why would—'

'Your clothes. Your hair. Your makeup.'

'What's wrong with my hair?'

'Nothing. I like it.'

Bailey adjusted her legs beneath the table and caught something with the point of her shoe.

'Ouch.' Jack bent beneath the table then reappeared, his face redder than before.

'Sorry, did I get you.' How old is he, she wondered. Thirty? Forty? She hadn't seen many tramps close up, but this one didn't seem to fit the typical profile. Beneath his rough appearance and abundance of facial hair, she could tell he had good teeth and decent skin. He also had good manners, spoke well and drank without slurping. A presentable tramp, if there was such a thing. 'What's your story?' she asked.

Jack held the cup between both hands and crossed his legs. 'My story?' he said. 'I like coffee. Actually, I love coffee. It's the one vice I have. Good coffee. There's a place across town ...'

His dog had curled into a ball and seemed happy enough beneath the table. A small, terrier thing with black and white patchwork markings, it was almost as scruffy as him. Bailey sighed, wondering how she was going to bypass the creepy waiter to speak with the manager about the job.

'Don't you think?'

She looked up. 'What? Sorry. What did you say?'

'Nothing. Forget it.'

The waiter loomed in the doorway and caught Bailey's eye. He reached their table in two strides. 'Is that it? Are you off? Or do you want something else?'

'Um.' Bailey hesitated, wondering if now would be a good time to ask him about the job. 'I don't suppose ...'

'Another coffee perhaps? Water for the dog?' He snorted. 'Or a cake and two forks?'

The waiter's words seemed coated with barbs and Bailey couldn't be sure if he was intentionally being a dick. The sneer on the side of his face suggested he was. 'No,' she said. 'That'll be all. Thank you.'

But he continued to loom. 'For how long will you require the use of my table? I'm keen to recover it.'

Jack smiled. 'Recover it?'

'Yes, I would like to retrieve it for my next patrons.'

Jack turned to Bailey and laughed. 'I can't believe this guy. Do you get this a lot? C'mon, let's go.'

The waiter reached for Jack's cup, but Bailey raised her hand to stop him. 'Hang on,' she said. 'He hasn't finished. So I think we'll be a bit longer, thank you very much.'

The waiter muttered something as he turned and left, but Bailey saw his nose appear around the door-frame moments later and he didn't look happy.

'You didn't have to do that,' Jack said.

'Take your time, enjoy it.' She watched the waiter watching them. 'You're a paying customer, just like everyone else.'

'Except you of course.'

Bailey surprised herself by doing something she hadn't done for a long time—she laughed.

'You've got a great smile,' Jack said. 'Nice dimples.'

'Do you think I can borrow some money?'

'Pardon?'

'Do you think I can borrow some money? I want to call my Mum and I gave my last bit of change to a man in the park.'

'A man in the park?'

101

'Yes. Can I borrow some or not?'

'Don't you have a mobile?'

'No,' she said, remembering how it fell into the meat grinder at the chicken factory. 'That's a long story.'

'How much do you need?'

'Just something for the phone box. And maybe some chocolate. And a Coke.'

'I could get you a Coke here.'

'No thanks. Although I am tempted because I'd love to see the look on our lanky friend's face.'

Jack got up, dug into his trouser pocket and presented her with a palm full of coins. 'Take what you need.'

She picked out a pound, a couple of fifties and some twenties. 'That should do, thanks.'

The waiter reappeared, but as Jack sat back down, he frowned and retreated through the doorway. Bailey grinned. 'I've gotta go,' she said. 'I've got things to do. But you stay here for as long as you want. Maybe get a refill, what do you think?' She stood, pushed her chair beneath the table and set off down the lane.

Stuff 'em, she thought, as she elbowed her way through the bustling bodies, they could keep their stinky job.

Chapter Three

Bailey leaned against a traffic light to catch her breath. The hill was steeper and longer than she remembered it, and her shoes pinched her toes.

Granny's Antiques occupied the ground floor of a three-storey house on the corner of a busy crossroads a mile to the south of Farnham town centre. It was easy to spot because the wide pavement outside overflowed with an assortment of furniture and bric-à-brac.

A fat old lady sat hunched in a chair in front of the shop, puffing on a cigarette. When the traffic lights changed and Bailey set off towards her, the old lady got up and shuffled inside. Bailey skipped onto the pavement and followed her into the shop.

A buzzer sounded when she stepped through the front door and it felt like she'd stepped back in time. Packed with furniture, it smelled smoky, old and damp. It had a humdrum feel with floorboards that groaned as she walked.

Bailey could see the old lady at the far end of the room —smoke ballooning around her—but there was no clear path to reach her so she sucked in her tummy and tried to squeeze between a bookcase and a wardrobe.

'Follow the carpet, pet.'

A thin strip of brown carpet headed off in another direction and Bailey followed it. Around a table and passed a clock that was taller than her by a foot or more, she found the old lady leaning against the edge of a gnarled counter, flicking ash into a bowl. Almost as wide as she was tall, and wearing an off-white dress that covered her ankles, she resembled a soggy dumpling.

'What are you looking for, duck?'

Bailey couldn't remember ever being called *duck* before. Was it complimentary or insulting? She held her nose against the smoke as she closed in.

'You all right, sweetie? Got something up yer?'

Bailey shook her head, still clutching her nose.

'Smoke a bother?'

She nodded.

'You'll get used to it.'

Bailey chanced a breath and her eyes watered. 'What *is* that?'

The old lady chuckled. 'Naval Shag. Imported. Best you can get.'

'Can you put it out?'

'Never waste what's wanted.'

'What?' Bailey pointed at the cigarette. 'That stinks. Please, put it out.'

The old lady mumbled something as she pinched the end of the cigarette and tucked it into a discreet pocket.

'Thanks,' Bailey said between coughs. 'Are you Granny?'

'What d'ya reckon?'

'I'm Bailey, I'm here about the break-in.'

The old lady nodded and rings of fat quivered around her throat. 'You the police?'

Bailey didn't know why people continued to mistake her for a policewoman—she might be tall, but she was seventeen for God's sake and sincerely doubted any policewoman had ever worn makeup the way she did. 'No,' she said.

'From the local papers?'

'Definitely not.'

'So what concern is it of yours?'

It wasn't really her concern at all. She wanted to find out if there was a mystery to solve, but she wouldn't be solving it for the old woman's benefit. 'I'm looking into it for personal reasons. Privately.'

'You're investigating the toe-rag who broke in?'

'Yes.'

'Privately.'

Bailey nodded.

Granny wiped a hand across her mouth, and Bailey noticed faded blue letters inked on her knuckles. 'So you're a Private Investigator?'

Bailey tried to keep a straight face as she refrained from denying or confirming the old woman's assumptions, but *Private Investigator* sounded good.

'Who hired you?'

'What?'

'Don't matter.' Granny sniffed. 'What d'ya wanna know?'

Bailey kicked herself for not having a notebook like the police used—she would be sure to get her mother to buy her one. She looked around cautiously and then leaned towards the old woman, stifling a gag at the residue of stale tobacco on her clothes. 'Tell me what happened.'

Granny retrieved the half-finished cigarette from her pocket with one hand and scraped a match across the counter top with the other. She puffed the cigarette back to life and let the smoke settle in around her. Then she told Bailey what happened.

Her grandson had opened early on Tuesday and found

the glass in the back window knocked through. The door between the kitchen and shop, normally locked for insurance reasons, had been forced open. The till had been emptied of the previous day's takings, an expensive lamp smashed and a dozen bits of jewellery taken along with a painting.

Granny stubbed the cigarette into the bowl. 'Sixty years of grind and grimace.'

'What?' Bailey tried to remember the list of things taken.

'I've travelled the world and always kept my own bed. Never did a bad deed to no-one.'

Money. Jewellery. Lamp.

'And this is what I get. Some toe-rag helps himself to my takings and my best silver.'

Painting.

'Without so much as a by your leave.' She produced a tin and fumbled the lid open. Then pinched a wad of tobacco, peeled off a paper and rolled with expert hands.

Bailey gestured to a stack of leaflets headed *Granny's Antiques.* She took one, helped herself to a pen alongside the till and started making notes. There might be a connection with the paintings taken from the warehouse, but she struggled to see any link between the break-in here and the car-boot theft that never happened.

She was about to ask if anything else was missing when the woman blew out a lungful of fresh smoke and pointed to a feather trapped beneath the literature dispenser.

'See that,' Granny said. 'He dropped it.'

The feather was three inches long, wispy and bright red. 'Who?'

'The thief.'

Bailey's heart raced. 'Are you sure?'

'Sure as eggs.'

Bailey didn't know any bird that had such bright feathers but guessed it had to be something exotic. 'Didn't the police want to take it as evidence?'

'Forgot to tell 'em.'

Bailey pulled it free. It was incredibly soft. Almost unnaturally so.

'Take it.'

'Really?' She lay the feather between the folds of Granny's flier and tucked them both inside her jacket.

'I suppose you wanna see the video?'

'Video?'

'TTCV or whatever it is.'

'You've got cameras in the shop?' Bailey looked around but didn't see them.

'Sure. Front and back.'

'In that case,' said Bailey. 'I'd love to see the video.'

Granny led her through a door into the kitchen at the rear of the property. One of the windows was boarded up with strips of wood and she crossed the room to inspect it. She opened the back door and looked outside. A narrow path followed the building and a tall fence topped with barbed wire followed the path. The thief must have been stupid to climb over that, she thought. Or desperate.

'I know what you're thinking,' Granny said. 'But I doubt he climbed over the fence. We keep the side gate open in case someone drops by on the spare and needs in.' She propped herself against the kitchen worktop and coughed her chest clear. 'Come here, chuck. This is it.' She handled a machine that looked too old to work. 'See, there's one camera here.' The woman pointed to a chunky black box above her head. 'And another at the front door.

But that didn't pick up anything on accounts he left through the back.'

A tingle ran the length of Bailey's spine as the woman pressed play and the monitor flickered into life. The machine clunked and whirred as a grainy black and white image appeared. Bailey leaned closer.

She saw the empty kitchen, then a shadow darkened the window seconds before it exploded. Shards settled across the room as a gloved hand cleared the frame of straggling fragments.

'Stop it. How d'you stop it?'

Granny pushed something and it stopped.

'Tell me, do you live on the premises?'

'Aye.'

'But you didn't hear a noise? I mean, the glass breaking must have been pretty loud.'

Granny shook her head. 'I sleeps with Gordon.' She winked.

'Who?'

Granny pointed to a cupboard and Bailey opened it to see a bottle and a half of gin.

'Ah, too bad,' Bailey said. 'Play some more.'

Granny set the machine to play.

A head and shoulders pushed through the window and then someone climbed inside. It looked like a man and his face appeared deformed. His nose was bigger than it should have been and his forehead pronounced to the point of exaggeration. And he seemed to have untidy hair.

If only it were in colour.

The man disappeared beneath the camera.

'Where did he go?'

Granny pointed. 'Through that door into the shop.'

Bailey reached to the monitor and swiped the screen

frantically with her fingers. 'It's not moving. Can't we follow him? How can we see what he's doing?'

'Don't work like that, love.'

She ran her finger across the screen a couple more times before giving up. Damn, she thought, old school. 'It's not very clear,' she said, unable to hide her disappointment.

'That's as may be.'

The man reappeared a few moments later with a painting under one arm. He lay it against the wall, climbed through the window and then reached back inside. As he lifted the painting, he caught his face on the frame and his nose twisted awkwardly—almost as if made from putty. He reset his face before making his escape.

'What's wrong with his nose?'

'Dunno, duck.'

'It's very big.'

'That's what I thought when I saw him. I thought, Christ, that fella's got a sizeable beak. Here ...' She pointed to the skirting beneath the window. 'That's where I found the feather.'

The shop buzzer sounded and Granny peered through the doorway. 'Be right with you, duck.' She turned to Bailey. 'Coppers.'

Bailey's stomach heaved.

'I'd better go see what he wants.'

He?

The old woman disappeared into the shop and a deep voice greeted her.

Tierney?

For some reason unknown to her, Bailey had managed to upset Police Constable Tierney during her involvement with the disappearing dogs. It was a mutual dislike and she'd gone out of her way to avoid him and his colleagues ever since. Whilst her mother held a soft spot for the police, Bailey didn't. She couldn't be sure if it was Tierney in the shop now, but decided not to wait to find out.

Slipping through the back door, she closed it quietly and followed the path around the building to the side gate. Holding her breath, she reached for the latch and almost cheered when it opened. She was about to burst through when she noticed a police car on the pavement in front of the shop. A woman sat in the passenger seat, apparently occupied by something on her lap. Bailey knew the moment she stepped through the gate the policewoman was sure to look up. There was no way she could escape without being seen, and any hope of staying put was crushed when voices echoed off the garden fence behind her.

She took a breath, smoothed back her hair and forced a n *I'm supposed to be here* look on her face. Then she stepped through the gate and onto the pavement in front of the police car.

Bailey tried to stop her body shaking, but when the policewoman looked up and their eyes met, she raised a trembling hand to her forehead and saluted.

Shit. What's wrong with you? Just a nod or a smile would be quite sufficient. Dickhead.

She heard the car door open.

Keep moving. Don't stop. Don't look. And don't fucking salute.

'Excuse me.'

She could be talking to anyone.

'Miss, please stop.'

Bailey stopped and as she swivelled to face the

policewoman, she felt an incredible urge to pee. The policewoman was smaller than her. She had a pretty face, slim waist and athletic thighs. Bailey waited for her to speak again.

'Wait there.' The officer stepped towards the gate and bent to pick something off the ground. She handed it to Bailey and said, 'You dropped this.'

She had kind eyes. Sharp, but kind. Bailey spotted the red feather poking out of Granny's flier as the policewoman handed it across. 'Thanks.' She grabbed it, turned and marched to the traffic lights where she hit the button and begged the lights to change. Hopping from foot to foot, the weight of the policewoman's stare increased her desire to pee.

It took an age for the little green man to show and when he finally did, Bailey was across the road and heading into town, long before he finished blinking.

Chapter Four

Perspiration tickled Bailey's neck as she tipped her head back and drank. She'd bought a bottle of Coke from a corner shop on her way down the hill and now sat on a bench in the meadow by the river to enjoy it. She had her legs stretched out, her shoes off and her jeans rolled up a far as they would go.

Had that really been Constable *Dickhead* in the shop? She couldn't be sure, but if it was and if he compared notes with his female colleague, it wouldn't be long before they joined the dots and came looking for her. She reached into her jacket and removed Granny's flier, opening it carefully.

The feather was so soft.

Was it the thief's calling card? Or had he dropped it by mistake? And why had he taken the painting at all? According to the old lady, it wasn't even an original.

The broken lamp puzzled her even further. She didn't think thieves were supposed to be that clumsy—but maybe he wasn't a good one. And the money? Granny could have told her any amount was taken, but exactly £500 … something didn't feel right.

She shuffled to the end of the bench when somebody sat beside her. Her thoughts were snapped away when he spoke.

'Hello, Miss.'

She turned to see an old man smiling.

'It's very nice to see you again.'

It wasn't until she noticed his walking stick that she recognised him as the old man she'd met in the park a couple of weeks ago. She nodded.

'It's longer than it looks,' the man said.

'What?'

'The hill.' He used his stick to point in the direction Bailey had come. 'I can walk down it fine, but getting home is a problem. Annie thinks I'm silly, but if you stop trying then you start dying—that's what I used to tell my men.'

'What?'

'Oh, don't mind me.' He gripped the top of his stick and fell silent, a vacant smile glazing his features.

Bailey considered things for a moment and then said, 'Have you been spying on me?'

The old man's smile slipped. 'Spying? Why do you say that?'

'Well, how did you know I've been up the hill?'

He chuckled. 'Where else would you get that from?'

'The feather?'

'No. The brochure for Granny's Antiques.'

Of course, Bailey thought, don't be so paranoid. He's just a lonely old man with too much time on his hands and not enough sense to know when he's not welcome.

'Granny's had the same leaflet for the past five years. She's a character.'

Bailey drank.

'I've known Granny since the fifties. I was a whippersnapper in those days, always getting into trouble. We'd ...'

Although Bailey couldn't see the river from where she sat, she imagined it to be shallow and slow and perfect for a paddle. She wiggled her toes in anticipation.

'Keep your spirits up and your head down.'

The old man was still talking. 'What?'

'That's what our drill instructor used to say.' He chuckled. 'He also said it wouldn't hurt to pray sometimes.'

She had never seen an old man grin before, but there he was, exposing a full set of teeth that were surprisingly clean. Was he simple? Or had he escaped from somewhere nearby? 'I don't mean to be rude,' she said. 'But I've got a lot on today.'

'Oh, yes. Just like me,' he said. 'We're both very busy people.'

'No, I mean, I've got a lot to think about.'

'Sometimes it's best not to.'

'What?' Bailey snapped, a little tired of his cryptic comments.

'To *think*. Sometimes, you can over-think a problem. And if you do, that mouse can turn into a monster. Sometimes, gut instinct gets you further and faster. It's never failed me.' He paused. 'Well, it did once, but—'

Bailey couldn't control her impatience. 'I don't know what the hell you're talking about? And I'm not sure you do either.'

'I'm just saying, you can do anything if you put your mind to it. In '87, some of the brass didn't want me for a position because they thought I was too old.'

Bailey scratched her head, conscious that her mouth was open as she tried to work out how long ago that was and how old he might have been at the time.

'I argued my case, they gave me the opportunity to prove them wrong and I grabbed it. One of the most satisfying things I ever did.'

Her thoughts turned to the job at the coffee shop—

perhaps she had given up too quickly. She sucked in her next breath and scowled as she wondered how that lanky twat of a waiter had managed to get the better of her. Was this old man missing a couple of batteries or was he actually talking a lot of sense?

'Sometimes you've got to hold your ground and fight your corner.' His grin returned. 'Even if that means standing against superiors. And with a bit of luck, they'll appreciate you all the more for it.'

He was right. Why was she intimidated by a gangly, middle-aged chicken serving tables? She pulled on her shoes with a groan and stood, then nodded to the old man and mouthed the words *thank you*.

If he could do it, then why couldn't she?

Despite the protest from her feet, she marched towards town, her elbows high and stride long.

A job waited for her.

And she was going to grab it.

* * *

Following the cobbled lane into Lamb Yard, Bailey sidestepped shoppers as she advanced to the coffee shop. All the tables outside the shop were occupied and the waiter busied himself between them. He seemed more flustered than before, and sweatier too. She tapped him on the shoulder and he turned sharply.

She hadn't previously noticed his crooked teeth. Or the hairs jutting from his nose. She straightened her back and said, 'Hi, I was here earlier with … a friend.'

'Yes, I remember you.'

That's a good start, Bailey thought, perhaps he'd mellowed in the time he had to think about his actions.

'I'd like to speak with the manager, please.'

'Do you wish to complain about something?'

She had forgotten how whiny his voice was. 'I should,' she said. 'You gave us the most appalling service. But I forgive you.'

'You forgive me?'

'Yes, but that's not why I'm here.'

'Is it not?'

'It hasn't escaped my attention that you're struggling to cope because you're so busy and understaffed.'

'Indeed. And I'm very busy now, so if—'

'Well, your problems are over.' She slapped her hands together. 'Because I'm here.'

'Okay,' he said slowly, a thick glaze of confusion covering his face. 'And what are you here for exactly?'

'To help, of course.'

The corners of his mouth puckered for the briefest moment. 'You're here to help?'

'Yes,' she said. 'So if you can take me to the manager, I'd like to discuss the terms of my employment.'

'Are you saying you would like a job?'

'Yes.'

'Which job would that be exactly?'

Bailey frowned. Was he actually stupid or just naive? 'The waitress job of course. The one advertised in the paper.'

'Oh yes, the advert in paper,' he said with a smirk. 'Do you have suitable experience for such a position?'

'Experience of what? Carrying things? Handling money? Being nice to people? Of course,' she said, unconvinced about the last point. 'I do that almost every day.'

He cleared his throat. 'Where have you *waited* before?'

Bailey wasn't sure what he meant. She spent half her life waiting on someone or another, but why would he want to know about that?

His face creased into an enormous grin that bared his gums and molars. 'You have waitressed before, haven't you?'

'Well, not professionally, but …' The pause extended to an embarrassing length, during which time Bailey stretched the back pockets of her jeans with her fists. 'Why am I telling *you* anyway?' Realising surrounding conversations had hushed and faces turned their way, she lowered her voice. 'I'd like to talk to the manager about it. In private.'

'The manager is extremely busy at the moment.'

'Well, I shan't leave until I see him. I mean it.'

He sighed. 'Very well. If you care to follow me.'

She followed him into the coffee shop where a dozen tables buzzed with customers. Behind a glass counter, a woman made a machine screech so loud it hurt Bailey's ears. The assortment of cakes and pastries on display took her fancy and she paused to admire them.

'This way, please.'

She followed the waiter through a beaded curtain, into a hall and up a set of stairs. At the top, they stopped outside a door with a golden placard that said *Mr Smeak - Manager*. Without knocking, he pushed the door open and stepped inside.

The office was small and smelled of cheese. A messy desk sat against the far wall with a lamp on one side and a bird cage on the other. In the cage, a parrot squawked once and nodded its head in her direction. The waiter reached for a window and opened it. Then he sat in the only chair in the room and swivelled round to face her.

117

'I am Mr Smeak,' he said. 'The Manager.'

Bailey steadied herself against a filing cabinet.

'Now permit me to enlighten you as to why, exactly, you'll never secure a job at this establishment.'

Chapter Five

Amid the incredibly annoying presence of her mother who buzzed around the lounge, cleaning and dusting, Bailey tried to compose her thoughts. She'd explained all about Mr Smeak and the job, but her mother didn't seem to appreciate the vile nature of the man, and it didn't help to be told simply that something better was sure to come along.

'Can I get you a drink?' her mother asked, folding the duster.

Bailey grunted.

Arrogant. Ignorant. Rude.

She associated herself with none of the phrases Smeak had used.

Inappropriate. Unseemly. Tasteless.

And she didn't agree with his attack on her style.

He had been so insulting it was all she could do not to kick his office door more than once as she stormed out.

She couldn't remember walking home from the coffee shop, but she'd woken in her bedroom twenty minutes ago with her face puffy from crying and her hair tangled from sleep. From there she had gravitated to the lounge.

A shadow fell across her lap when her mother returned with a plate of biscuits and a glass of Coke. 'Here,' she said. 'For my little girl.'

Bailey took the glass and drank, fighting back a wave of tears.

'I spoke with Mike today,' her mother said, almost

skipping to the sofa.

Her mother appeared to be suppressing a smile.

'He explained everything.'

Bailey wanted to scream.

'He's coming round tomorrow night.'

Smeak had such a whiny voice. And a beak for a nose.

'I want you to meet him.'

A beak for a nose.

'You'll like him.'

Something sparked inside Bailey's mind and she looked up.

'Do you want to join us? We'll probably go for a meal. You're welcome to come too.'

Her mother sat forward on the sofa, apparently unable to hide her joy any longer. With her hair tied back, her elegant neck raised her head like a jewel on a sceptre.

'Perhaps we can get you something nice to wear?'

Bailey held up a hand and said, 'Can you stop talking please.' She reached for a thought and swore when it vanished.

'Is everything okay?'

Bailey huffed. 'Not really, but who cares? What were you going on about?'

'Would you like me to buy you something?'

She nodded. That sounded a good idea. 'I need a note pad and pen.'

'A what?'

'Something to write in,' Bailey said.

'Okay, anything else?'

Bailey thought. 'I still don't have a mobile phone.'

'I was thinking of something to wear.'

She had her eye on a pair of new boots in town. It seemed a fair exchange: a pair of boots for putting up with her mother's incessant drawl. 'Yeah, sounds great. Something to wear, I'd like that.' She stood, sending the plate of biscuits tumbling to the carpet. 'Oops, sorry.'

The front door opened and she heard male voices.

'Fuck.'

'Language, Bailey,' her mother said as she helped her pick up the biscuits.

'Is that Martin?' Bailey tried desperately to untangle her hair. 'Don't let him see me like this.'

'It's all right, they'll probably go upstairs.'

But they didn't, their voices grew closer and a moment later Timothy stepped into the lounge. 'Martin's here,' he said.

'Hello, Mrs Jacobs.' Martin's thick, rich voice flowed into the room like a jar of spilled honey.

'We're going to do some coding again,' Timothy said.

'Okay, darling.'

'Where's the creep?'

Bailey couldn't see from her position behind the door, but guessed brother-Dickhead was pulling a boneheaded face to impress his friend.

'Hurry upstairs and I'll call you when tea's ready,' she heard her mother say.

When their footsteps faded and she was sure they were safely out of the way in her brother's bedroom, Bailey peeled herself from the wall and hurried upstairs. In the bathroom she washed and applied a new layer of makeup. When she descended the stairs half an hour later, she felt clean and refreshed and in better spirits.

Martin and her brother sat next to each other at the dining table.

Timothy grinned like a fool. 'Martin's staying for tea,' he said.

Bailey met Martin's eye and nodded. *Policemen, computer nerds and sporty types. Leave 'em be.* She sat opposite and forced a smile.

'So, Bailey,' Martin said, apparently surprising Timothy as much as he did her. 'I hear you're getting a new job.'

His voice was intoxicating. What colour were his eyes? Blue? Green? Or a blend of both? She tried to see.

'Don't mind her,' Timothy said, pushing up his glasses. 'She's only ever grasped the basics of table manners.'

Bailey realised she was leaning forward too far and pulled back. 'Don't mind *him*,' she said. 'He masturbates into his socks.'

Timothy's face flushed and he spluttered defiance, lashing out with a wild hand that knocked the pepper-pot off the table just as their mother appeared. She lowered a dish of lasagna onto a mat, picked up a spoon and began to serve.

'What are you kids talking about?' Mrs Jacobs asked as she filled Martin's plate.

'Socks,' Bailey said, delighting in the smile on Martin's face and the maroon colour of her brother's.

'Oh,' said her mother, sounding a little confused. 'Timmy's very hard on socks. And they're forever going missing.'

'Mum!'

The meal was a lively affair. Martin and her mother engaged in polite conversation about school and family, while Bailey found ways to insert items of clothing into the conversation. Timothy glared at her throughout with obvious passion.

Only when everyone had finished did her mother turn

to Timothy and say, 'Timmy, that reminds me.'

Bailey grinned at her brother's discomfort. He hated being called that.

'Give Bailey one of your old phones.'

Timothy looked as if she'd grown a set of horns.

'You must have one you don't use.'

She touched his hand and he recoiled. 'All right,' he said. 'She can have one. But not one of my best ones.'

'Be a sweet and get it now, would you?'

Bailey caught a twinkle in Martin's eye and warmed inside. Her brother pushed back his chair and stomped out of the room.

'Do you have lots of unused phones, Martin?'

'A few, Mrs Jacobs.'

'I bet you do. But they're so expensive. I don't know where you kids get the money from these days.'

'We get quite well paid for all the coding ...' Martin stopped mid-sentence, his face changing from olive to ashen.

There was only the briefest pause before, 'Paid?' Mrs Jacobs steepled her fingers together and began drumming them lightly. 'What do you mean, darling?'

Martin fidgeted with his napkin and Bailey leaned forward close enough to see that he had green eyes. 'Do you get *paid* for doing those things upstairs?' she asked.

'Er, yeah. When they use it we do.'

Bailey shared a look with her mother that said: *Did you know about this? No, neither did I, but I look forward to hearing what Timothy has to say on the subject.* It only lasted a few seconds, up until they heard a noise and turned together to see Timothy standing in the doorway carrying a mobile phone.

'What?' he said, looking perplexed. 'What have I done

now?'

Bailey grinned. It was going to be a good evening.

* * *

For the previous six months, Timothy had been earning money from coding computer games in his bedroom—that was commendable. But he had done it in secret and continued suckling the family purse—that was not.

Although he wasn't earning a full-time wage, he had amassed two thousand pounds from the code he'd sold to software companies. It turned out that he was very good at what he did and in much demand. He'd brought Martin on board to help him juggle the paid work alongside his school work.

'It seems they've got a nice little business going on up there,' Bailey said to her mother when Timothy finished explaining things.

Martin had made his excuses and departed before the conversation got started. He apologised before he left, but Timothy looked pretty sour and didn't speak to him as he went. Bailey wasn't sure where that left their friendship, but hoped she'd see Martin again.

'It's not a *business*,' Timothy protested. 'I've just been selling bits of code.'

'You've got two thousand pounds stashed away,' Bailey spat.

'Actually, it's a bit more than that.'

'How much more?'

'More like five.'

'Five thousand?'

'Yeah.'

'I call that a business.'

'That's because you're used to working for peanuts plucking chickens.'

She reached across the table and slapped the top of his head.

'Oi,' he cried.

Her mother watched in silence, rubbing her thumbs together.

'We're going to have some changes around here,' Bailey said. 'First off, I want a cut.'

'Of what?'

'What do you think?'

'No way.' Timothy wiped spittle from his mouth.

'I want ten percent of everything you make.'

'You're crazy if you think—'

'Or,' Bailey said with dramatic effect. 'I'm going to tell your headmaster what you've been up to. Personal projects in school time. Using school equipment. They might expel you on the spot.'

Bailey noticed her mother nod and Timothy noticed it too. 'But, Mum,' he said.

Her mother stopped nodding and looked at him. 'Ten percent sounds fair, Timmy. Ten for Bailey and ten for the house. Everyone has to pay their way.'

He pointed at Bailey. 'She doesn't.'

'She will when she can spare it.'

'That's not fair, Mum, you can't.'

'Timmy, darling. You're the man of the house, you're almost an adult and you're learning adult things—this is one of those lessons. Anyway, we've all got to pull together to make this work.'

'But why should I give *her* some?'

'Whatever arrangement you have with your sister doesn't concern me.'

Bailey was sure he was about to cry. He removed his glasses, wiped his eyes and screwed up his face as his shoulders slumped. She held back a laugh and said, 'Good, now we have the first item agreed, let's have a look at the rest of my list.'

Chapter Six

Drawing a line through Timothy's name on the cover of a nearly new A4 pad, Bailey leafed to a clean page and wrote: *The Case of the Red Feather Thief.*

Fortunately for her, Timothy's reprehensible deceit gave traction to her list of demands which included some stationery, a mobile phone, a laptop, a writing desk, a swivel chair and the pair of boots she'd been coveting in town for the last two weeks. Timothy had opposed each one, but she swatted away his objections as her mother looked on apathetically. Bailey didn't expect to get everything she wanted, so she wasn't disappointed when she didn't.

In her bedroom, sitting at a worn-out Ikea desk on a chair that squeaked when she moved, she pushed the feather around with the end of a pen and chewed over what she knew. Then she made notes about the case.

CLUES
- *Car-boot garage lockup ... nothing taken. Really?*
- *Antique shop ... £500 taken from till. Broken lamp. Painting. Jewellery. Red feather (very soft). CCTV shows man with deformed face.*
- *Warehouse ... three boxes of paintings taken.*
- *Police ... think the thefts are related. Why?*

Further down the page she created another list.

ACTIONS

- *Identify the feather.*
- *Ask Mum how she knows so much.*
- *Talk to the car-boot man.*
- *Find the thief.*

She stared at a poster of Kurt Cobain for inspiration. Looking unwashed and unshaved, his sultry features did nothing but distract her. Beneath the poster, an old picture frame leaned against the wall with her father's photo inside.

My two favourite men, she thought. Both dead.

Why did the police say the crimes are related? And how come Mum knows so much about it? The newspaper that evening had an article on the antique shop break-in, but no mention of the surveillance tape or the feather. Their description of the thief suggested he was tall and male but not much else.

It was no use. She needed someone to help her examine the case and discuss ideas. Someone to be a Watson to her Holmes. Every good detective had a side-kick, but what were her options? Jack, the tramp? Her mother? Definitely not her brother.

Kurt sucked on a cigarette with a guitar under his arm. He looked tired.

The phone Timothy had given her was old and slow. He hooked it up to the Wi-Fi and she used it to try to identify the feather online, but the screen was too small and too frustrating to be any use. She had persuaded Timothy to climb into the loft and retrieve her bird books, but she had no idea there were so many types with a red plumage, and after twenty minutes leafing through the pages, she gave up.

Scratching her nose, she wondered what Kurt was thinking.

The information in the weekend's newspaper said the car-boot man lived on the Green Hill Estate—a rough estate on the outskirts of town and not the sort of place she cared to go without good reason. Bailey knew that to solve the case, she would have to pay the car-boot man a visit.

So now she needed a map.

Leaning back in her chair, she arched towards the half-open bedroom door and yelled, 'Muuum.'

A moment of silence was followed by muttering from the kitchen and then the muted steps of her mother climbing the stairs. Bailey counted slowly, reaching eight before her mother's face appeared at the door. They exchanged smiles. 'Are we still going shopping tomorrow?'

Chapter Seven

Shortly before ten o'clock on Friday morning, Bailey pulled on a fresh pair of socks and slipped her feet into semi-clean trainers. Although her mother had approved most of Bailey's demands, she'd rolled her eyes at buying her a new pair of boots. But that was just a minor detail and Bailey was confident that with a manipulative squeeze or two in the right places, the boots she'd been coveting in town for the last two weeks would soon be hers.

A car horn blared and her mother called up the stairs, 'Taxi's here.'

Bailey attempted to push her brother's old mobile into the rear pocket of her tight jeans. 'This phone's like a brick,' she said as she trod the stairs down to join her mother at the front door. 'Dickhead didn't do me any favours when he let me have it.'

Her mother grimaced. 'Have you got your list?'

'Yes.' She tapped her pocket. 'Stationery and boots.'

'I told you, I'm not buying you any more boots.'

Bailey smiled as she stepped through the door.

The taxi driver greeted them as they settled onto the back seat. The fat on his neck rolled as he turned his head towards them. 'Where to, love?'

If he calls *me* love, Bailey thought, I'll fill his ear with my fist.

'Franzine's. West Street.'

Bailey groaned. 'Really? I thought we'd have a nice

walk around first. Just the two of us. A casual stroll and some window shopping before lunch and then go to Franzine's after. That way we'll have plenty of energy and loads of time.'

Her mother didn't protest.

'Change of plans,' Bailey said. 'Can you drop us off at the bottom of Castle Street?'

'No problem, love. Buckle up.'

She fumed as she fastened her seatbelt. If he calls me that again, I'll—

'Here, aren't you that woman?' he said, straining to catch a better look at her mother. 'The one who ate those dogs.'

Bailey stabbed her toe into the back of his seat. 'Shut up and drive.'

'No need for that, love.'

She stabbed again. 'And I'm not your fucking *love.*'

The journey into town seemed longer in silence. When they eventually pulled up to the curb in Castle Street, Bailey was first out and slammed the door behind her. 'Did you tip him?' she asked as her mother joined her on the pavement.

Her mother didn't answer.

'Oh, Mum. You've got more money than sense.' Which is great, she thought, but don't give it away to strangers. 'Can we go to the stationer's first?'

'What about our stroll around town?'

'Sure, in a minute, but follow me first.'

Half an hour later, after a heated discussion with her mother about who would carry the four-foot whiteboard if they actually bought it, Bailey left the stationer's feeling mostly satisfied. Clutching a plastic bag bulging with stationery—coloured pens, notebooks, two maps, Blu

Tack and a calculator—she reflected on the whiteboard as they left the shop without it. It could wait for another time and anyway, she would need her hands free to carry the boots.

Her mother stopped at a shop window and pointed to a headless mannequin wearing a green dress. 'What do you think?'

Bailey paused long enough to give her the impression she was actually considering the garment and then said, 'I've seen something much nicer elsewhere. Let me show you.'

Bailey headed off along the pavement and down a side alley where she stopped outside a shop window and pointed through the glass to a pair of lace-up boots.

'Shoes?'

'No, look there.' Bailey stabbed the glass. 'Boots. Aren't they fantastic?'

Her mother squinted. 'How long are those laces?'

'Fourteen holes. Great, eh?'

'They don't look very sensible.'

That wasn't the reaction Bailey had hoped for, but she didn't give up 'Buy me those and I'll love you for ever.'

'Have you seen the price?'

'An investment,' said Bailey, selecting a smile she felt right for the situation.

'Sorry. I'm not buying you boots.'

'But they—'

'I'll buy you something else. But not boots. Something to cheer you up a bit.'

'The boots will cheer me up,' Bailey said.

'That's not what I meant.' Her mother turned and walked away.

'My other boots are old and worn and grubby.' Bailey

chased after her. 'If I'm to get a new job, I'll need new boots.'

She didn't stop.

'I'll be a happier, nicer person.' Bailey struggled to maintain the pace. 'I'll even take the tablets.'

She slowed and turned. 'What?'

'I'll take the tablets,' Bailey said again. 'I mean, I can't promise they'll work or that I'll take them long-term. But I'll give them a try. For you.'

Her mother took hold of Bailey's arm and rubbed it. 'Oh, darling, will you? For me?'

'Absolutely.' Bailey nodded earnestly, whilst inside, she danced. The boots were hers, she just knew it.

'It's so nice to hear you say that. I know you think I'm silly, but I think they'll do you a lot of good. Now, how about we find somewhere to sit and have a cup of coffee?'

'Whatever you say, Mum.'

They headed for an Italian restaurant in an old building across the road, and their footsteps echoed off a flagstone floor as they stepped inside. An olive-skinned man was quickly upon them and they followed his sashay to a table by the window. He presented a chair to each of them with a smile and Bailey duly sat, then scraped it across the floor as she tucked herself in. They appeared to be the only customers.

The waiter drew closer, followed by an alluring musk.

'Coffee, please.' Mrs Jacobs coughed. 'Cappuccino.'

The waiter's pen danced across his pad and when he'd finished writing, he turned to Bailey. 'And for you, bella ragazza?'

His melodic voice was silky smooth and filled with hidden intentions. She quivered. 'Coke please.' He nodded, turned and left, and she watched his shiny black trousers tighten around his bum as he went. The moment evaporated when she turned to see her mother enjoying the show as well. Disgusting. 'So what's up with Mike?' Bailey asked.

'What?'

'Why has he been so mysterious these last two weeks?'

Her mother's face lit up. 'Oh, everything's fine,' she said. 'He explained it all. Apparently, he had some urgent business to attend to. Did I tell you he owns a car showroom in Doncaster?'

'Maybe.'

'Well, he had a shipment coming in from abroad that he wanted to manage himself and that meant spending time in Europe. He's ever so sorry …'

Pedestrians flowed by the window in a hazy blur and Bailey nodded at intervals as her mother droned on. Her concentration was occupied by events taking place over her mother's shoulder, where the Italian busied himself at the bar. His black hair shone and his white shirt bulged in all the right places. She wondered how his lips tasted.

'… about eight o'clock. He's looking forward to meeting you.'

Bailey registered the pause and nodded again. 'Great,' she said, watching the Italian head towards them with drinks on a tray and a smile that could melt chocolate.

'For you, bella ragazza.' He lay down a napkin and set a glass on top of it. 'And for you, bella donna.' He presented her mother with a cup and saucer and a side plate of sugars. 'Buon appetito.'

They both watched him leave.

'Tell me,' Bailey said, annoyed that her mother probably had more chance of pulling the waiter than she did. 'How do you know they're all related?'

Her mother seemed confused.

'The thefts. You said they're related.'

'No, I said the police think they're related.'

Bailey put down her glass and leaned forward. 'So, how do *you* know that *they* know?'

A red hue blossomed across her mother's face and her left eye twitched once.

'There's no connection mentioned in the newspaper and I couldn't find anything online. So ...' Bailey waited for the second twitch. 'How do you know?'

'I must have read it somewhere.'

'Where?'

Her mother took a sip of coffee.

'Where?' Bailey persisted.

'Or maybe I over-heard it.'

'Okay, where?'

She picked up a napkin and dabbed her lips. 'I'm not sure. I don't remember. I could have been wrong.'

'Hang on,' Bailey sat back and sipped her Coke. Her mother had mentioned it straight after being dropped off by that mysterious black car yesterday morning. Was that a connection or a coincidence? 'Who dropped you off yesterday?'

She didn't answer.

'Mum. Look at me. Who dropped you off yesterday?'

'Dropped me off? Where dear?'

'I saw you get out of a black car yesterday, at the house. The same car you climbed out of a couple of weeks ago.'

'Did you, dear? Tell me, what haven't we got from that list of yours?'

Easily sidetracked, Bailey considered the boots—shiny black leather, embossed with red stitching in the shape of a thorny rose—but she knew how to play this game. 'A laptop,' she said. 'I was saving that for another time, but we could go together now if you want. The shop's not so far from here.'

Mrs Jacobs coughed and the cup nearly slipped from her grasp.

Bailey continued, 'Just a small one. They've come down in price so much.'

'Why didn't you ask for any of these things in March on your birthday?'

'I didn't want them then?'

'Doesn't Timmy have a laptop you can use?'

'He said I can borrow one if I pre-book it, but I need to have my own.'

A shadow fell across the table and Bailey looked up to see the back of a man standing against the glass outside. Sandy hair spread wild beneath a brown hat and when he turned his head, she recognised the tramp.

She tapped her mother on the arm. 'Have you got a few quid I can borrow?'

'Borrow?'

'Well, you know. C'mon, quick.'

Her mother peeled a five-pound note from her purse. 'Will this do?'

'If that's all you have, sure. Thanks.' She scraped her chair as she stood and headed to the door. Outside, the dog noticed her first. It wriggled over and lifted a paw. Bailey knelt and tickled its tummy, then straightened to face the tramp.

He removed his hat and scraped back his hair. 'Are you following me?' he asked.

'Here,' she said, handing him the money. 'For that coffee and stuff.'

'You don't have to,' he said with a straight face, though his eyes twinkled.

'Then I'll keep it, shall I?'

He snatched it from her. 'That'll get us both a decent supper tonight.'

'Us?'

He pointed to the dog. 'Us homeless folk.'

'Well, enjoy.' She turned and left and by the time she regained her seat in the restaurant, he had moved on.

'Who was that?'

Bailey shrugged.

'Bailey, who was that man?'

She shrugged again. 'I guess you're not the only one with secrets.'

'Well,' her mother said. 'He looks like a druggy.'

'A *druggy*?' Bailey wanted to respond with something quick and snappy, something about Paul, her ex-boyfriend, and how he liked to smoke weed at the weekend. But antagonising her mother now could prevent a *good* day becoming a *great* one. She continued before the pause became too uncomfortable. 'Can I go and try those boots on now?'

Chapter Eight

Bailey had gained another inch since acquiring her new boots. They squeaked when she walked, but that was a small price to pay for looking great.

She put down a knife, picked up a fork and caressed it with a tea-towel as she watched children playing on the road in front of the house. They didn't bother her as much as they used to. Maybe they were beginning to grow on her? Or maybe the pill she'd taken was kicking in.

'Not finished yet?'

'Chill, Mum. It's not even three.'

'He hates tardiness.'

'Tardiness?' Bailey stifled a laugh.

'Are you going to change before he gets here?'

Bailey turned. Her mother had on the trouser-suit she'd worn earlier that day. 'Are you?'

'Here.' Mrs Jacobs took the tea-towel from her and began drying a plate. 'Let me finish this up. You go and get ready.'

Bailey was half way up the stairs when the phone rang. 'I'll get it,' she said, darting into the lounge. She lifted the receiver on the third ring. 'Hello.'

Nobody spoke.

'Hello.' She held her breath and hoped it wasn't *him*.

'It's me.'

She froze at the sound of his voice.

'How are you?' he asked.

He spoke in a sultry tone, his voice as warm and sweet

as cherry pie.

'Bailey, I—'

She slammed the phone down and stood over it, hands trembling. She had rehearsed that conversation countless times, when she was alone in her bed with thoughts of him keeping her awake at night. She wanted to tell him so many things. *Fuck off. You're not forgiven. I never want to see you again.* But he had taken her by surprise and the sound of his voice had unsettled her. She didn't want to fall under his spell again. Not *ever* again.

'Who was that?' Her mother called from the kitchen.

'That was Paul.' She stopped halfway up the stairs and added. 'My ex-boyfriend.'

In her bedroom, Bailey dropped into the chair behind her desk and the red feather fluttered across the surface. She opened a pad to the page headed *The Case of the Red Feather Thief* and drew a line through the item *Ask mum how she knows so much.*

The clues were drying up and the action items leading nowhere. The next one on the list was *Talk to the car-boot man.* The estate where the car-boot man lived wasn't too far away, and according to the phone her brother had given her, it was a quarter past three—plenty of time to get there and back again before Mike turned up.

She spread last weekend's paper on the desk and found the article about the break-in at the garage lockup. *Gary Blunt, Grainger Way, Green Hill Estate.* She reached for the maps her mother had bought and put the one marked Ordnance Survey to one side. She opened the other, found her house and circled it with a red pen. Then she searched for the Green Hill Estate and marked that with a blue pen.

It was almost a full hand-span between the two points. Too far to walk perhaps, but not too far to cycle.

Bailey peeled her leather jacket from the chair and put it on. She picked up her phone and a notebook and pen, then left.

In the kitchen, she gave her mother a hug. 'Love you, Mum. Can I borrow your sunglasses?' She reached into her mother's handbag and retrieved them. 'Thanks. I'm just popping out for a bit. Is Tim's bike in the garage?' She was through the side door and in the garage before her mother could reply. She found the bicycle, forced the garage door open and pedalled away to the sound of her mother calling her name.

She hadn't been on a bike for years but didn't remember it being quite so difficult. Her new boots clipped the frame as she pedalled, the seat hurt and the steering felt precariously loose. But she didn't stop. At the top of Folly Hill, she turned right onto Upper Hale Road and followed it all the way to the Green Hill Estate. After twenty minutes of cycling, a couple of near misses with passing cars and an exchange of insults with a group of lads outside the corner shop, Bailey arrived.

A dreary place made more so by the tint of her sunglasses, the estate stretched out before her and she pedalled into it slowly. A row of seventies flats had more satellite dishes than windows. She could see inside many of the homes and, as far as she could tell, most of them had giant televisions and tropical fish tanks.

She cycled along Grainger Road, looking for Grainger Way. An un-signposted lane led to a block of concrete garages where a pocket of youths had gathered. She continued on to the end of the road, turned around and rode back. Grainger Way had to be somewhere off Grainger Road. Didn't it? She should have checked the map before she left. Or better still, brought it with her.

As she passed in front of a row of shabby-looking terraced houses, a child ran into the road, forcing her to stop. She dropped a boot to the ground and removed her sunglasses. 'What?'

He was small and scruffy with dirty face and dirty clothes. He pushed a finger into his nose, excavated something dangly and grinned as he popped it into his mouth.

Other children appeared and they formed a circle around her. One carried a stick. Another a piece of rope. The all looked like they could turn a good bath black.

'What ya doing, skank?'

Skank? She took a breath and counted to three. 'Does your mother know you speak like that?'

'Skank's making a bootie call.'

Bailey turned to see who had spoken, but the dirty faces grinning back at her gave nothing away. Some of them might have been female. She couldn't tell.

'Nice boots, skank.'

One of them kicked the front wheel of her bicycle. 'You got a flat tyre.'

She turned sharply. 'Piss off.'

Their laughter unsettled her.

Little fuckers.

They were half her size and probably half her age. Too cocky by far. She wasn't going to take shit from a bunch of gobby children, no matter how feral they looked. Bailey got off the bike and lay it down. Then she stepped towards the nearest kid with her fists raised. It was either a boy or one butt-ugly girl. When he didn't run away as expected, she grabbed his jumper and pulled him close. 'Look here, fuck-face.'

Someone yelled behind her. 'Got it.'

Bailey turned as a chorus of shouts and screams followed.

'See ya, skank.'

A child who could barely reach the pedals was trying to ride Timothy's bike away. She started after him, but something caught her foot and she fell with a slap to the tarmac. Her brother's mobile flew from her pocket and scraped along the ground. A lad with a shaved head saw it, laughed and kicked it back to her.

Her cheek hurt and her head spun. She was picking grit from the side of her face when she felt someone grappling with her boots.

A savage creature of no distinguishable sex held a knife to her laces. 'Fuck off.' She kicked out and caught it beneath the chin.

'Argh,' it cried. 'I'm gonna tell my daddy.'

Definitely a girl, Bailey thought. Or an effeminate boy.

She tried to stand, and although a blow to the head slowed her, it fuelled her anger and as her temper rose, so did she. She stood tall, filled her lungs and bellowed phrases she didn't remember learning.

This time they scattered.

When she eventually exhausted her repertoire of swear words and curses—and realised she needed to stop to catch a breath—she found herself alone on the road. Timothy's bicycle had vanished and her hopes of retrieving it faded as the last child disappeared over a garden fence.

'Shit.' She massaged the side of her face and pulled another piece of grit from her cheek. The sunglasses lay smashed on the ground and she kicked the pieces into the gutter. She found the mobile and picked it up, hit the *on* button and waited for something to happen. She tried again without success and shook it. 'Fuck.' She slapped it against her thigh, tried to switch it on for the last time and then stuffed it into her jacket pocket, cursing her brother for giving her such a shitty phone.

She groaned and headed home on foot, wondering how she was going to explain things to her mother.

Chapter Nine

Bailey filled the bath half way and eased through a creamy layer of bubbles that covered everything from her shoulders down. She lay back with a flannel over her face and groaned.

Everything always went wrong and no matter what she did, she did it badly. Was she really that dumb? She sighed. But what could she have done differently? Cycled on and not engaged the little brats? No. What she should have done is not go in the first place. Had she really expected to poke around and ask a few questions that would magically unlock the case? Stupid girl.

A knock on the bathroom door made her jump.

'Are you in there?' Her mother's voice sounded wary.

Bailey didn't answer.

'Is everything okay?'

She lifted the flannel in time to see the handle turn and the door open. 'Go away.'

Mrs Jacobs walked in and knelt beside the bath. 'Lucky for me you're still funny about locked doors.'

'It's not *funny*.'

'No, it's not.' She ran her fingers through Bailey's hair. 'What's wrong?'

Bailey wanted the bath to swallow her. She felt such a fool. Tears gathered and tumbled and she wiped them away.

'Oh, Bailey Bee.'

'I screwed up again, Mum. Someone took Timmy's

bike. And they broke your sunglasses.' She covered her face with the flannel. 'I'm so sorry.'

'Don't worry, sweetie. As long as you're okay.'

Bailey nodded between sobs.

'And as long as you're still feeling up for meeting Mike tonight.'

She'd forgotten about him. 'Oh.' She peeled the flannel from her face and frowned. 'I'd forgotten about him.'

'Bailey, please. It's important to me that you both meet. He's been looking forward to it and I—'

'I don't know if I'm up for it, Mum.'

Her mother stood.

'Don't be mad,' Bailey said through her tears.

Her mother stiffened. 'Then perhaps we can come to some arrangement?'

Bailey's sobs slowed and she cocked her head.

'If I buy you a laptop.'

She held back the urge to grin.

'I want you to do two things.'

She wiped her eyes with the flannel and nodded.

'Meet Mike this evening.'

'Okay,' she said. 'And?'

'Go back to that coffee place and ask for that job again.'

'What? I couldn't. You didn't see the man there. He was so rude and—'

'I know. You've told me. But I want you to do it anyway.'

'Why?'

'Just because.'

'Because what?' A high-pitched inflection reminded her of Smeak and she hated herself for it.

'Because it'll be good for you.'

'That's not fair.'

'Fair or not, that's what I want you to do. And in return, I'll buy you a laptop.'

'Can I think about it?'

Mrs Jacobs shrugged. 'If you really have to.'

She so wanted a laptop. Her birthday had recently passed and Christmas was an age away … but she didn't savour the thought of seeing Smeak again—the tall man with the beaky nose—hell, she would rather kiss a tramp.

Bailey's thoughts jolted. *Tall man. Beaky nose.* The thief had a beaky nose. And he was tall and thin just like Smeak. On top of that—she could hardly contain her excitement—Smeak had a parrot. Was it blue or purple? She hadn't seen its tail so it might have had red feathers at the back. Could Smeak be the thief? It was looking very likely.

Her mother knelt and touched her arm. 'Do we have a deal?'

Bailey nodded furiously. 'Oh yes,' she said, thinking it would be a great opportunity to confirm her suspicions about the despicable Mr Smeak. 'We definitely have a deal.'

* * *

Mike was taller than she expected—even in her new boots, he towered over her by three inches. Mildly handsome in a polished, refined way, he had the sort of style that only money could buy. Lots of money.

Bailey took his hand and shook it heartily. 'Nice to meet you,' she said. His grip was no stronger than hers but his skin felt noticeably softer. 'I've heard so much about you.'

'Good things, I hope.'

'Mostly,' she said, leading them into the lounge.

He seemed familiar with the room and sat without being asked, resting one arm along the back of the sofa. He had expensive-looking shoes and neatly pressed trousers that shimmered when he crossed his legs.

Her mother sat next to him. Close, but not touching.

'So, Mike,' Bailey said. 'You're down for the weekend?'

'I go back first thing Monday morning.'

Bailey wanted to ask what he got up to during the days —and the nights—he spent away from Farnham. 'And you're into cars.'

He smiled and she noticed the whiteness of his teeth. 'Yes,' he said. 'You could say that.'

'Is that a good business?'

'Very good.'

'Do you make lots of money?'

'Bailey.' Her mother stood and straightened her dress. 'Would anyone like a drink?'

Mike nodded. 'A gin and tonic would be lovely, Valerie.'

Did he know they had a bottle of gin in the house or was he guessing?

'Bailey?'

'Coke please.'

Her mother lingered. 'Anything in it?'

'Such as?'

She hesitated. 'Ice, or something stronger?'

'No, thanks.' Bailey gave a buoyant smile that lasted until her mother left the room. Alone with Mike for the first time, she filled the silence with a question. 'Where do you live, Mike?'

'I've got a flat here in town and a house just outside Doncaster.'

'Any children?'

He looked surprised. 'None.'

'Previously married?'

That seemed to amuse him. 'Never.'

'But you like to travel,' she said.

'Doesn't everyone?'

'Not me.'

He adjusted the fold in his trousers.

'So, your business is in Doncaster and your home is there too. Interesting. Look, I don't know what plans you have for the future, but you should know that I don't like Doncaster.'

'No?'

'Don't get me wrong, I've never actually been, it's just the way it sounds. Doncaster—not very appealing. Have you ever thought about moving your business to Farnham?'

'Yes I have, Farnham's a lovely place and my—'

'You could do a lot worse than moving your business to Farnham. There's so much going on here. I mean, you must have other interests aside from my mother, otherwise you wouldn't be here already. What are they? What brought you to Farnham in the first place?'

She heard the rattle of ice and looked up to see her mother walking in with a tray of drinks. Mike seemed pleased to see her.

'What have you been talking about?' her mother asked, handing out the drinks.

'I was about to explain that my mother lives nearby,' Mike said.

He had a charming voice, so charming it clung to the edge of slimy.

He turned to Bailey. 'She has a cottage in Rowledge. She's seventy-two and still plays tennis. Do you play any sports, Bailey?'

She shook her head. 'Not so much. The only sport I can stand is swimming.'

'Where do you swim?'

'Oh no,' she said. 'I don't swim. But it's the one sport I can stand watching. You know, when the Olympics are on.'

'I heard about your role in the dogs fiasco last week.'

Fiasco? What an odd choice of word. 'That was two weeks ago actually.'

'Sorry, I've been away.'

She wanted to ask him about that as well.

'Do you see yourself as an amateur sleuth, Bailey?'

She wondered whether the twinkle in his eye meant he was laughing *at* her or *with* her. Either way, she didn't like it. 'I like solving mysteries,' she said.

'Can you make a living doing that?'

She wished she could. 'Doubt it. Who would pay me to solve mysteries?'

'You could write about them.'

'Maybe.'

'Or live off the reward money.'

Fat chance.

'Or charge people for your services.'

'I'll think about it,' she said, fighting the urge to tell him she thought he was talking out of his arse. 'Actually, I'm going to be a waitress.'

'Really?'

'Yes. If all goes well I should start tomorrow.'

'Fantastic ...' He took hold of her mother's hand and Bailey thought she saw the first hint of a blush darken her cheeks. 'So are you joining us to celebrate your new position?'

'What?'

'I take it you're coming out with us to celebrate getting a new job.'

He obviously hadn't heard. 'I'm not going out with you tonight.' She looked at her mother. 'That was the deal, right? Just to meet him?'

Her mother responded with the faintest of nods, but her cheeks crimsoned.

Mike uncrossed his legs and leaned forward. 'The *deal*?'

Bailey wondered why they looked at her that way: Mike with an intense quizzical stare and her mother through the gaps between her fingers. She felt a little awkward and decided to change the subject. 'So, Mike. Where have you been these last two weeks?'

* * *

Sitting at the kitchen table, Bailey scraped a spoon inside a bowl to catch the last pieces of puffed wheat.

The feather puzzled her. Had the thief intended to leave it? Or had it been dropped by somebody else and had nothing at all to do with the break-in?

Her phone was plugged into the wall and she was disappointed to see it had only reached 30% charge.

The more pieces she put together, the more obvious it became that Smeak was the thief. He was tall and thin, he had a long nose and he owned a bird that probably had red tail feathers. But why steal a painting? She could understand if it was an original by a famous artist, but a cheap print? It didn't make sense.

At the moment it was all just guesswork and she knew the police would tear her to pieces without some sort of evidence. She had to take a closer look at the parrot and maybe tease a confession out of Smeak.

She tipped the bowl to her face and drank the remaining milk, then stood. 'I thought it went well.'

Her mother paused at the sink, hardly turning.

'Meeting Mike. He seemed okay.' Bailey elbowed her mother aside and dropped the bowl into the water. 'Is he coming over tonight?'

Her mother didn't answer.

'When are you guys going out again? I'm not saying I want to join you, but I wouldn't mind if he called in next time you guys hooked up.'

Finally she turned and Bailey noticed her tears.

'What's wrong?'

Her mother shook. 'He's gone back to Doncaster.'

'Oh,' Bailey said, wondering if it was something she'd said. 'Was it something I said?'

'No, sweetie. I don't think so.'

'Then what?'

'He said it was an emergency and he had to go.'

'When's he coming back?'

'He didn't say.'

'That's a shame,' Bailey said. 'I was going to ask him to teach me to drive.'

Chapter Ten

According to the disappointing mobile phone her brother had donated to her, it was twenty-five minutes past five when she activated the voice recorder.

'One, two, three, lemon tea.'

She played it back and barely heard it, but it would have to do.

Slipping the phone into the breast pocket of her leather jacket, she stepped from the shadows of the bus-stop.

'Are you sure you're not a secret agent?' Jack stood there beaming. The patchwork dog by his side.

'Are you stalking me?'

'That hurts.'

'I'm very busy,' she said and walked away.

The road to Lamb Yard lay quiet with no traffic and just a sprinkle of evening shoppers. Avoiding the pavements, she walked along the middle of the road at a brisk pace, her tied-back hair bobbing with every step. Above the muffled conversation of a passing couple, she heard the clip of feet and paws behind her.

'Hold up,' Jack called.

She turned abruptly and snapped, 'Can't you leave me alone.'

'I thought you should know that—'

'What?' Although marginally shorter than Jack, in that moment she felt a lot taller. 'Why do you get in my business all the time?'

His face dropped and he stared at her open-mouthed.

'You don't know me. We're not friends.' Her voice rose and the dog moved between Jack's legs. 'I've told you I'm busy and I've asked you to leave, so do me a favour and go away.'

'But—'

'Yeah, blah, blah, blah,' she said as she stomped away.

The tramp was a definite distraction and she could do without having him around when she confronted Smeak. If the tramp hadn't been there last time, she might have got the job already. Determined not to let him ruin things for her again, she flipped him the finger as she headed for an opening in the wall near the Waitrose supermarket. From there it was a short walk through the courtyard to the coffee shop, and her showdown with Mr Smeak.

When a car rolled slowly into view up ahead, she noticed it and dismissed it in the blink of an eye. She was so wound up by the meddling tramp's intrusion, that its yellow and blue markings didn't register with her immediately. It wasn't until she heard the siren that she took more interest.

A police car rolled slowly towards her. Inside was Constable Tierney and the policewoman she'd seen outside the antique shop.

Instinct took over and she ran, darting along the pavement towards the gap in the wall, startling a woman carrying more bags than she could manage. Bailey ran until she hit the cobbles in the courtyard and then stopped behind a shop to catch her breath.

She panted fiercely and felt the first drops of sweat form on her chin. Studying her reflection in the shop window, she checked her makeup and adjusted her hair. Something tapped the window and she noticed a strange-looking man on the other side of the glass. Small and bald with a peanut head, he reached between a display of paintings to shoo her away. She pulled a face and then turned and left.

The courtyard was almost empty with just a sprinkle of tardy shoppers ambling about. A handful of teenagers cycled by—so intent were they to avoid the uneven cobbles, they went without jibe or joke in her direction.

As she neared the coffee shop, she noticed a man walking towards her wearing blue jeans and a matching hoodie. There was nothing out of the ordinary about him, but with his head covered and his hands thrust deep into his pockets, he looked a bit shifty. Tall and thin, the way he moved seemed familiar, but she couldn't place it. She stepped aside and caught a waft of tobacco and beer as he passed.

Up ahead, Smeak wiped tables. She knew exactly what would happen after she exposed him: he'd get fired and she'd get hired, he'd go to prison and she'd get a reward for catching him. It was all going to be so easy.

His head twitched and he looked up, locking eyes with her almost immediately. He arched his back and rolled onto the balls of his feet as she approached.

'Hello again, Mr Smeak.'

He nodded.

Despite the silent snarl creasing his face, Bailey felt confident she could manipulate him sufficiently to get the result she wanted. 'Can we talk?'

'I'm very busy,' he said brusquely.

'Indeed, and I can help you with that problem.'

His expression didn't change.

'Can we go upstairs to your office?'

'Why?'

'So we can talk in private.'

He looked around and Bailey followed his gaze. Apart from the Denim Man loitering outside the art gallery, there was nobody in sight. 'Can't we talk here?'

We could, she thought, but I want to take a look at your parrot before naming you as the thief. 'I'd like to see your parrot.' Why did she say that?

'Pardon?' He seemed as stunned as she was. 'I'm sorry, but it's been a long day and I want to finish up for the night.'

Everything was going wrong again. Shit. She rubbed her eyes. 'Hang on. Can we start again? Look, I'd really like a job here, I'd make an excellent waitress and I'm such a hard worker.'

'And our previous conversation meant nothing to you, did it?'

Bailey tried to recall the conversation and the list of reasons he had for not giving her the job. 'I'm sure you didn't mean all the things you said and even if you did, we both know that most of them weren't entirely true anyway.'

His face flattened.

If she couldn't inspect the parrot now, the next best thing would be to secure a job at the cafe so she could see it another day. 'Let me serve your customers. It'll take the pressure off you and it'll be great for business. You'll see an increase in sales, happy customers, everyone wins.' She held her breath and waited for him to process the offer. It didn't take very long.

'The position has been filled already.'

'Oh.' She hadn't expected that. 'You've found someone?'

'Exactly.'

'To be your waitress?'

'Indeed.'

'Are you sure?'

'The new girl seems adequately suited. Yes.'

Well that was that then. She turned and started down the lane, but the sight of Jack and his dog at the bottom, made her stop. Damn. She had the tramp at one end and Tierney at the other. A picture of the old man in the park sprang to mind and she recalled his dogged tale of never giving up. She turned back to Smeak. 'Do you collect pictures, Mr Smeak?'

'Excuse me, what?'

'Pictures. To look at. Specific pictures. Do you collect them?'

'Well ...' He seemed uncomfortable. 'Why do you ask?'

'And jewellery? Do you have a particular fondness for silver?' Bailey opened her jacket, leaned in and said, 'Because I know what you've done.'

He twisted the dishcloth in both hands and looked at her through uncertain eyes.

'I know you're collecting pictures, Mr Smeak.' Was that sweat forming on his lip?

Then he took her by surprise as his brows furrowed and he stepped forward, finger first. 'Listen here—'

'STOP.'

The cry echoed off the surrounding buildings and she wasn't sure where it had come from. By the look on Smeak's face, neither was he.

'THIEF.'

At the bottom of the cobbled lane, Jack pointed over her shoulder. 'Behind you,' he called.

Bailey and Smeak turned to see a man at the top of the lane jumping up and down outside the art gallery, waving his hands wildly. 'Stop him,' he cried.

About mid-way between them—and making awkward progress on the cobbles—Bailey saw Denim Man running. His hood had fallen back around his shoulders and a crop of bright red hair crowned his face. He carried something, but from that distance, she couldn't see what.

'Stop him,' the gallery-man called again.

About twenty feet wide at the coffee shop, the width of the lane was narrowed by tables and chairs and the presence of Bailey and Smeak. She wasn't sure where the thief was running, but if he wanted to escape that way he would have to pass between them.

She heard a dog bark and Jack screamed, 'Duncan, wait.'

Bailey turned to see the dog running towards her, and Jack chasing after it. Behind her, the slap of Denim Man's steps grew louder as he closed in. The dog barked again and she stepped in front of it, but it changed course and made a beeline for the red-headed figure bearing down upon them.

'Stop him.'

Bailey's instincts took over. She threw herself to the ground, grabbed the dog and tucked it inside her jacket. Then she jumped to her feet and, with the selfish intention of saving both herself and the dog, she headed towards Smeak and the safety of the coffee shop.

Everything happened quickly after that.

Pain exploded as something slammed into her shoulder, knocking her down amid the sound of raised voices and the crescendo of breaking glass.

* * *

Something licked Bailey's fingers and she looked down to see the patchwork dog on her lap. On the other side of the room, a girl she'd never seen before shovelled glass into a bin.

Bailey felt groggy, but her senses cleared the longer she stroked the dog. 'Why did you call him Duncan?'

'So, we're on speaking terms now.' Jack grinned.

'Sorry, I was a dick.' She shrugged. 'Again. Why did you call the dog Duncan?'

'A lad from school bullied me rotten. Now I can tell Duncan off without getting thumped.'

She wanted to laugh but the pain in her shoulder told her not to. She nodded towards the girl sweeping. 'What happened there?'

Although she didn't think it possible, Jack's grin widened. 'You were great.' He pulled up a chair and sat beside her. 'Turns out, that bloke had stolen a painting and was making good his escape when you shoulder-charged him through the window. The police are outside now.'

'I was just saving the dog.'

'So you say. What I saw was a nifty tuck and bump. An old rugby move we learned at school. And, I might add, extremely well executed. He went flying.'

'Did he get away?' she asked.

'Not a chance. He was knocked out cold. The police have him. One of the coppers will pop in for a chat with us soon.'

'Man or woman?'

'Who?'

'The copper.'

'Man. Tall. Thick-set. Didn't catch his name.'

Bailey groaned. Tierney. 'Any chance of a drink? A

Coke or something?'

'I don't know,' Jack said. 'The waiter didn't seem very impressed with you using his window to stop the thief.'

'I was saving the dog, I mean Duncan. I thought he'd be trampled.'

'Yeah, well. Keep that to yourself. There might be a reward for catching this fella.'

Bailey's mood brightened. 'What did he steal?'

'A Constable.'

'What?'

'A painting by John Constable.' Jack laughed. 'The policeman commandeered the Constable. Get it?'

Bailey didn't, but it intrigued her that another painting had been stolen. 'Did he really have red hair?'

'No. That was a mask. A bird mask. One of those fancy-dress things. Beak, feathers, you know.'

Of course, Bailey thought, that would explain the big nose. Had she really stopped the thief? Her first thought had been to save the dog. But if in the process she helped solve a crime then—

A shadow fell across the room and Bailey looked up to see Constable Tierney enter. He took off his hat, reached for a chair and sat in front of her. Turning to Jack, he said, 'I'd like to speak with the young lady in private, sir. If you can wait outside, I'll be with you shortly.'

Jack lifted the dog off Bailey's lap and was about to go when she caught his arm. 'Don't go.' She turned to Tierney. 'I want him to stay.'

'Sorry, miss. You're both witnesses to a crime and I need to interview you separately.' She nodded to Jack and he left.

Bailey fidgeted herself comfortable as Tierney pulled out a pad and turned a few pages. When he leaned towards her, his face had tightened. 'Spare the bullshit, Jacobs,' he whispered through narrow lips that sprayed as he spoke. 'What's your relationship with Danny Douglas?'

She backed off and wiped her face. 'Who?'

'Don't piss about, Jacobs. The man you pushed through the window twenty minutes ago.'

Chapter Eleven

As the police car eased to a stop outside her house, Bailey hid her face from the gaggle of kids who had gathered around to watch. She would rather have walked home, but Tierney and the policewoman Mundy, had insisted on driving her. She was only thankful they hadn't used the flashing lights.

Children closed in and some pressed their faces against the glass. She could hear them laughing and jeering. One of them slapped the window and Tierney swore, then he flicked a switch and Bailey cringed as the siren blared and the children cheered.

Her mother met them at the door, her face apparently drawn by concern. She stepped aside to let Bailey and her two police escorts into the house.

Bailey ran upstairs and crumpled on her bed. They hadn't spoken in the car but she could hear them now, Tierney and Mundy, talking with her mother in the hallway. She didn't know what they were saying, but their voices seemed curiously calm and relaxed.

Tiredness took hold and she drifted. She wasn't sure how long she had been asleep but when she opened her eyes, she was lying on her back with Constable Mundy holding one arm and her mother holding the other. Tierney sat on top of her with a knife, its blade cold against her face as he toyed with her flesh.

She stretched her mouth wide and screamed.

'It's all right, darling.'

Bailey opened her eyes again and sat up, almost knocking her mother off the bed.

'You were dreaming.'

'What?'

'You've been dreaming. I heard you moaning from the kitchen.'

Her chest heaved. 'The police?'

'They've gone.'

'Am I in trouble?'

Her mother pushed back a strand of Bailey's sweat-soaked hair. 'Everything's going to be all right,' she said. 'They know you're not involved.'

'Good. But then who?'

'Relax.' She wiped her forehead. 'They caught a local lad. Not much older than you.'

'It was definitely him then?'

Her mother nodded. 'His wife was wearing jewellery from the antique shop when the police called round to inform her.'

'And the paintings?'

'They didn't mention any paintings.' Her mother adjusted her position on the edge of the bed. 'But,' she said in a harsher tone. 'They told me that you stopped him by hurling him through a window.'

Bailey remembered.

'What were you thinking?'

She closed her eyes and waited for the lecture that was sure to follow.

'I mean, you could have been hurt.'

She felt her mother caress her cheek.

'My sweet, Bailey Bee. What would I do if anything happened to you?'

Not quite the reaction she had expected.

'Constable Mundy said they have a witness who says you saved the life of a dog and stopped the thief all by yourself.'

Jack.

Her mother beamed. 'I'm so proud of you.'

She wanted to explain that her first thought was to save the dog and then herself—she hadn't considered the painting or the thief—but her mother seemed so happy and … *proud*. That was new. She'd never been proud before.

'But not everyone thinks you're a hero. The manager of the shop wasn't very pleased when I spoke with him.'

Bailey cleared her throat. 'You spoke with Mr Smeak?'

'He was very curt.'

Bailey could describe him in other ways.

'But I talked him round and it turns out he's not such a nasty man after all.'

'Is he not?' Bailey asked.

'No. But he's very upset about his window and he's got an insurance excess of £200 to cover.'

Bailey grinned.

'Anyway, we came to an arrangement.'

Her grin faded. That didn't sound good.

'Yes,' her mother said. 'He's decided to give you a job after all.'

Bailey's eyes widened. Great, she thought, a waitress at last.

'You start Monday morning at nine.'

She nodded. 'I think I'll be a good waitress.'

Her mother looked surprised. 'Oh no, darling. Not as a waitress. As a washer-upper. You can work there until you've paid off the cost of the window. And after that, well, he said to wait and see.'

She was about to protest when—

'It's better than plucking chickens,' her mother said.

'But—'

'It's all settled, Bailey. You start Monday.'

'It's quite a way to walk each day.' Bailey frowned. 'Is there any way that Mike could—'

'I don't think we'll be seeing Mike again.'

She waited and when no explanation followed, she asked, 'Why?'

'He's gone back,' her mother twisted her sleeve as she spoke. 'To his husband.'

'I knew there was something—' Bailey stopped. '*Husband?*'

'Yes,' her mother said. 'He dances around a different tree.'

Bailey spluttered, shocked and impressed that her mother knew such a phrase.

'He said he had no intention of us ever being a couple.'

Bailey rubbed her shoulder. 'Are you okay with that?'

'Sort of. I can't believe I didn't see it. I suppose you were right when you said there was something too perfect about him.'

That's not exactly what I said, Bailey thought. 'Weren't you both? I mean, didn't you ever, you know—'

'What?'

'Couple.'

'No. I would never.'

'Oh,' Bailey said. 'I assumed you had.'

Her mother bit her lip. 'If there was an understanding between us, that would be different. But I'd only known him a few weeks and anyway, the subject never came up.'

A few weeks? It had only taken a Paul a few hours to

164

find the clip on her bra. She shrugged. 'Why did he bother to see you at all? If not for that?'

Her mother dropped her head and shook it slowly.

'Mum?'

'He said he felt sorry for me.'

'Sorry?'

'He said he enjoyed taking care of me because I reminded him of his mother.'

'But why leave now? Is it because of me? Something I said?'

'No, darling. Not you.'

'Then what?'

'It's nothing, forget it.'

Bailey took her hand and squeezed. 'Please, tell me.'

Her mother hesitated for what seemed an age before, 'It's your father.'

Bailey glanced at the photo on her desk as the touch of her past pressed its fingers to her chest.

'I told him about Connor.'

'Why should that upset him?'

'He wasn't upset,' her mother said, faltering. 'Just ... a bit scared.'

Bailey didn't understand. Why should he be scared about her dead dad? She asked, 'Why?'

'Because, darling, the thing is—'

Christ. Bailey let go of her mother's hand and gasped. 'He's not dead.'

Her mother didn't respond.

'Is he? He's not dead. How? Why?'

'It was such a long time ago. You were young and I didn't want to hurt you.'

'You didn't want to hurt me?' she spat.

'Any more than we had done already.'

Bailey hardly remembered her father. Following his untimely death, they had moved to Farnham when she was three. 'How do you know he's still alive?'

'Because they would have told me if it was over.'

Bailey wanted to know *who* would have told her, but her mind was a scramble of questions tumbling over each other to be asked first. 'So, the car crash was a lie?'

'Not a complete lie. He did crash the car.'

'He just didn't die in it.'

Her mother nodded.

'When you told me that he beat you. Was that true?'

'Yes, everything else I've told you is true. Except …'

'What?'

'Well, you know that he's Irish.'

Bailey nodded hesitantly.

'The thing is, he got himself into a bit of trouble.'

But he's *alive*.

'He got mixed up with some bad people.'

Bailey moved her hand away when her mother reached for it.

'He left us, Bailey.' Her voice wavered. 'He might have been young, naive and stupid, but when it came down to it, he just wasn't a very nice man.'

'Does Timothy know?'

Her mother hid her face in her hands.

If her brother didn't know then maybe it was time he found out?

Her father died in a car crash fourteen years ago. He had been drunk and left the house in a rage after getting into a fight with her mother. That's the truth she had lived with and the truth her mother had just smashed apart. She had lied to her all these years. Lied to them both. Bailey's head throbbed and a vice-like grip squeezed her heart. She

166

wondered what other secrets her mother was keeping.

'Go.' She pointed to the door.

'Let me explain.'

'Don't.' Bailey stiffened. 'Just go.' She watched her mother leave, hunched and slow, older than she'd ever looked before.

When she'd gone, Bailey sat at her desk, took her father's picture frame and held it until her fingers numbed.

Then she wiped her eyes, leafed to a new page in the pad and carefully wrote at the top, *The Case of the Resurrected Father*.

Episode Three

Bailey Jacobs
and the
Bungled Burglary

Prologue

He placed a golden vase on a coffee-coloured rug and crushed it with the heel of an over-sized boot.

Then he lifted a gilded frame from the wall and carried it stealthily into the garden.

The evening air was gloomy and dry, and that suited him fine. He closed the door behind him, weighed up a brick and hurled it through the glass.

Inside the house, a woman screamed.

Chapter One

Bailey took a deep breath and held it, savouring the pleasing scent of freshly cut grass. Things were looking up. She'd stopped the Bird Thief, got a new pair of boots, secured a job and discovered her dad wasn't dead. The weekend was turning out to be a good one, and it was still only Sunday.

She sat with arms stretched along the back of a park bench as the midday sun warmed her face. Lifting the hem of her dress, she raised her legs and beamed at her shiny black boots. She loved how the red stitching embellished both sides, wrapping each ankle with the shape of a thorny rose. The best boots she'd ever owned.

Her leather jacket creaked as she twisted around. The park was busy. Some people cruised about with dogs, others had children. A couple fell to the grass in a playful embrace then scrambled to their feet, patting away patches of wet. The sun hadn't dried away all of the overnight rain, but it was trying.

She couldn't see the old man anywhere.

Whilst they hadn't exactly arranged to meet, she knew he was bound to show at some stage. But when? She'd been there almost an hour already, there was no sign of him yet and her bottom ached. She didn't know if she could put up with it much longer.

Bailey had no paternal male friends to turn to and she desperately wanted to talk to someone about her father. Finding out he was alive after believing him dead for the last fourteen years, she needed help to process that kind of information.

A fat boy on roller-blades puffed his way along the tarmac path, almost clipping the toe of her boot as he passed. She watched him go, his lycra covered backside struggling like a sack of angry cats. She squeezed her stomach to check the state of her own plumpness. Just about satisfactory.

Her brother was still pissed off with her, but she didn't mind that at all. Winding up Timothy was one of life's little pleasures. She'd recently embarrassed him in front of his friend, got his bike stolen, and blackmailed him with a list of demands because he was using school time and equipment to code for commercial projects.

The two years between them gave Bailey an edge over her brother that she happily exploited. At five foot eight they were the same height and similar build, but her extra years and combustable temper gave her the upper-hand—at least for the moment. She knew he'd be stronger than her one day, but that day wasn't yet.

Bailey counted down from ten, deciding to leave when she got to zero if the old man hadn't shown. When she got to three, she heard gravel crunch in the car park at the end of the path and looked up in time to see a beige car come to a stop. A woman got out, pushed a white-gloved hand through blonde hair and moved to the passenger side.

Seconds later, the old man appeared clutching a walking stick. The woman helped him from the car, then pecked him on the cheek and left him to cover the distance alone. Bailey was sure his pace quickened when he looked up to see her sitting on the bench.

'Hello, Miss.'

She smiled and moved across to make room for him.

'What an unexpected pleasure to see you again.' He sat, positioned the walking stick between his legs and placed both hands upon it.

'Where have you been?' Bailey blurted and wished she hadn't because it wiped the smile from his face.

'Did we have an appointment?'

'No, but ...' Bailey shuffled round to face him.

'I go to church every Sunday. And then come here to visit—'

'Listen, I've got to ask you something.'

'First, tell me, did you attend to your business last week?'

Bailey had met the old man by the river a few days ago. In an abstract, roundabout way, he'd given her advice about a difficult problem she had. At the time, it happened to be bad advice, but later when the dust settled, things worked out well for her.

'Yes, kind of.' She waited until the pause that followed felt ready to pluck. 'Can I ask you something?'

'Of course.'

She suddenly felt a bit stupid for being there. The old man was almost a complete stranger and she knew very little about him. Except perhaps, that she liked him. He might have been old and doddery, but he made her feel comfortable. 'Are your children still alive?'

He held a smile, but topped it with a frown. 'Margaret and I were never fortunate with children.'

'Oh.' She had assumed he had a bunch of them. Didn't all old people have a string of children or grandchildren following them around all the time?

'Why do you ask?'

'Nothing really. It's just that, well, my dad's dead. Or at least he *was*.' She bit her lip. 'Sorry, this is so stupid.'

His expression didn't change all the while she bumbled. 'I mean, you're an old man and I'm ...' She wondered how to end that sentence.

'A beautiful young woman?'

She stopped and stared at him, her mouth open. 'What?'

'Ask me anything. But let's be clear, a dalliance isn't within my power or intention.'

She didn't know what that meant, but thought it sounded lovely. 'Well.' She took a breath. 'I'm seventeen.' He looked like he was about to speak so she held up a hand and continued. 'Dad died when I was three. At least, that's what I thought until yesterday when Mum said he was still alive. She said he wasn't a very nice man and we're better off without him.' She sucked in another breath. 'Thing is, I can't stop thinking about him and I know I won't be able to stop until I find him or at least speak with him about everything that's happened since he's been gone.' Her chest pounded, but it felt good to tell someone, if only a stranger.

She could see him thinking, mouthing words that were yet to form. She knew it was a lot to take in but her patience ran out before he responded. 'What do you think?'

He hesitated and then said, 'You look older than seventeen.'

'Is that all you've got to say?'

He nodded.

'I thought you could help me. Aren't you supposed to be wise as well as old? I thought—' Bailey stopped talking when he held up a hand.

'What is your name?' he asked in his soft, clear voice.

'Er.'

'It's a simple question.'

'Bailey.'

'Is that your birth name or your family name?'

'It's my first name.'

'Hmm,' he said. 'My neighbour gave his dog the same name.'

She scowled.

'Well, Bailey. Out of all the things you said, the only part I find incredulous is your age.' He cleared his throat. 'You seem older than your years. You have good stature, intelligent eyes and, beneath that …' He hesitated on the next word. 'Exterior, I can see a beautiful woman waiting to get out.'

She wasn't sure if he had complimented her or not. 'What about my dead dad?'

'You said he wasn't dead.'

'Exactly.'

'I find it easy to understand and appreciate. Your mother told you he was dead to protect you. That seems a genuine if not rather drastic solution to the problem of him not being a very nice person. You, however, *do* seem to be a nice person. I therefore assume she did it because she didn't want him to hurt you or damage your chances of a better life.'

He seemed to have grasped the situation fairly well. 'But I can't stop thinking about him.'

'That's only natural. He's your father and your memories of him are tainted by the age you were when you knew him and the time that has since elapsed. You probably didn't experience his nasty side. Or, if you did, you simply don't remember.'

One of the few dreams she had of her father was him carrying baby Timothy across a muddy field. She didn't know how the dream ended, but if the accompanying screams and tears were anything to go by, it wasn't good. 'Maybe you're right,' she said.

The quiet between them lasted for the length of a bird's song.

'Should I contact him?'

'Yes.' He turned steely blue eyes onto hers and nodded. 'I think you should.'

'How?'

'Do you have a phone number? Or an address?'

'No.'

'Well, I assume you know his name and his last known location. So, use that big G-machine in the sky to research and identify his present whereabouts.'

'You mean I should Google him?'

'Yes.'

'And if that doesn't work?'

'Are you so incapable of using your intellect?'

She shrugged.

'It's not difficult. Simply gather intelligence and interrogate. Concentrate on the primary or closest source —whichever is opportune—then work from there. Collate information and review. Do you have someone who can help you consider the options?'

Consider the options. She used that phrase often herself when she needed to think things through. 'Not really,' she said. 'Except you.'

He coughed. 'Nobody else?'

She shook her head.

'Speak to your mother. See what information she can provide. Then if you still need help, we can talk again.'

'How will I find you?'

'By using your intelligence. It's in there.' He pointed

to her head. 'You simply have to harness it.'

She was about to rise when he took her arm.

'You're always in such a hurry, Bailey. Please, do an old man a favour and sit. Just for a while. In silence. Enjoy the day, the park, the moment.'

'Okay,' she said, settling back down. 'Do you want to —' He held up a hand again and Bailey liked him all the more for it. Spirited old man.

They sat in silence and he seemed to lose himself in memories. His face glazed and his breathing slowed to the point she thought he'd died. She wondered how long an appropriate time was to wait before leaving. She wanted the old man's help, but it didn't mean they had to hang out together in public like friends.

He cleared his throat. 'Thank you,' he said, wiping an eye.

Bailey stood. 'I guess I should be—'

He caught her by the arm again. 'Colonel.'

He had a good grip for an old fella. 'What?'

He released her. 'You didn't ask. But I'm sure you meant to. People call me Colonel. Or Sir. Either one is fine. I'll see you around, Bailey.' He kissed his fingers and lay them on the bench, then stood and shuffled back along the path.

Bailey had seen him kiss the bench before and wondered for the briefest moment *why*, but the thought quickly faded. She was up and away, heading home to find her mother and to make sense of the questions building inside her head.

Chapter Two

Bailey pushed the front door open and stepped into a house saturated with chicken-infused humidity. Steam seeped from the kitchen as her mother's head appeared round the door. 'Ten minutes to lunch.'

'No problem,' Bailey said as she ran upstairs, her boots thumping every step.

When she reached the top, the bathroom door opened and her brother stepped out. He mumbled something incoherent as they passed each other on the landing.

In her bedroom, Bailey sat at her desk, opened an A4 pad and flipped to a page entitled *The Case of the Resurrected Father*. The page had a list of actions that comprised just one item.

- *Find Dad.*

She reached for a tired-looking photo frame leaning against the wall—old and crooked, the glass front shifted so much she thought it would fall out. It was the only photo she had of her father. He sat astride a motorbike with three year old Bailey in his arms. She didn't remember the moment, but her three year old self radiated happiness. She put the frame down, picked up a pen and added another item to the list.

- *Talk to Mum about Dad.*

She sucked the end of the pen and shivered. *Resurrected Father*. It sounded pretty sinister, but she knew she wouldn't rest until she discover the truth about what happened. No matter how long it took.

'Oi, creep.'

She didn't bother turning around because she knew who the sinewy voice belonged to.

'Mum says you've got to come downstairs.'

She waved her brother away with the flick of a hand. When she didn't hear him leave, she turned and her temper flared. 'Get the hell out.' She shot across the room.

Timothy backed off quickly. 'What?'

'Your foot was over the line.'

'What line?'

Bailey closed the distance between them. 'Don't be a smart arse.' She poked a finger into his chest. 'Keep out of my room. Don't even look inside. And next time, make sure you knock. Got it?'

'Yeah, right, whatever.'

She poked him again. 'Now piss off.'

Timothy crept away and mumbled something she barely heard. 'I shan't tell you ...'

She pulled him back by the shoulder. 'What?'

'Get off.'

'What did you say?'

'Nothing. Argh.'

Bailey held him by the throat. 'Tell me what you said.'

He wrestled with her hand and she tightened her grip, his face growing redder the more she squeezed. 'Okay,' he gurgled, massaging his neck. 'I said ...' His words were spiked with acid. 'I shan't tell you what I know.'

'Are you seven?' she spat. 'You've got yourself a

secret and you're dangling it around so people take notice of you. Trust me, it's nothing compared to the secret I've got.' She stopped herself in time. Timothy didn't know about their father being alive and she wasn't sure she wanted to tell him yet. 'Come on then,' she said. 'What is it?'

His eyes narrowed. 'I saw Paul.'

Bailey felt cold and hoped it didn't show.

'Around the corner. Looking shifty.'

'Shifty?'

He nodded. 'Probably surveying his next job.'

'What are you talking about?'

'I bet he's planning another robbery.' Timothy stepped back as she stepped forward.

'What the hell do you mean by that?'

'Argh,' he cried. 'He's out there, hanging about, looking shifty. Everyone knows he's a thief. What would you—'

'He's not a thief.'

'No? What about the off-licence last year? And his new car?'

'What car?' Bailey pushed him towards the stairs. 'You don't know what you're talking about. Go on, bugger off and tell Mum I'll be down in a minute.'

'You'll see that I'm right.' He stopped at the first step and turned. 'So, what's *your* secret then?'

Bailey rolled the words on her tongue, contemplating whether to share them. 'Nothing. Piss off.'

If Paul was hanging around the house, that meant he only wanted one thing. And it wasn't to plan a burglary.

At least, she hoped not.

* * *

Bailey wrapped a towel around another plate and patted it dry.

Tea had been a subdued affair: Timothy hardly spoke, Bailey hardly ate and their mother sat between them trying unsuccessfully to encourage conversation.

Now Bailey stood beside her mother with tea-towel in hand wondering how to ask the many questions queuing up inside her brain. The old man was right, she had to use her intelligence. 'So,' she said, adopting an impassive tone. 'Dad's alive then?'

Her mother paused at the sink for a single beat without reply.

Bailey picked up a spoon and polished it dry. 'Why did you change our name to Jacobs?'

'That's my maiden name.'

'I know, but what's wrong with Kelly? Bailey Kelly. It's got a nice ring to it.' She continued drying. 'Where do you think he's living now?'

Her mother stopped and let bubbles drip from a sponge. 'I really don't want to think about it right now.'

The old, impetuous Bailey wanted to jump in and argue the point. But the new, intelligent Bailey held her back. She nodded. Dried. And hummed. *Gather intelligence and interrogate.* After a plate and a bowl, she said, 'Do you think he's still in Ireland?'

Her mother spun round, eyes fierce. 'Drop it. Please.'

New Bailey wanted to, she really did, but the effort to silence *Old* Bailey was just too much. 'How can I?'

'Keep your voice down. Timothy's upstairs.'

'I want to know about my father,' Bailey whispered. 'Maybe I'll ask Aunt Liz.' She saw her mother stiffen. 'I still don't know why you two fell out.'

'Don't bring her into it.'

Bailey sensed she'd found a nerve. 'I bet she knows enough about Dad to help me find him.'

'Stop it.' Her mother's eye twitched. 'For me.' Twitch. 'For Timmy.'

'But—'

'No, Bailey. Not this time.' She turned back to the sink. 'Unless you want us to have to move again.'

'What do you mean?'

'Nothing.'

'Mum?'

Tears stained her mother's face. 'Please,' she said, her chin quivering. 'Don't.'

Bailey didn't. She desperately wanted to find out more about her father, but the interrogation hadn't been as easy as she hoped. Fourteen years had elapsed since he left them, but it was clear as crystal that her mother still had a thing for the man. Bailey threw the tea-towel down and left.

Upstairs at her desk, she opened the pad to *The Case of the Resurrected Father* and read.

ACTIONS
* *Find Dad.*
* *Talk to Mum about Dad.*

She picked up a pen and scribbled through the second item—*Talk to Mum about Dad*—then she added two new items.

* *Talk to Aunt Liz.*
* *Research Connor Kelly (Dad).*

Bailey reached for her dad's old picture frame and the

loose glass rattled in the surround as she inspected it. Her mother had offered to replace the frame many times in the past, maybe she should let her. She added another item.

* *Identify Dad's motorbike.*

Further down the page, she started a new list.

CLUES
* *Lives in Ireland (probably).*
* *Likes motorbikes.*
* *Mum moved to get away from him.*

Bailey gazed up at the sultry face of Kurt Cobain and felt herself drawn to his torment. If *he* had used his intelligence, she thought, he'd probably still be around making music. Such a waste.

She put the pen down, stood and walked across the landing to her brother's bedroom where she knocked, waited, then knocked louder.

He opened the door and pulled a face.

'I'm sorry,' she said. 'Are you all right?'

He grunted and rubbed his neck.

'I flipped. I'll try not to—'

'What do you want?'

'It's like this,' she said.

'Just tell me.'

'I need a laptop.'

'Yeah, and I need twenty-four hours notice.'

She pointed to the desk behind him. 'What about that one?'

'I'm using it,' he said without looking.

'Come on, you've got at least three of them.'

'I know.' He wiped his nose. 'And I'm using them all.'

Diplomacy, Bailey thought. Use your intelligence. 'If I borrowed just one for a short while, could you work around it?'

He didn't answer.

'I really need one,' she said. 'Not for long. Just this evening.'

'Well you can't.'

Having taken a moment to consider her options, and realising there were desperately few, she formed what she hoped was an intimidating scowl. 'How would you like to go to school tomorrow with no eyebrows?'

Timothy huffed, turned to the laptop and tapped some keys. He gathered a cable and handed the bundle to her. 'I want it back by the morning.'

A few minutes later, Bailey was at her desk, typing *Connor Kelly* into Google. She had begun to scroll through the results when a gentle knock at the door distracted her. She slapped the laptop shut as her mother walked in with an armful of clothes.

'Here,' she said, dropping the clothes onto the bed. 'Clean things for tomorrow.'

Bailey stared. 'Tomorrow?'

'Your first day at work.'

'Ah, I thought maybe …'

'No,' her mother said flatly. 'Your new job starts tomorrow and you're going to be there. Have you decided what to wear?'

Bailey sighed as she sifted through the pile. 'Black jeans and that silk blouse you bought me last year, the black one.'

'To wash up in? Are you sure?'

'Why not?'

'Because I imagine it will be hot and humid. Probably dirty as well.'

'D'you think?' Bailey selected a t-shirt from the pile and held it up. 'What about this one?'

Her mother cringed. 'Disturbed?'

'They're a group.'

'A group of what? No,' she said. 'Save that one for later. For when they get to know you better.' She lifted a plain blue t-shirt from the pile. 'What about this with your old jeans and trainers?'

'But if they want me to serve tables as well then I've got to be ready, right?' It was very likely, she thought, even if the new waitress did bother to turn up, she might be completely useless at the job. In which case, they would probably swap roles: she would do the waitressing while the other girl did the washing up.

'It's up to you, darling. It's your day. Just be sure not to wear your new boots.'

'Wouldn't dream of it,' Bailey said, wondering how she was going to smuggle them out of the house.

Chapter Three

Climbing out of the taxi at ten past nine, Bailey mumbled her thanks to the driver, slammed the door and ran to the coffee shop, careful not to turn an ankle on the cobbled lane.

Getting ready that morning had been a struggle. She'd slept badly and risen late, her head foggy with remnants of faded dreams and the anxiety of a first day at work. Having picked at her breakfast, she took time to apply a fresh layer of makeup and dressed slowly, insisting her mother iron her blouse twice before agreeing to wear it. Finally, at quarter to nine, she was ready.

'It's hardly worth going now,' she had argued after explaining to her mother that she had a thirty-minute walk into town and it was better not to arrive at all than to arrive late. Her mother had agreed and much to Bailey's annoyance, she phoned for a taxi.

Mr Smeak was standing in front of the coffee shop when she arrived. He checked his watch, rolled onto the balls of his feet and wrote something down on a clipboard.

Bailey wanted to project a confident smile and hoped the nausea she felt at being so close to Smeak again, didn't distort it too much.

Five tables with accompanying chairs had been set in front of the shop and their chrome edges gleamed. The large window—through which she'd pushed an escaping thief two days earlier—was covered with clear plastic sheets held in place by lashings of grey tape. She tried not to look at it.

Smeak pointed to the side of the building. 'There is a side gate that you will use on future occasions to access the premises. For now however, and this being the only time it will occur, I permit you to enter through the customer entrance. This way please.'

Bailey followed her new boss inside.

Arrogant. Ignorant. Rude. That's what the despicable Mr Smeak had called her last time they met when she applied for the waitressing job. She had ended up storming out of that interview. It had only been last week, but it seemed a long time ago now.

The cafe smelled of coffee and cinnamon with a hint of mint. Two girls busied themselves behind a glass counter. The younger one smiled at Bailey, but the other didn't. Neither of them spoke.

Smeak led Bailey through a swing door into the kitchen and she moaned inwardly at the sight. It was bleak and basic with shelves in one corner and the biggest sink she'd ever seen, set beneath a frosted window. A worktop and cupboards occupied the opposite wall and a door at the end of the room appeared to lead outside.

Being a washer-upper wasn't high on her list of priorities. She'd only taken the job to keep her mother quiet and because Smeak insisted she pay something towards the cost of a replacement window.

'This is where you will work.' Smeak spread his arms wide as if the sight should impress her. 'Waiting staff place dirty crockery and cutlery on the bottom three shelves here. You wash them, dry them and stack them neatly on the top three shelves, here.'

Bailey nodded and wondered if she would be paid for

the ten minutes she was late.

'Waste food goes into the bins, here.' He pointed to a pair of plastic barrels beneath the sink. Neither barrel had a lid and remnants of waste stained the rims.

Disgusting, she thought, as she scoured the room for rats.

'Be sparse with the washing-up liquid, but keep the water piping hot. Hot water is the domestic servant's friend. It cleans better and dries faster. In time, you'll come to appreciate that. New towels are in the drawer, here. Do you smoke?'

I was thinking about starting, she thought. 'No,' she said.

'Good. It's a repulsive habit. Undeniably bad. But there's a bench in the yard if you wish to use it for … other things.'

She wanted to ask about comfort breaks, but wasn't sure how to pose the question.

Smeak looked at her and frowned. 'Is something troubling you?'

'No,' she said, scratching her head.

'Remove your rings and tie your hair back. There should be rubber bands upstairs.'

'My rings?'

'Yes.'

'All of them?'

'Yes. I don't want my crockery chipped by the metal on your fingers. And after an hour doing this job, you'll be quite pleased you discarded them.'

'Can't I wear gloves?'

'Did you bring any?'

'No.'

'Well,' Smeak said. 'Perhaps you will tomorrow. But I

still want rings removed.' His mouth turned up at the
sides for the briefest moment, but his eyes remained cold.
'Arthur comes in at eleven. That's when business picks
up. You can work things out between yourselves.'

'Where's the toilet?' she asked.

'The lavatory is upstairs next to the snug.'

Bailey pointed to the swing door. 'Through there and
—'

'No,' Smeak said. 'Don't ever go into the serving area.
Stay in the kitchen where nobody can see you. Do you
understand?'

She wasn't sure if she did understand, but thought he
probably didn't want her distracting customers from
spending their money. 'Then how do I ... you know ...
go?'

He opened the back door. 'Follow the path left, take
the first door on your left and you will see a staircase
directly in front of you. The lavatory is at the top on the
right.'

'Great,' Bailey said. 'Can't wait to start.'

'Not so fast, Miss Jacobs.' Smeak flipped the top page
of the clipboard over and handed it to her. 'This is the
contract and indemnity waiver you have to sign before
starting work at Cafe Luga.'

Bailey took it from him and squinted at the print. 'I can
hardly read it.'

'I'll give you a copy to take home this evening. Please
sign it, here.'

She signed and handed it back. 'I'm all yours.'

'Indeed,' Smeak said. 'Now let me introduce you to
the others.'

Bailey followed him back through the swing door.

'Ladies, this is Bailey. She's starting work here today

for a trial period.'

Yeah, she thought, as short a period as possible.

'She's a Special NT, so please keep a special eye on her.'

Special NT? Bailey wondered what he meant … Special New Trainee, perhaps?

'Karen's been here for three years. She's in charge if I'm not available.'

Bailey smiled and the taller of the two women returned a nod.

Smeak placed a hand on the shoulder of the younger girl and she grinned like captured prey. She had a naive face and short blonde hair styled like a boy. 'This is Christine. It's her first day as well. She's our new waitress.'

The prey giggled.

Bitch, Bailey thought. She's got to know, hasn't she?

'Continuing on …' The girls parted and Smeak stepped between them.

Bailey followed him into a hallway she recognised from the time she applied for Christine's job. They headed upstairs and when they reached the landing, Smeak turned right.

'This is the snug,' he said. 'Hang your jacket with the others. You can leave your rings here too. It's very secure. Only staff have access to this area.'

The room looked comfortable enough with a sofa and two chairs facing each other across a low table. At the far end was a sink, a fridge and a simple run of cupboards. Bailey removed her jacket and hung it next to a mauve fleece that smelled of oranges. She began pulling off her rings and tucking them into the inside pocket of her jacket.

'If you don't mind me asking,' Smeak said, hovering over her shoulder. 'Why do you wear so many rings?'

Surprised by his change in manner from abrupt boss to caring co-worker, she said, 'I just like them.'

'You realise, of course ...' He grunted. 'They're not a good accessory for your new profession.'

Profession? She wasn't sure a few weeks washing-up counted as a profession.

'Best not to wear them again, thank you. And if you decide to wear less makeup in future, that would be appreciated also.'

Bailey hesitated with the last ring, a mottled gold thing with simple blue markings. Not that one, she thought, pushing it into the pocket of her jeans.

'Now, please select an apron and make your way downstairs. Work awaits.'

Bailey chose the largest from a cluster of aprons, put it on and tied it at the front. 'Tell me,' she said. 'Am I being paid for the time it's taken you to explain all of this?'

Smeak snorted so loud his nose-hairs fluttered.

* * *

The sink was uncomfortably low. She'd decided not to wear her new boots, but her old pair still raised her a sufficient distance off the ground to make the sink awkward to reach. That hadn't been too much of a problem at first, but after twenty minutes of stooping to lift things from the basin, her back ached.

Karen and Christine—the evil sisters from front-of-house—kept her busy with a steady flow of plates, cups and cutlery. Neither of the girls volunteered conversation, electing instead to deposit dirty items and hurry out with the clean ones. Bailey supposed Christine had bad breath because a minty smell followed her everywhere, but she didn't risk getting close enough to find out.

Hot water scalded her hands and the temperature in the room rose each time she filled the sink. Sweat dripped from her face as she washed, rinsed, dried and repeated. Even though she had rolled up her sleeves and unfastened the top two buttons on her blouse, the heat still stifled her, making the silk cling to her body in patches.

A hesitant flow of air pushed through the slim gap in the window above the sink. She tried to force the window wider, but it held fast. Her view of the back yard was hampered by the frosted glass and all she could see through the gap was the edge of something wooden.

The morning lengthened and the noise through the swing door escalated. Muffled conversations increased and the chink of crockery and scrape of chairs intensified, all punctuated by the screech and grind of the coffee machine. The sounds competed with a backdrop of dreary music she couldn't identify and wouldn't be caught dead listening to.

As Bailey filled the basin again—making sure there were plenty of bubbles—the back door opened and a man walked in. He was shorter than her and older than her mum. His round face beamed and she noticed a couple of teeth missing.

'Hello there,' he said, wedging the door open.

She dried her hands and held one out. 'You must be Arthur?'

'Sure am. And you must be the new girl. Sorry, they didn't tell me your name.'

'Bailey.'

He took her hand and shook it, but seemed distracted

by something on her face. 'That's alarming,' he said.

'What is?'

'Your makeup. Nobody mention it?'

'No,' she said, turning around as the swing door opened.

'Morning, Arthur.' Karen placed a cup and saucer on the shelf. 'Good weekend?'

'Top weekend. Yourself?'

Bailey turned to the sink and checked her face in the back of a spoon. Although small and obscured, the reflection was sufficient to see her mascara had spread, giving the impression of a startled panda peering back at her. She splashed her face with water and it turned the bubbles black. Someone tapped her shoulder.

'I'm gonna take the readies out,' Arthur said.

'Readies?'

'Yeah,' he said. 'The clean stuff.'

Bailey watched him load a tray with clean plates and head to the swing door. 'What are you doing?' she asked.

'Taking this lot to the counter.'

'I thought we weren't allowed out there?'

He laughed. 'Let me guess, you're an NT right?'

'I'm a *Special* NT apparently,' she said.

His laughter faded as he pushed through the swing door. He returned a few minutes later with the tray covered in dirty crockery. 'Not Trusted.'

'What?' Bailey said.

'That's what it means. NT. Not Trusted.'

'So, if I'm a *Special* NT, that means I'm …'

Arthur nodded slowly. '*Specially* not trusted.'

She returned to the sink. Did everyone know what that meant and had they been laughing about it behind her back? She guessed they had.

'I see the window's getting fixed. Couple of guys doing it at the moment. Peter's been sleeping here in case someone breaks in.'

'Who?'

'Peter. Mr Smeak. Has he given you the tour?'

She shrugged.

Arthur flicked a switch on the wall and the room filled with music. 'Did he show you that?'

She shook her head and inspected speaker vents in the ceiling.

'You're a tall one, aren't you? Near six-foot, I reckon.'

'It's the boots,' Bailey said.

'Don't they give you gyp?'

'Gyp?'

'Yeah,' he said. 'Don't they make your feet sore?'

'Not so it matters.'

'I bet your back hurts though.'

'Yes,' she said. 'How did you guess?'

'Look at me, five foot six with shoes on. I'm the perfect height for this sink. Tall girl like you needs a taller sink. Stands to reason.'

'You're probably right.'

'Take them off.'

'What?'

'Take them boots off.' He opened a cupboard beneath the worktop and pulled out a pair of slippers. 'I wear these when my feet hurt. Give them a try.'

Bailey slipped her boots off and placed them by the back door. She took the slippers and sniffed them before putting them on. They were more comfortable than her boots and she was probably a couple of inches closer to the sink. 'Hey, thanks.'

'No problem. What about your hands?' From the same

cupboard appeared a pair of yellow gloves and he threw them to her. 'Come on,' he said. 'Let's get the dirties done, then you can take a break to sort your face out.'

'Sounds good to me,' Bailey said.

'Course it does. Stands to reason.'

Chapter Four

Arthur hummed as he worked. He was fast and light-footed and danced around Bailey when she got in the way. He had time for everyone, making Christine giggle and engaging Karen in conversation about the smallest things. Although some of his lustre faded when Smeak showed up, Arthur still shone. 'Hello, boss. All ship-shape here.'

Smeak nodded at Arthur, but addressed Bailey, 'I'd like a word please.'

'Sure,' Bailey said, flicking the worst of the wet from her gloves.

Smeak turned the music off and took her to one side. She stood before him with her yellow gloves, half-cleaned face, sticky shirt and old-man slippers—he seemed not to notice. 'There's a reporter outside,' he said. 'He wants to interview you about catching the so-called Bird Thief.'

Arthur turned his head from the sink.

'You're not obliged to speak with him, of course, but it would be excellent publicity for the cafe. And it would be good for your ... development, within the cafe.'

Bailey shrugged and looked across to Arthur who had his ear angled towards them.

Smeak noticed and moved sideways, breaking her line of sight. Then he leaned closer. 'Some people think you're something of a hero,' he whispered. 'And that's all very well.' He cleared his throat. 'Let them continue to think you're a thief-stopping vigilante and it will be good

197

for everyone. What do you say?'

Bailey stepped back, putting fresh air between them. 'Is he from the *Echo* or the *Herald*?'

'The *Farnham Echo*.'

Bailey recently had a bad experience of the *Echo* when they ran a story about an unsavoury episode her mother had at a local restaurant. They treated her terribly, twisting the truth and printing blatant lies. It was all still clear in her mind. She shook her head. 'They weren't very nice to my mum.'

'But this is—'

'No thank you, Mr Smeak. I don't wish to talk to him.'

'That's rather a shame,' Smeak said. 'Because doing so could make your time here significantly more pleasant.'

She could tell by his grimace that Arthur had over-heard Smeak.

'No,' she said again. 'Final answer.'

'Very well.' Smeak snorted and left, the heel of his shoes clipping the floor as he strode from the room.

'What was that about?' Arthur gaped, dribbling for details.

She switched the music back on and returned to the sink. Christine brought in a tray of dirties and Bailey waited for her to leave. Then she said, 'You know the window they're repairing?'

Arthur nodded.

'I was the one who broke it.'

He chuckled. 'How so?'

'I was trying to save a dog from being trampled. I bumped into a man and he went flying through the window. A complete accident, but it turned out he'd stolen something from the gallery up the road and was trying to make a getaway.'

'So,' Arthur said, looking delighted with the tale. 'Peter gave you a job to thank you?'

'No. He gave me a job so I can pay off the cost of the window.'

'That's a very big window.' Some of the fun had left his voice. 'And it's going to take a long time to pay off.'

'I know,' she said. 'Do you think I could take that break now?'

Arthur nodded. 'I'll call you if I need you.'

'Thanks.' Bailey pushed hair from her face with the back of her arm. 'I suppose I must look a bit of a state.' She headed to the side door and stepped outside.

Having followed the path along the side of the building to a glass door, she was about to go in when the latch on the side gate lifted. Curious as to who it might be, she waited for them to appear and moments later, a man stepped through, his face hidden by a camera that clicked repeatedly as he spoke.

'Bailey.' Click. Click. Click. 'Can I have a word?' Click. 'We want to know about your crime-stopping exploits?'

She hesitated, wondering who …

Click. Click. 'How did you know he was the Bird Thief?'

A badge hanging from his neck showed a face she didn't recognise beneath the words *Farnham Echo*.

Bailey turned to the side door, losing one of Arthur's slippers as she pivoted.

'Did you have to use a window to stop him, Bailey?' Click. Click. Click. 'Seems a bit extreme.' Click. 'Do you have anything to tell our readers?'

She wanted to pick up the slipper, but he had his

camera in her face and forced her against the door.

Click. Click. Click. 'Tell us what happened.'

The name on his badge was *Lawrence Williams*—the dickhead journalist who had written the libellous article about her mother.

That was it. She exploded.

Spinning like a whirling dervish, she knocked his camera to the ground and yelled, 'Yes, I've got something to say.' He reached for the camera and she kicked it away. 'You're disgusting. The things you do. Harassing people. Making up stories.' She advanced on him, poking his shoulder with every screeching syllable. 'You're a nasty man and you should be ashamed.' Catching her breath, she wiped spittle from her mouth with the back of a yellow glove. 'Now, piss off.' When he didn't, she retreated to the side door and went inside, standing with her back to it, panting furiously.

Behind her, the reporter called her name, tapping the glass like a persistent pigeon. In front of her, looking tall and menacing with his arms folded, Smeak stared down the length of the hall, a grim expression etched upon his face.

She ran upstairs in tears.

* * *

The afternoon dragged by like a lingering chore on a hot day. After cleaning her face and fixing her hair, Bailey swallowed her pride, found Smeak in his office and apologised. He sat in his chair, fingers steepled beneath his chin and flinty eyes watching as she told him about the story the *Farnham Echo* ran on her mother. When she'd finished explaining, he told her that he didn't condone the way she reacted, but he understood why she had done so. Then he had reached for a pad, wrote something down and handed it to her.

'Are you okay?' Arthur fussed as she stepped through the side door into the kitchen. 'I couldn't believe it, I mean, I heard this commotion and then ... are you all right?'

Although she wasn't feeling conversational, she eventually gave in to Arthur's incessant pestering and told him what happened.

'You got a written warning on your first day? I've been working here six years and he's only issued one written warning in that time.' He leaner closer and whispered. 'And *that* young lad came to a very sticky end.'

But she didn't care and she told him so. And conversation dried up after that.

Arthur left at two and although Karen and Christine remained aloof for the rest of the afternoon, Bailey felt they did so with a little more consideration. The dirties didn't clatter so much when they set them down and Christine even thanked her before exiting in giggles with a tray full of readies.

Time dragged and when five o'clock eventually arrived and the cafe closed, she grabbed her jacket and left feeling exhausted. The walk home took longer than she had ever known it to. Her head hurt, her back ached and her legs protested as she climbed the hill to the top of the park.

Her mother must have been watching through the kitchen window because the front door opened as soon as the house came into view. 'Well,' she said, her face a field of smiles. 'How was it?'

Bailey almost fell inside the door and dropped onto the stairs. 'Exhausting. You've got no idea. I can honestly say that's the hardest job I've ever had.'

Her mother laughed. 'My poor baby. I've done moussaka for tea, your favourite.'

'I need to take a bath.'

'That's fine. There's plenty of hot water and I'll keep your food warm.'

Bailey ran a bath and undressed. She climbed in and the hot water claimed her, relaxing her muscles and easing away her stress. She woke sometime later to a knock at the door.

'Are you okay in there?'

The water had chilled. 'Yeah.'

'Are you ready to eat?'

Muscles protested as she stood. 'Be right down.'

A few minutes later, Bailey sat at the dining table wearing pyjamas while her mother sat opposite and watched her eat. 'Where's Tim?' Bailey asked between bites.

'At Martin's.'

She loaded up another mouthful, chewed and swallowed. 'That was a tough day, Mum.'

'I'm sure.'

'Arthur's nice. I might introduce you.'

'Okay.'

'The boss is a dick, but I suppose all bosses are.'

'Hmm.'

'He gave me a written warning.'

Her mother's mouth fell open.

'Yeah, I know, what a knob. That dickhead journalist Lawrence whatsisname from the *Echo* came round looking for a story. He made me cry, Mum. I actually ran upstairs in tears and Mr Smeak—he's got a massive nose —gave me a written warning. Can you believe it? Just for refusing to talk to the journalist.' Bailey waved an empty fork between them. 'Oh, that reminds me, why did you have to tell Mike about Dad?'

Her mother closed her mouth and sat up.

Last Friday, Bailey had met her mother's boyfriend of six weeks. The day after their meeting, the boyfriend ended the relationship. Apparently, his being gay had nothing to do with it.

'I've been thinking about it,' Bailey said, 'and I just don't understand why you told Mike about Dad. I mean, why?'

'I had to.'

Bailey chewed and swallowed. 'But why?'

'It's not that easy to—'

'Whether he's alive or dead, why bring Dad into the conversation at all?'

Behind cupped hands, her mother said, 'Because I like to do things properly.'

'What does that mean?'

Her mother took a deep breath and exhaled. It was almost as long as the breath she'd let go when Grandad died. 'Because your father and I are still married.'

Bailey stopped, fork poised.

'I'm afraid it's true,' her mother said. 'We never got divorced. But that aside, tell me more about this written warning.'

Chapter Five

Bailey woke early on Tuesday morning and despite an ache in her shoulders, she felt strangely relaxed and refreshed. The intermittently reliable mobile phone her brother had donated to her, suggested the time was quarter past seven. Having gone to bed just after nine the previous evening, that meant she'd slept uninterrupted for ten hours—something she couldn't remember ever having done before.

A peaceful night's sleep: unspoiled by restless thoughts and intrusive dreams. She settled back to enjoy the new-found benefits of waking early.

Things with her parents were developing. *Parents*— she couldn't remember the last time she'd used that term. But the fact was, Dad wasn't dead and Mum was still married to him. Why her mother hadn't filed for divorce was a mystery—she sure had good enough reason to do so. They'd been separated for fourteen years because her father's temper was quicker than he was. Maybe she had no intention of remarrying? Or, Bailey grinned at the thought, maybe she still loved him.

The pieces began to fit together.

Her mother was a good-looking woman who'd had a succession of suitors in recent years. But none of them ever lasted. In fact, at six weeks, Mike was the longest boyfriend she'd had. Too bad he turned out to be bisexual.

And *that* had to be it. Sex. It all came down to sex. The boyfriends wanted it, but her mother didn't. Instead, she was probably waiting for the right man and the right commitment. It all made perfect sense.

So, Bailey assumed, when the subject eventually came up, she probably thought they deserved an explanation, and told them about her current husband. For some men that wouldn't have been a problem, but for her mother, it must have been a line she wouldn't cross.

Poor woman, she thought. No sex for fourteen years.

* * *

Early morning sunshine blazed across Farnham's rooftops, creating a collective simmer of radiant reds and burnt ambers. Bailey didn't think she'd ever seen it look so beautiful.

She'd dressed casually that morning for her second day at work, and made good progress through the park wearing comfortable trainers and baggy jeans. Keeping things casual included tying her hair back and limiting her makeup to eyeliner and lipstick. It felt strange leaving the house wearing such little makeup, but stranger still not to be wearing her full accompaniment of rings. Bailey had left all but the blue-dotted gold ring at home, slipping it onto her little finger and turning it round to hide the stones.

In a large field surrounded by trees, a group of people exercised. A dozen women followed a man as he trotted this way and that, barking orders that resulted in them pulling shapes and throwing themselves to the ground. Some were having more success than others.

Bailey hated exercise—even at school she was first with a sick note or an excuse to avoid it. One time in winter, they'd been forced to play hockey on a frozen pitch with iced-over puddles and a rock hard ground. She'd stood like a lemon on the sideline wearing a short skirt and long socks as a vicious wind tested her resolve. A girl called Sharon twisted an ankle on a hard piece of sod which brought an end to the lesson—and that was the last sporting activity Bailey had ever taken part in.

The exercise man broke off from the group and ran towards her, flagging her to stop. Dressed in lycra bottoms and a rugby shirt that hugged his chest, he was hardly out of breath when he reached her, despite having run half way across the field.

'Hi,' he said, falling into step beside her.

He seemed familiar, but she couldn't place him.

'How are you doing?'

He had a nice smile.

'Last time I saw you,' he said. 'You were covered in mud.'

She liked the way he pushed back his wavy blond hair. He had a strong jaw and a Roman nose.

'That guy was laying into you. Remember?'

Bailey did remember. During her investigation into the disappearance of local dogs a few weeks ago, a man had assaulted her. At the time she was sure he wanted to kill her and it was only with the help of a stranger—a handsome stranger as she recalled—that she survived. She hadn't realised who that stranger was until now.

'Oh yeah,' she said.

'I wasn't certain it was you.' He pulled back his sleeves. 'When I saw you from over there, I couldn't be sure because you look so,' he mouthed a few words before selecting one. 'Different.'

Different good or different bad? She wanted to know. 'How so?'

'You look kind of ... healthy.'

Bailey shrugged. 'Thanks, I suppose.'

'Do you want to get some breakfast, or a coffee?'

She looked over his shoulder at the group of women who now stood watching them. 'I think you need to get back to your ladies.'

'We've almost finished.' He waved to them and shouted, 'One minute of star-jumps.'

Bailey heard the women groan.

'There's a cafe in the golf club over there,' he said.

'I don't think so.'

'Come on, what's the worst that can happen?'

The worst? Probably a pissed off Smeak, she thought, who would make it his job to make her day a living nightmare. 'Sorry, I've really got to go.' Careful not to break into a trot, she picked up her pace and left him behind.

Bailey didn't know his name, but he seemed nice. Too sporty for her of course, but nice enough. She had a rule about dating men—no policemen, sporty types or computer nerds. Although, she thought as she recalled his thick golden curls, she was prone to breaking the odd rule.

Once out of the park she picked up the road into town, passing a queue of cars along Castle Street. Turning into a side alley, she followed a lane all the way to Lamb Yard.

The pedestrian shopping area was alive with people scurrying around and moving with purpose. Shutters despatched as shops opened and signs and stock went on display. Everyone seemed in good spirits.

On the bench near the coffee house, she spotted Jack and Duncan, the homeless man and his dog she'd recently befriended. She waved as she approached and the dog stood to greet her with a wagging tail.

'Hey, love the new look,' Jack said. 'And what a great morning.'

She heard a clock chime and wondered why it felt important.

'The warm weather makes sleeping outside almost enjoyable.'

Bailey plugged her hands into her jeans and waited until his eyes settled on hers. 'Thank you,' she said.

'What for?'

'For saying what you said to the police.'

'No problem. I only told the truth. Anyway, from where I was standing, you were great. You saved the dog and stopped the thief all in one go.'

She nodded towards the coffee shop and the new window gleaming in the sun. 'But I took out the window.'

'A little collateral damage. Who cares?'

She smiled. 'I started work there yesterday.'

'I know,' he said. 'I saw you. How's it going with Beaky?'

She cut her laugh short when she noticed Smeak looming in the doorway holding a clipboard. 'Sorry, better go. Thanks again.'

Smeak tapped his watch as she walked passed him towards the side entrance.

* * *

The drab morning brightened when Arthur arrived at eleven with a wide grin and a tall tale about his journey to work. 'Stands to reason,' he said, 'if you're young enough to wear orange, you don't need a seat more than I do.'

Until his arrival, the kitchen had been filled with a sombre atmosphere that did its best to sap her strength and her willingness to communicate. Maintaining parity between the dirties and the readies, Bailey had so far avoided any serious conversation with her colleagues. Smeak hadn't done more than grunt and Karen and Christine kept their distance.

'What's her problem?' she asked Arthur when Christine rushed out of the kitchen for the umpteenth time, the swing door flapping in her wake.

Arthur chuckled as he stacked a tray with clean cups. 'I think they're afraid of you.'

'Of me?'

'Stands to reason,' he said. 'Yesterday you turned up in black, all six feet of you.'

'Five foot eight.'

'Not in the boots you had on.'

Five foot ten at best, she thought.

'You had this menacing war-face.'

'What?'

'You didn't see it. Black stuff smeared all over like a …' He sucked air through the gap in his teeth. 'Like an Amazonian warrior.'

'A what?'

'You screamed like a demon at that newspaper guy, and you told me the new window is down to you pushing a fella through the old one,' he said. 'What would you think of you if you were them?'

She could see his point. Maybe she hadn't made such a good first impression. 'But I'm not *scary*, am I?'

'Huh. Not for me to say.' Arthur turned and left. She heard the clutter of cups and voices and a few moments later he returned with a tray of dirties and placed it on the shelf. 'You could try talking to them.'

'Why?'

'Why not?'

'They're not talking to *me*,' Bailey said.

'Don't mean you can't talk to them. Does it? Stands to reason, one of you've gotta make the first move.'

It did stand to reason, Bailey thought. And just after lunch when she saw Christine hurry past the open kitchen door, Bailey pushed aside her dislike of the girl and followed her into the yard.

She found Christine sitting on a bench facing a leafless bush that did its best to cover a grey fence. The girl turned around as Bailey approached.

'Hi,' Bailey said as cheerfully as she could.

Christine giggled and looked away.

Bailey sat beside her, but didn't speak immediately. She smelled mint and saw the girl playing with something in her hands. A bird settled in the bush and they watched it in silence until Bailey asked, 'How do you like it here?'

Christine shrugged.

Bailey waited to see if she had anything to add and when it was obvious she didn't, she said, 'Arthur's nice.'

'I suppose.'

The sound of crunching disturbed the quiet that followed and Bailey wondered what the girl was chewing that could be so noisy. She persevered. 'Karen seems okay.'

'Yes, she is.'

Bailey thought she saw Arthur peering through the gap in the kitchen window. 'The boss is a bit …'

Christine's mouth puckered and she turned sheepishly until their eyes met. 'Difficult?'

Bailey laughed. 'I was going to say lanky.'

Christine held out a packet of extra strong mints. 'Want one?'

'No,' Bailey said. 'But Thanks.'

'Um,' Christine said, focussing on the bird again. 'I heard you wanted my job.'

'Yeah, I did.'

'Sorry.' Christine played with her mints. 'I only found out this morning.'

Maybe she had misjudged the girl? She seemed nice enough, perhaps a little sweet and simple, but not the bitch she'd initially taken her for. 'I don't want it now though,' Bailey said. 'I'd rather be in the back with Arthur than out front with Smeak.'

'Which one?'

'Huh?'

'Which Smeak? Him or her?'

'There's more than one of them?'

Christine's smile lit her face and Bailey liked her a little bit more. 'Mrs Smeak works here as well. Didn't you know?'

Bailey shook her head.

'Thursdays and Saturdays. There's a roster upstairs.'

Who the hell would marry Smeak? 'What's she like?'

'Karen doesn't like her,' Christine said. 'She didn't say as much but I can tell.'

'I thought he was, you know … I mean, he's so …'

'Odd?'

'Yeah,' Bailey said. 'Creepy.'

'Creepy? You should've seen some of the customers we had yesterday. Karen said she gets more odds than evens in here. Just like my last place, I suppose. There's always someone to watch out for.' Before Bailey could ask what she meant, Christine continued. 'Um, did you really push a man through the window?'

'Yeah.' Bailey grinned. 'But he wasn't a very nice

211

man.'

'And that commotion with the newspaper reporter?'

'He wasn't a very nice man either.'

Christine finished her mint with a series of crunches and then asked, 'Did you get your slipper back?'

'What?'

'You lost your slipper, didn't you? At least that's what it says.'

Bailey jolted. 'What *what* says?'

Christine's pale face grew paler. 'The, um, newspaper article,' she said, pointing over her shoulder to the coffee shop. 'Haven't you seen it?'

* * *

Bailey sat forward on the sofa, the newspaper trembling in her hands as she read the headline on page five.

Cinderella Heroine Spits Fire

Three photos accompanied the article and she was in two of them, looking a complete write-off. Her face was a state, her hair tangled and you could clearly see damp patches where her blouse clung to her body.

But it was the combination of yellow gloves and a feral snarl that made her appear positively certifiable.

She read the first paragraph again.

Do-gooder, Bailey Jacobs unleashed a tirade of abuse as our intrepid reporter attempted to interview her today. Bailey—a local heroine since capturing petty thief, Danny Douglas—attacked our reporter physically and verbally in a manner unbecoming any young lady.

She'd been alone in the snug for ten minutes and although Smeak was nowhere to be seen, she guessed he wasn't too far away.

Do-gooder?

'Are you okay?' Christine moused her way into the room and closed the door behind her.

Bailey snapped, 'Leave it open.'

'Would you like some water?' Christine scuttled to the sink, filled a glass with water and held it out. 'It'll help with the, um, shock.'

Bailey drank until the glass was empty, then handed it back and stabbed the paper with her finger. 'How could they?'

Christine edged closer. 'See the picture in the bottom right-hand corner? I'm in that one.'

Bailey growled. 'Do-gooder? That's so not me.' She pulled in a breath to scream, but released it as a moan. 'It makes me so mad?'

'What's wrong with being a do-gooder?'

'It doesn't feel right, I mean, it's just not *me*.'

From downstairs, Smeak barked Bailey's name and Christine scurried out of the room like a frightened hamster. As her quick, light footsteps faded, they were replaced by slower, heavier ones and moments later, Smeak emerged carrying a newspaper.

'With me, Jacobs,' he said.

Bailey rose unsteadily and followed him across the hall to his office. She could see his pink ears twitching from behind and could tell he wasn't happy.

* * *

Arthur kept his own company for the rest of the day.

When Bailey joined him in the kitchen following Smeak's curt lecture, he had changed. It was obvious straight away that something was wrong: no quips, no jests, even his posture was flat.

And Christine—who Bailey had started to warm to—distanced herself at every opportunity, scampering in and out faster than she had done previously. Bailey didn't know how or why Christine's attitude had changed so quickly, but she decided it was her loss. They could have been friends.

Thoughts of Smeak plagued her. Being so close to him in that tiny office made her skin crawl. His beady-eyes had scrutinised her every move, and his sneering mouth spat saliva as he delivered his lecture. She cringed.

It's your final chance, Jacobs. He'd repeated over and over. *Your absolute final chance.*

At two o'clock, Arthur left without a word and Bailey switched to automatic. The afternoon dragged, but eventually the flow of dirties eased and noise through the swing door faded. When the clock reached five, she peeled off her gloves and hurried upstairs to the snug.

The door to Smeak's office was closed, but she could hear him talking to someone. She grabbed her jacket from the peg and slipped it on, then headed downstairs. Outside, she edged to the gate, poked her head through and looked around. When she was sure the coast was clear, she stepped out and headed home across the cobbled courtyard.

As she passed the art gallery near the top of the lane, someone tapped her on the shoulder causing her to jump.

'Miss Jacobs.'

Her instinct was to run, but indecision and curiosity made her stop and turn. A small man stood before her.

Slim, with black hair greased back over a peanut-shaped head, he carried a folded newspaper.

'I've not had the opportunity to thank you for your assistance.'

She didn't recognise him. 'Sorry, what?'

'The value of the picture may have been insignificant,' the man said, gesturing with his arms as he spoke. 'But the value of your actions was insurmountable. The courage and fortitude you showed in preventing the criminal's escape …' He drew breath. 'Was magnificent to say the least.'

And then it dawned on her that he was the man from the art gallery whose painting she'd recovered when pushing the thief through the coffee shop window.

He waved the newspaper. 'Not until I saw this reprehensible attack on your person, did I realise how to locate you.' He gave a long, meaningful bow and then rose with a smile. 'Were I wearing a hat, I would salute you with it now.'

He had a strange way of speaking that Bailey liked. 'No problem,' she said, and turned to be on her way.

'Ah, Miss Jacobs, one further moment if I may.'

She was beginning to feel a little less tolerant. It had been a long day, she'd been chewed up by Smeak and ostracised by her colleagues. All she wanted to do was go home, have a bath and soak away her troubles.

'If there is ever anything that you need, anything at all, just say the word and Clemence will be there.'

'Who's Clemence?'

'It is I. And I am at your service'

'Sorry,' she said. 'I'm exhausted and I just want to go home.' When his face dropped she added, 'But thank you. That's very kind of you.'

'Think nothing of it, my friend.'

Friend, she thought as she continued on, at least someone thinks so. But a reward would have been nicer.

Bailey reached the top of the courtyard and passed through an opening onto the road which she followed towards the park.

'Psst.'

She slowed and looked around, but couldn't see anybody near her.

'Over here.'

The voice seemed to have come from behind one of the trees on the other side of the road. As she edged towards it, the tree giggled. 'What the hell?'

'Shhh.' Christine's excited face appeared from behind the trunk and she ushered Bailey closer. 'Quick.'

Christine's appearance was surprising and unexpected. After her standoffishness that afternoon, Bailey assumed she wanted nothing more to do with her—and yet here she was, instigating a clandestine meeting beneath a tree. 'What's going on?' she asked.

'Are you being followed?'

Bailey turned around to check. 'I don't think so. Why?'

'Um, Mr Smeak,' Christine said. 'We've got to watch out for him.'

'Again, why?'

'He told us to stay clear of you.'

Bailey stepped closer. 'What?'

'Yeah, the paper said you're a do-gooder but Smeak said you're a bad influence.' Christine giggled. 'Arthur thinks it's because Smeak thinks you'll turn us all to the dark side.'

'Arthur as well?'

'Yes, and Karen. Mr Smeak told all of us not to associate with you.'

Bailey fumed. 'Where does that bloke get off?'

Christine shrugged and handed her a small pink box. 'Here,' she said. 'For you.'

Bailey prised open the lid to see a perfect slice of cake with an extra flange of icing spooned across the top. Her stomach cheered.

'A peace offering. I hope you like carrot cake.'

'Love it,' Bailey said, dipping her finger into the icing.

Christine pulled a packet of mints from her pocket and pushed one into her mouth. 'What did you do to upset him?'

'Smeak?' Bailey closed the lid of the box and licked her finger clean. 'You mean, aside from pushing someone through his window?'

Bailey knew exactly why Smeak hated her. Last week she had suspected him of being the Bird Thief and tried to goad him into a confession. But he'd turned on her sharply. Too sharply, she'd thought, for an innocent man. Did Smeak really have something to hide and was that the reason he reacted so harshly towards her? The only thing she was sure of was that she'd make it her job to find out.

'Bailey?'

'What?'

Christine seemed worried. 'Are you all right?'

Bailey felt a spot of rain wet her cheek and looked up. The clouds had thickened over Farnham. 'Where are you heading?' she asked.

'Adams Road, bottom of the park.'

'Come on,' Bailey said. 'I'll tell you all about it as we go.'

While they walked, she told Christine about her

amateur investigations, solving the case of the disappearing dogs and her role in stopping the Bird Thief. She didn't mention her run-ins with the police, getting beaten up twice, or the seriously dark suspicions she had of Smeak.

By the time they reached the edge of Farnham Park, the spots of rain had turned to a drizzle and they sheltered beneath the reach of an oak tree.

'How old are you?' Bailey asked.

'Seventeen.'

'Me too. Did we go to the same school?'

'Don't think so. I went to a girl's school in Godalming.'

'Oh,' Bailey said. 'That explains it.'

Christine blushed. 'Explains what?'

'Nothing really. Just your good manners, courteous nature and, you know ...' Lesbian hair, she thought.

Christine nodded. 'Do you want to go out tomorrow night?'

Things were moving quickly—strangers in the morning, best friends at night. She'd seen an unsavoury documentary about picking up strangers in a park in London, and although she was pretty sure Christine wasn't that sort, she thought now was an appropriate moment to test her theory. 'Are you a vagitarian?'

Christine spluttered. 'A what?'

'You know, do you prefer women?'

'Sexually?'

'Yeah.'

'Um, no.'

'Sorry. I assumed because of your hair ...'

'What's wrong with my hair?'

'It's okay. It's just a bit ... manly.' Bailey grinned at

Christine's obvious discomfort. 'But to answer your question, no, I can't go out. I've got a lot on at the moment.' And then she added, 'It's not because you're not a lesbian. I like lesbians. Not in that way of course, but … shit. You know what I mean.'

'I think so,' Christine giggled. 'But I'm not entirely sure. Look, can I go now? Mum will be expecting me.'

Bailey watched her hurry past a row of tiny cottages and disappear around a corner.

That, she thought, could have gone better.

She headed home through the park, using the trees as cover and the wing of her jacket to shield the cake box from the rain.

Home seemed so far away. Farnham park was only a mile long, but the trek was mostly uphill and some days she found it a bit of a slog. All this walking was fine, but it was too much like exercise, and it always took so long to get anywhere. But what were her options? She couldn't use Timothy's bicycle, since a gang of kids stole it from her. Perhaps she could buy a pair of roller-blades? Or learn to drive? But Mike was out of the picture for good and her chances of getting a cheap car had disappeared with him. Maybe her mum's next boyfriend would stick around long enough for her to wangle a car out of him? And some lessons.

By the time she reached the top of the park and stepped into a narrow alley lined with fence panels taller than herself, the rain had stopped, but she was already wet through. The evening air darkened as the alley walls closed in and she hurried to the end where she turned right and followed the pavement home.

She wasn't far from her house when a hooded figure lurking alongside a neighbour's property caught her eye.

She stopped and watched the suspicious figure begin to climb the Lancaster's garden fence.

Her heart raced.

Even from two-hundred feet away and with dusk descending, she could tell it was her ex-boyfriend Paul.

If he turned around now, he would be sure to see her.

She ran, covering the distance to her house at a sprint. When she reached the door, she fumbled the key into the lock, barged inside and stood with her back to the glass. What the hell was he doing? Her chest heaved. Was Timothy right about him being a thief?

Bailey steadied her breathing before carrying the crumpled cake box into the kitchen. There she found her mother sitting at the table with a copy of the *Farnham Echo*. She frowned as she pointed to the article on page five and the picture of a scary-looking girl reaching for the camera with yellow rubber gloves.

Chapter Six

Bubbles slid from her skin as she rose from the bath and reached for a towel. The conversation with her mother had escalated into an argument that ended in Bailey storming upstairs amidst a furious barrage of abuse. She would have soaked for longer, but hunger drove her, and now it steered her towards the kitchen.

Wrapped in towels, she tiptoed downstairs, pausing at the bottom where the TV flickered through the glass lounge door.

She found the oven turned to low and the remains of a pie inside. She removed it with a towel and placed it on a tray alongside the cake box and a spoon. Then she headed back upstairs, her stomach voicing approval as she went.

At her desk, she ate with one hand and leafed through her pad with the other. She'd solved the case of the disappearing dogs and wrapped up the case of the red feather thief. The only case that remained open was the resurrected father.

Since starting work, Bailey had hardly spared a thought for her dad. She pulled his picture towards her now and grazed on her memories.

She hadn't seen him since she was three and her recollections were limited to colouring in her mother's stories of Christmases and birthdays. But recently, her dreams had yielded other details.

One repeated dream was of her father struggling across a muddy field with Timothy bundled in his arms, while

Bailey and her mother watched from the car. There were tears and screams and the definite presence of fear.

Another dream had her locked in a dark place she didn't recognise. A confined and suffocating space with a dull strip of light on the floor that she couldn't reach. It panicked her to be there and the terror often woke her.

Bailey pushed the pie dish aside and pulled her brother's laptop towards her. She lifted the lid, opened a browser and typed *Connor Kelly*. She was about to scroll through the results when a blue light flashed across Kurt Cobain's face on the wall. Holding tight to her towels, she walked across the landing and stood on tiptoe to peer through the dormer window at the front of the house.

A police car blocked the road, its lights flashing across a crowd of people who had amassed outside the Lancaster's house. A second police car pulled to a stop and Constable Wendy Mundy climbed out.

Although still a copper, Bailey liked Wendy Mundy. They hadn't spoken much but she seemed a kind, reasonable person—unlike that dickhead, Tierney, who hated her guts. She looked for him in the crowd and when she didn't spot him, she decided it was safe for her to take a closer look.

Dressed in jumper, jeans and trainers, she stepped through the front door a few minutes later and headed for the crowd.

There were faces she knew with names she didn't. There were hysterical voices and angry ones. A man pushed past her, elbowing his way through the bodies. Bailey was about to follow when someone caught her arm and pulled her back.

'Not so fast.'

Bailey was shocked to see the sleeve of a uniform, but

pleased to see it belonged to Wendy Mundy. The constable led her away from the throng while Bailey looked around for her police colleagues.

'If you're looking for Tierney …' Constable Mundy pointed to the crowd. 'He's got his hands full with that lot.'

Bailey felt her heart settle and turned to the policewoman who was bathed in the pulsing blue light.

'I don't know what's going on between you two,' Mundy said, 'but you'll do well to stay away from him. There's only a short list of people he doesn't like, but you seem to be at the top.'

Bailey knew that already, but thanked her anyway.

'Here.' The policewoman handed her a card. 'That's got my mobile number on it. If ever you need me, for anything, please call.' She stiffened. 'Now, I'm not going to go to the bother of asking if you were involved in the goings on here tonight, but do you have any information about what happened?'

'What did happen?'

'Burglary.'

She thought of Paul climbing the fence, looking every bit a burglar. 'What was taken?'

Mundy's eyes fixed on her's. 'A painting.'

'Another one? What a coincidence.'

The playful blue light contrasted the serious look on the policewoman's face as she drew closer. 'Now,' she said. 'With that in mind, let me ask you again. Do you know anything about what happened here tonight?'

Bailey thought she did. And she told her.

* * *

Sitting at her desk, one leg bouncing to a beat playing in her head, Bailey opened the pad to a new page and wrote, *The Case of Another Painting Theft*. Beneath it, she made a list.

CLUES
- *Paul ... outside the Lancaster's house.*
- *Painting stolen ... how related to other painting thefts?*

She created another list further down the page.

ACTIONS
- *Talk to the Lancasters.*

As she considered how a professional investigator might tackle the case, a cold realisation hit her. No matter which way she looked at it, she would have to talk to *him*.

Biting her lip and with her inner-self screaming *no*, she added another item to the list of actions.

- *Talk to Paul.*

It wasn't that she *wanted* to speak with Paul—she *needed* to. And whether or not he was involved in the burglary, it was inevitable she would talk to him at some stage. She sighed. But not tonight.

She reached for the old frame with her dad's photo, kissed the loose glass and took it with her to bed. Tucking it beneath the edge of her pillow, she switched off the bedside lamp and settled down to sleep, trying not to think about Paul and the bad dreams that waited for her.

* * *

Sausages. And bacon.

Bailey wiped crusted tears from her eyes and took a moment to savour the smells seeping through her bedroom door. She stretched and yawned, excited at having a day off work and another crime to investigate.

The bad dreams hadn't found her last night. But thoughts of her dad, Paul and the burglary, all scrapped for her attention.

When she switched the bedside lamp on, something on the floor caught her eye. The photo frame with her dad's picture had fallen and lay broken on the carpet. She eased herself out of bed, picked up the pieces and carried them to the desk, making a mental note to repair it later.

Dressed in an over-sized black t-shirt and thick blue socks pulled up to her knees, she descended the stairs to the kitchen and sat at the table.

'Here,' her mother said, setting a glass of Coke in front of her before resuming her place at the cooker.

'Thanks, Mum.'

'Got anything nice planned for the day?'

Bailey finished half the glass and then said, 'This and that, you know. It's just great to finally have a day off.'

'Terrible thing about the Lancasters.' Her mother forked bacon from a pan. 'Some people have the worst luck.'

Bailey eyed the bacon expectantly.

'You never think it will happen so close to home, do you? That could easily have been us you know.'

A car horn sounded in front of the house.

Her mother set down a plate of fried breakfast and washed her hands. 'That's my taxi,' she said.

Bailey looked up from the plate, her mouth half-filled with sausage. 'Where are you going?'

'Here and there, you know.'

Bailey manoeuvred an egg onto a piece of fried-bread and cut into it, conscious that her mother was still buzzing around. She attacked a strip of bacon and added beans to the fork. Somewhere around the mushrooms, the buzzing stopped and she heard the front door snap shut. She finished eating to the sound of cutlery scraping china and then licked the plate clean.

She was about to refill her glass when a boisterous knock at the front door made her jump. Her mother had obviously forgotten something and was in a hurry to get it back, but still, that was no excuse for knocking in such a rude manner.

Bailey dragged herself to the door, pulled it open and froze when she saw Paul standing there.

'Hello, Bailey.'

She slammed the door and stood with her back to it.

'I can still see you.' The letterbox squeaked open. 'I just want to talk.'

'Go away,' she screamed as she ran to the lounge and folded into an arm chair.

Had he been watching the house? Out there waiting for her mother to leave? He looked so different, so angry. Her hands shook and she cursed herself for it. Why was she so afraid of him? And why was she acting like a helpless victim?

The veins in her forehead throbbed.

When was that bastard going to leave her alone? As if breaking her heart wasn't enough. Now he wanted to torment her.

A noise in the garden startled her and she looked up to see Paul peering through the window. She ran to the patio door, twisted the handle and pulled it open with a whoosh.

'What the hell are you doing?'

'Don't be mad.'

'Get out of my garden.'

'Bailey, listen.'

She stepped outside, grabbed a garden hoe and advanced across the patio.

'Please,' he said, parrying the sharp end.

'Piss off.'

'Please.' He grabbed the handle and pulled it from her. 'I just want to talk.'

Bailey spotted a rake. If she was quick—

'Don't.' Paul must have seen it too because he stepped between her and the weapon. 'Why did you grass me up to the police?'

She hesitated.

'I know it was you.'

How could he possibly know that? 'Who told you?'

'Don't play games, Bailey. Not now.' He threw the hoe down. 'After all we've been through, why did you do it?'

'Because I saw you,' she spat.

'What?'

'I saw you outside the neighbour's house just before the burglary.'

'I was waiting for *you*. I—'

'You were climbing over their fence.'

He moved towards her. 'I wasn't. I would never—'

'But that's not true, is it? You're a thief. And a bad one at that.' The wind chilled her knees and she was conscious of wearing so few clothes. 'I know you robbed the off-licence last year.'

'I told you I never—'

'But you did. The police were right. I know how much

227

you took home each week, and it wasn't enough to buy all those cigarettes and alcohol.'

'Eddie gave me—'

'Stop lying.'

Paul raised his hands and took a breath. 'Okay, I did it, I admit it. But I've changed, you've got to believe me. I've been promoted, I'm working in the freezer department now. No more plucking chickens for me.' His face showed the first crack of a smile and his eyes twinkled. 'People still talk about that day. After you left, they were picking your phone out of that grinder for ages.'

Bailey recalled the event. They'd argued, he'd slapped her and the phone flew from her hand into the machine. 'It was your fault,' she said.

'How come? You weren't supposed to have a phone in there in the first place. I got a warning because of that.'

'Yeah, and I got sacked,' she said.

'Look, I'm sorry. I really am. But you've got to believe me, I had nothing to do with the burglary last night. I was waiting for you, I heard a commotion and tried to look over the fence to see what was going on.'

She wondered if he was telling the truth. 'So?'

'What?'

'What did you see?'

'Nothing. The fence was too high for me to climb. But I heard glass smash,' he said. 'And a woman scream.'

'What time was that?'

'Half an hour before the cops came.'

He seemed sincere enough, she thought, but he was a very good liar. 'So why *are* you here? I mean, if you weren't involved in the burglary then why were you hanging around in the first place?'

He closed the space between them and had time to touch her arm before she pulled away. 'I want you back.'

Bailey felt her legs weaken.

'I want you back and I want us to have another baby.'

She wiped away the crown of a tear. 'We didn't have the first one.'

His expression changed but he didn't break eye contact. 'I know, that's why—'

'No,' she said flatly.

'But I'm earning good money now. I've got a car. A career.'

'No.' She sucked in a breath and stood tall. 'We're finished. Get over it and get out.'

'Can't you just forgive me?'

Anger flashed inside her. 'No,' she said again. 'You made me lose that baby. I was going to have it because I loved you.' Her chest heaved with rasping breaths. 'But you ruined everything.' A moment of quiet passed between them as she wiped her eyes, then she straightened and said, 'Now get the fuck out.'

She marched him through the house, opened the front door and pushed him through. Before he had a chance to turn and say any more, she slammed the door and ran upstairs, her face creased with pain.

Why did he have to mention the baby?

Chapter Seven

Bailey didn't know what time she woke. Her mobile phone was dead to the world, but the sun had shifted far enough to excite the dust particles hovering in front of her bedroom window. She guessed it was a bit after midday.

Forcing herself to rise, she showered, put on a new face and slipped into a black dress. Sitting at her desk, she tidied her nails and applied a fresh coat of blue varnish.

Her dad's broken photo frame lay on the desk, looking beyond repair. Two of the joins had come apart and the glass and picture had dropped through one corner. Careful not to smudge her nails, she pressed her thumb on the edge of the photo and pushed the frame clear.

The picture appeared brighter without the smeared glass to blemish it and when she looked closer, she noticed something new—the faint shadow of a dimple winking from the edge of her father's smile. She gently touched her own dimples, doing her best to subdue her emotions. But when she flipped the photo over, what she saw on the other side made her cry.

To my darling, BeeBee.
I'm sorry.
Know Too Late, Mine Waits For One at Heaven's Gate.
Thee Also.
21 Botanic.
Love, Daddy

She read it three times before breathing again.

To my darling, BeeBee.

She couldn't remember having heard him speak those words before, but she tried to recall his voice and how he might sound. She imagined a rich baritone.

I'm sorry.

She blew on her nails to quicken their progress.

Know Too Late, Mine Waits For One at Heaven's Gate. Thee Also.

Was it a quote from the Bible? Or Shakespeare?

Or a cryptic suicide message?

She was desperate to find out.

But first, the Lancasters.

* * *

Number twenty-six Brampton Road was a detached house in the same seventies style architecture as all the others on the estate. Sitting on the corner of Brampton Close, its long back garden was hidden by a tall fence that reached all the way to the next property.

Bailey pressed the doorbell then stepped back and waited.

An attached garage on the right opened to a tarmac driveway as wide as the house. Plastic planters dotted the perimeter and a grass verge edged the property on one side.

From inside, she heard a muffled sound and the front door opened to the length of a chain. A woman peered through the crack, her puffy eyes bulging beneath a mop of curly white hair.

'Mrs Lancaster?'

'Yes.'

'I'm Bailey.'

The woman squinted and said, 'Are you the girl from across the way?'

'Yes I am.'

She removed the chain and let the door swing open. 'You've grown.'

Bailey was sure she had. The last time she had anything to do with the Lancasters was when she was twelve, and Mr Lancaster chased her off their property at Halloween. At the time, she didn't think going back for *thirds* warranted the level of abuse she got.

'I guess you're here about last night?'

Bailey wondered how she knew. 'How d'you know that?'

'People talk. They say you're some kind of vigilante now. I say we could do with more like you.'

She liked the woman instantly. 'Yep, I'm here about the burglary.'

'Terrible thing to happen, dear. It scared the willies out of me. I didn't sleep one bit last night. Even though I took Frank *and* Winston to bed, I was so frightened I didn't get a wink of sleep. Of course, both of them snoring away like a couple of hogs didn't help.'

Bailey wasn't surprised. No doubt sharing a bed with two men would make sleeping difficult. She coughed. 'Which one is your husband?'

'Frank, silly.'

'Well, Mrs Lancaster. I'm pleased to say that I'm happy to take your case.'

'What case is that, dear?'

'I mean, I want to solve the crime for you.'

'You and me both. Apparently some shifty-looking miscreant staked out the house before it happened.'

'Don't worry about him,' Bailey said. 'I've already dismissed him from my enquiries.' She removed a notebook and pen from her jacket. 'Can I come in and ask you some questions?'

'Sure, love, this way.' Mrs Lancaster left the door open and headed inside. 'I'll put the kettle on.'

The kitchen overlooked the back garden and Bailey scanned it keenly. Down the left hand side was a small shed flanked by a row of generous bushes. Down the right, a tall wooden fence fronted by an embankment of rockery. A perfectly mown lawn with precision stripes, ended at the gable wall of another house.

Mrs Lancaster handed her a mug of something hot and green.

'Oh,' Bailey said. 'Do you have any Coke?'

'Don't you like tea?'

'Sometimes, but that doesn't look much like tea.'

'Green tea. It's good for you. It'll look after your insides.'

Bailey took a sip and gagged as her insides protested. She put the mug down and turned the notepad to a new page. 'Can you tell me what happened?'

Mrs Lancaster eased herself onto a stool. 'I was terrified. There was this almighty crash, I screamed and came down. The mess, you wouldn't believe. Glass and china everywhere.'

'What time was that?'

'Ten to seven.'

'That's quite exact.'

'To be honest I can't be sure, but that's what Frank told the police so it must be correct.'

Bailey scribbled away.

'I was in the bath. I thought Frank had an accident so I

put on my dressing gown and rushed down. Winston hadn't budged, silly old man. He's getting on a bit now. He's rather slow and smelly. Poor thing doesn't always make it outside to do his business.'

'Who is Winston exactly?'

'Our Labrador. Fourteen next month. He's deaf too, but that's probably a good thing because Frank's always shouting at him these days.'

'Where was Frank, er, Mr Lancaster when it happened?'

'In his study with his headphones on. He didn't hear a thing.'

Bailey tried to get her bearings. 'Can you show me the lounge and the study?'

Mrs Lancaster slipped off the stool and led her into the hall. Situated at the front of the house, the study was no more than eight feet square. A laptop and a newspaper covered a mahogany desk. Bookcases lined one wall and a low settee lined another.

The lounge was a great deal bigger with three large windows and a door facing the garden. The door had a glass pane in the lower section and a piece of cardboard in the top. The room smelled of dog and Bailey noticed a bundle of blond fur in an armchair.

'Frank's gone into town to sign on and to get a new piece of glass. I don't expect him back for a while yet— he said the queues in that dole office are far worse than they ever used to be.'

Bailey inspected the door. The lower pane was single glazed which would make it easy to smash through, reach in and unlock it. She turned her attention to the wall above the fireplace where an empty hook jutted. 'Was that where the painting hung?'

Mrs Lancaster nodded. 'I can't believe that's the one they took. Frank only got it last week. It was quite nice, I liked it.'

Bailey glanced at the photo frames on the mantlepiece and pointed to one showing a dozen smartly-dressed people standing together in a garden. She identified Mrs Lancaster wearing a large yellow hat. 'Is your husband in this picture?'

'That's at a friend's wedding last year. Lovely day it was, but the champagne was bit too warm for my liking. Frank's in a grey suit on the end, he's the one who looks like he single-handedly finished off the buffet.'

She saw a fat man with too many chins to count and a belly that put his shoes in the shade. And then a thought struck her, something the woman had said earlier. 'Did you say, glass *and* china?'

'What, love?' Mrs Lancaster said.

'In the kitchen, you said there was a terrible mess of glass and china.' Bailey motioned to the door. 'I understand the glass,' she said. 'But where did the china come from?'

Mrs Lancaster pointed to a waste-high metal stand near the door. 'That's where I kept my Mum.' She sniffed. 'We had her there for three years—up until last night when I found her spilled all over the carpet like a bag of dust. She was in this beautiful golden vase we picked up in Morocco—she would have loved it. Not Frank though, he and Mum never got on. Unfortunately neither she or the vase could be saved, so Frank ended up throwing them both away. I loved that old thing.'

The metal stand stood tight against the wall and a thick, beige rug covered much of the room, but there was at least two feet of wooden floor between them. 'So the vase was on the stand?'

'Yes.'

'And the stand was against the wall?'

'Yes.'

'Then how …' She frowned as she sketched the position of the door, the vase and the carpet. How did the vase fly two feet across the room and land on the carpet? 'Never mind,' she said. 'Can I take a look outside?'

Mrs Lancaster opened the door and a wave of fresh air permeated the stale room.

Bailey stepped outside and looked around. The back of the garage was much like their own, with a door at the rear that Bailey assumed led through to the front of the property.

'We take our bins out that way,' Mrs Lancaster said.

'Is that how the thief got in and out?'

'No. The police say he climbed over the fence just there.' She pointed to the rockery where the earthen border had been raised a considerable height and topped with ornate stones the size of buckets. 'The police found footprints in the earth which they think belong to the burglar.'

In the earth between the rocks, Bailey found three perfectly clean footprints much larger than her own. She hunkered down and sketched one into her notebook. When she'd finished, she stepped onto the first stone and made her way across the others to the fence where she gripped the top and peered over. Just as she expected, cigarette ends littered a patch of trodden grass on the other side.

'You okay up there?' Mrs Lancaster asked.

Yes, Bailey thought, everything's perfectly fine. 'Tell me,' she said. 'What time will your husband be home?'

Chapter Eight

'Shakespeare was never my favourite,' Jack said as he took the paper from her.

Bailey watched him unfold it, sit forward and read. She'd copied out her father's message and gone looking for the Colonel to help her make sense of it. When she found Jack sitting at a table in the park, she had stopped to ask him instead.

Duncan sat beside him on the bench and stared at her across the table.

'Does Duncan like cake?' she asked.

'What? No. Well, I'm sure he does, but it wouldn't be good for him.'

'Oh,' she said. 'I was going to sneak some from work.'

Jack's face twisted with apparent thought. '21 Botanic. Is that a biblical reference?'

She shook her head. 'Don't think so.'

'You could ask a priest.'

'I've already asked Google.'

His mouth moved with silent words.

'I know chocolate's bad for dogs,' she said. 'But I thought maybe cake was okay.'

'No,' he said, eyes still fixed to the paper. 'Not really.'

'Neither are foxes.'

Jack looked up.

'They're bad for dogs too.' Bailey leaned across and stroked Duncan's head. 'That's how I lost my Powder.'

'You had a dog?'

'Long time ago.' She remembered finding it dead on the doorstep, the fresh December snow stained with its blood. 'Foxes killed it. Ripped its throat. It died in front of the house.' She pushed back a lock of hair. 'That's one of the few things I remember about life in Ireland.'

'You're Irish?'

She had always considered herself a home-counties girl, having lived in Farnham the best part of her life. 'Dad's Irish and Mum's English.'

'Know too late, mine waits for one at Heaven's Gate. Thee also.' Jack shook his head. 'If not Shakespeare, it's got to be one of the old poets.' He handed the paper back to her and asked, 'Why didn't the foxes finish off your dog?'

'What?'

'If it was dying, or dead. Why didn't they drag it away and eat it?'

'Urgh,' she said. 'Why would you say that?'

'Sorry, but foxes are scavengers and they don't give up a meal easily. Trust me, I know.'

She pocketed the paper.

'We might be leaving soon,' Jack said.

'I'm leaving *now*.' Bailey swung her legs from under the table and stood.

'No, I mean we might be leaving Farnham.' He pulled Duncan onto his lap. 'Moving onto somewhere else.'

'Oh,' she said. 'Where?'

'Don't know yet.'

'When?'

'Sometime soon. Maybe in the next few weeks.'

She didn't know whether to be happy because he was planning a new adventure, or sad because she was losing a friend. She enjoyed Jack's company and things wouldn't be the same without him. 'All right,' she said. 'Thanks for letting me know.'

Chapter Nine

Thursday proved to be a difficult day for Bailey. She was desperate to talk to someone about her father's message, but Christine had the day off and Mrs Smeak turned out to be less than friendly.

'So, you're the thief-catcher.'

Mrs Smeak had crept up on Bailey at the sink.

'The *special* girl.'

Her voice was slippery with a lisp on her s's.

'I saw you in the newspaper.'

Her breath smelled of cinnamon coffee.

'That's not good for business,' she hissed.

Bailey could feel the woman's hot breath against her cheek as words flicked from her tongue.

'Don't let it happen again.'

Bailey shivered as a cold drench of doom swathed her. This second Smeak was almost as horrible as the original. As soon as she paid off what she owed for the window, she was out of there. Guaranteed.

Arthur arrived at eleven and Bailey pinned him to the wall, thinking how light he was. 'Fuck Smeak,' she said. 'I don't care what he said about you keeping out of my way. I need your help.' She pushed her father's message into his hand. 'What do you make of this?'

Arthur whistled as he read the paper.

'It might be Shakespeare,' she said.

'What's a fella like me gonna know about Shakespeare?'

'I'm not saying it *is* Shakespeare,' Bailey added. 'I'm just suggesting it might be.'

Arthur looked at it again and shook his head. 'Just seems like a mixed up note. Are you BeeBee?'

'Yes,' Bailey held up a finger. 'And don't you dare consider ever using it.'

Arthur laughed and handed the paper back. 'Might be an address of some sort. 21 Botanic. Sounds like the start of an address.'

Indeed, Bailey thought. But where? And whose?

'Have you asked Karen?'

Having never properly spoken to the girl and only exchanged uncomfortable looks, Bailey didn't know whether or not she wanted to ask Karen. But her options were limited, so when she next entered the kitchen, Bailey was onto her.

'Did you do Shakespeare at school?'

Karen put down a tray of dirties and faced her like a cornered animal: shoulders back, ready to fight.

'Know too late, mine waits for one at Heaven's Gate. Thee also.' Bailey gave her time for it to sink in. 'Does that mean anything to you?'

'Really?' Karen's shoulders eased, but her face didn't soften. 'I thought you were kidding. No,' she said. 'That's not Shakespeare.'

'Are you sure?'

'Some of us,' she said, pushing past Bailey with her nose in the air, 'went to University and got a degree in English Literature.'

'Oh,' Bailey said. 'Why are you working here then?'

Karen left with a huff and as the swing door swung behind her, Bailey caught sight of Mrs Smeak glaring through.

* * *

She missed her rings. And her makeup. But mostly her rings. Aside from the small one Paul had given to her last year, she didn't wear them to work anymore. The blue dots on that ring matched her eyes, at least that's what he'd said at the time. She hated Paul now, but she still loved the ring and often wondered what stories it could tell.

As the sun slid between the clouds, Bailey hauled herself up the hill beside the golf course in the park. With her leather jacket over one arm, she slouched her way home. It had been a bleak day.

Where the path split at the top of the golf course, her mood lifted and her pace quickened when she saw an old man with a walking stick sitting alone on a bench. She reached him out of breath. 'Hey,' she said, wheezing slightly. 'Colonel.'

The old man met her eyes and smiled. 'I was miles away. Do you want to sit?'

Bailey sat, pulled the piece of paper from her pocket and thrust it at him. 'What do you make of this?' He mused over the message for longer than she felt comfortable. She had half-expected him to decipher it straight away and it annoyed her that he didn't. 'Is it a quote? Or an address?'

The old man folded the paper. 'Where did you copy it from?'

'I found it written on the back of my Dad's photo. The one he gave to me just before he died. Well, just before I *thought* he'd died.'

He nodded. 'Was there anything else with it?'

'It came in a frame,' Bailey said. 'An old wooden

thing that's falling apart now. Mum's wanted to replace it for years but I—'

'Did it come with a key?'

'What?' She tried to think if there'd been a key. She hadn't completely taken the frame apart so she could have overlooked one. 'I didn't see one, but I didn't really look.'

'Then go back and look,' he said, handing her the paper.

Excitement pulsed through her. 'Do you know what it means?'

'Not what it means.' He shook his head. 'But what it says.'

'How come?'

'It appears to be the contact details for someone,' he said. 'Or some *thing*.'

Bailey looked at the paper again. She could see *21 Botanic* as the start of an address, but the rest of it made no sense at all.

'Read it again,' he said. 'Out loud.'

'Know too late,' Bailey mumbled.

The old man poked her boot with his stick. 'Annunciate.'

'What?'

'Speak clearly,' he said.

'Know too late, mine waits for one at Heaven's Gate. Thee also.' She read it twice more, each time more slowly than the last. Then she puffed. 'This is stupid.'

'No,' he poked her boot again. 'If you think that, then the only stupid element is you. Read it again and this time, think phonetically.'

'What?'

'Consider,' he said. 'The sound the words make.'

She read it again.

'Do they remind you of anything?'

'Like what?'

'Numbers, Bailey. Numbers and rhymes. People use many techniques to disguise messages. This one is neither clever nor complicated which suggests it was made by someone of modest intelligence. The real codes ...'

Bailey looked at the passage again.

Know Too Late, Mine Waits For One at Heaven's Gate. Thee Also.

Some of the numbers appeared. *Too* was obviously two. *For* was four. She could also guess at one, eight and three. Quivering with excitement, she pulled out her pen, lay the paper across her pad and replaced the words with numbers.

Know 2 Late, Mine Waits 4 1 at 7 Gate. 3 Also.

She showed it to the Colonel.

'Good,' he said. 'Now what about the others?'

'*Know*?' Bailey frowned. 'That doesn't sound like anything.'

'Sometimes, the literal phonetic link is overlooked to create a more purposeful message. So, try being liberal with your interpretations.'

Bailey continued. '*Late*. That's got to be eight. What about *Waits* and *Gate*? Are they both eights as well?'

'Most probably,' the Colonel said.

Bailey scribbled the numbers in place.

Know 2 8, Mine 8 4 1 at 7 8. 3 Also.

'Tell me, Bailey. What do you make of the last word?'

'*Also*?' She mused. 'It doesn't sound like any number.'

He nodded.

'So, what?'

'Think, girl. Look at the word. Not just its *sound*, but its *meaning*.'

'Is it also three?'

'Good. Now you've started to use some intelligence. Continue.'

'*Mine*, well that has to be nine. And *Know*,' she sucked on the end of the pen. 'Is that nought?'

'Well done.'

Bailey filled in the rest of the numbers.

0 2 8, 9 8 4 1 at 7 8. 3 3

The Colonel leaned across. 'Notice how all the words have a capital letter except *at*. I suspect that is a filler word, one used to enhance the flow of the sentence without affecting its meaning.'

'So I can scrub it out?' Bailey asked.

'Yes,' he said. 'You can scrub it out. And remove the punctuation whilst your at it.'

Bailey did, then she copied the complete number into her pad.

0 2 8 9 8 4 1 7 8 3 3

'That looks to me,' the Colonel said, 'like a telephone number.'

Bailey could hardly contain her excitement. She was ten pence and a phone box away from speaking with her dad. She jumped when the Colonel's cane fell across her lap.

'Be careful, Bailey.' His blue eyes flicked across hers as he leaned closer. 'That number is from the past. From your father's past. And you might recall that your father is not a very nice man.' His lip quivered ever so slightly. 'Tread carefully, child. Tread very carefully.'

Chapter Ten

Bailey sat next to her mother in the back of the taxi, drumming blue-painted nails on the lid of a box. When she arrived home from work a couple of hours ago, she had been forced to eat then herded out again to go shopping. Apparently, Timothy had kicked up such a stink about her borrowing his laptop that her mother finally agreed to buy her one. Now they were on their way home from the computer store with a brand new Apple MacBook on her lap and a two-dimple grin on her face.

She couldn't believe it. Things really were looking up.

A thought struck her and she turned to her mother. 'Didn't you once tell me that Dad's insurance had been providing for us all these years?'

Her mother didn't answer straight away and when she did, it was in a cautious tone. 'Why?'

'Well,' said Bailey. 'If he isn't actually dead, why did the insurance people pay out?' Bailey saw the driver turn his eyes to the rear-view mirror.

'Not now, darling,' her mother whispered. 'Some other time.'

The laptop had suppressed Bailey's belligerent bent and she was happy to drop the subject for now. 'Okay,' she said.

When they reached home, Bailey was inside and upstairs before she heard her mother close the front door.

Timothy stepped out of his bedroom. 'You got one then.'

She showed him the box. 'Better than yours.'

'Apple, pah. Should have gone for a Unix.'

'You're just jealous.'

He followed to her bedroom, but didn't enter. 'Can you give mine back now?'

Bailey put the box on the bed and unplugged her brother's laptop. She gathered the lead and handed them to him. 'Thanks,' she said. 'I know that I was a bitch but, thanks.'

'Whatever.' Timothy marched off.

Alone in her room, Bailey dismantled the rest of the photo frame on her desk. It smelled old and mildewy, and dust spilled from the sides when she pulled them apart.

A piece of brittle sticky-tape dangled from a key-shaped indentation in the cork backing. She checked the rest of the frame again, but there was definitely no key. Disappointed, she reached for her mobile phone.

Tread carefully, child.

Bailey tapped her dad's number into the phone and with each new beep, her stomach churned.

She hit *connect* and pressed the phone against her ear to stop it shaking.

The numbers pulsed in turn and the line started to ring.

She let it ring twice before ending the call—then she released the breath she'd been holding.

Chapter Eleven

Having finished two glasses of Coke before calming down, Bailey stepped into the cool night air and crossed the road to the Lancaster's.

A car sat on the driveway with a *For Sale* sign in the rear window. The house stood in near darkness, a single soft light glowing behind the front door.

She rang the bell and stood back.

Inside, someone shouted and a second light switched on. A figure lumbered along the corridor towards her, distorted by the frosted-glass. The door opened to the sound of a chain and a man peered out.

'Mr Lancaster?' Bailey said. 'It's Bailey, from across the street.'

He spent an awful long time scrutinising her.

'I was talking to your wife yesterday about the—'

'I know,' he said. 'What do you want now?'

Bailey would rather have the conversation inside, in private, where he might feel less confrontational. 'I'd like to talk to you if I may.'

'So talk. But be quick.'

'Okay,' Bailey said. 'If that's what you want.' She swallowed. 'I promise not to tell the police, if you tell me why you did it.'

There was a moment of confusion on his face before an instant of clarity. 'Piss off,' he said before slamming the door shut.

That could have gone better, Bailey thought. She

considered ringing the bell again, but could still see his bulky frame behind the glass. It moved and she heard a rattle as the door opened, this time fully. Mr Lancaster stood there, obese and ugly, a brown jumper stretched over his ample waist.

'You'd better come in,' he said.

Bailey wasn't sure she wanted to anymore.

'Come on.' He gestured. 'I'm not going to eat you.'

She stepped inside, squeezed past him and headed for the lounge.

'No,' he said. 'In here.' Opening the door to the study, he flicked on the light, then squeezed into the chair behind the desk. Bailey followed and closed the door behind her. 'How much do you know?' he asked.

She knew he'd faked the break-in and stolen his own painting—probably because they had money problems—but she didn't know if it went any further than that. 'I know you did it. I know you burgled your own house.'

'How?'

'The footprints, the vase and a lucky break with a dickhead I know.'

'What are you on about?'

'The footprints in the rockery were just too convenient. Any half-decent thief would have stood on the rocks, it's easy enough to do. My guess is you used someone else's shoes, a different size from yours, then planted the prints for the police to find and draw their own conclusion.'

'And the vase?'

Bailey previously wondered how the vase smashed on the carpet when it would have hit the hard floor had it toppled over during the break-in. 'Your wife said you didn't like her mother or her vase. My guess is you took the opportunity to get rid of them both.'

He fidgeted. 'She was a cow. And that hideous piece of china was insured for much more than we paid.'

'That doesn't interest me.'

'So what do you want?'

Bailey lowered herself onto the settee but wished she hadn't. It was too low and the awkward position meant she had to lean forward. 'I think this is all linked to something else, something bigger. But tell me, does your wife know you stole the painting?'

'Christ no. She'd tear my throat out.'

Bailey shifted herself comfortable. 'So why do it?'

'Money,' he said. 'I lost my job last month. Things have been tight, but Daphne's talking about a trip to Spain.' He balled his fingers into fists and pushed them together. 'I can't afford it, but I'd hate to let her down.'

'Where is it now?'

'The painting? I threw it away. Smashed it up and put it in a skip.'

She edged forward. 'Why?'

'It wasn't worth anything. I paid twenty-quid for it from an antique place the other side of town. Doogie said it was tat.'

'Doogie?' Bailey took out her notebook for the first time and wrote the name.

'My mate's nephew, Doogie. He heard a local fella was interested in getting hold of some paintings. He said there'd been a mix up with an estate clearance. An old man died and left everything to charity—all his furniture, jewellery, paintings, everything. The removal company started clearing it cheap, before they realised some of the stuff was original.'

Bailey recalled her mother telling her about three crates of paintings that went missing from a warehouse a few weeks ago. 'Was any of it stolen?'

'Don't know about that. Doogie found out that a local trader was peddling some of them around town, so he started tracking them down. He gave me a list and I looked them up online. Old stuff, you know. I didn't recognise the names, but one of them was just like the painting I bought last week. So I thought well, it's worth a try. But when Doogie took it to this dealer guy, he said it wasn't even worth what I paid.'

'Who was the guy?' Bailey asked, pen poised.

'I never met him. But apparently, he's connected. To tell the truth, I was pleased when my painting turned out to be worthless. You don't want to get mixed up with the likes of him. Oh yeah,' he said. 'Doogie told me the dealer drives a red Mercedes. Top of the range. Expensive. That's all I can tell you.'

Bailey finished writing and looked up. 'Do you know a man named Danny Douglas?'

He shook his head. 'Can't say I do. Listen, do the police suspect me?'

She pocketed the notebook. 'I don't think you need to worry about them. They're not as clever as they want you to think they are.'

'So, am I in the clear?'

She rose awkwardly. 'I think so. I mean if the police are occupying themselves searching for an agile, fence-hopping burglar, then you've got nothing to worry about. And who knows, maybe the insurance money on the vase will be enough to pay for your holiday.'

'Yeah.' Mr Lancaster stood and tugged at his belt, hoisting his trousers higher. 'Sorry I was a bit short with you earlier.'

'Don't worry,' Bailey said. 'I'm used to it.'

Chapter Twelve

Taping up the picture frame was only a temporary fix, at some stage she'd have to replace it, but tape would do for now. She stood the patched up frame against the wall beneath the poster of Kurt Cobain.

My two favourite men, she thought. One dead, one disappeared.

Her brother had her new laptop in his room, fitting anti-virus software and downloading other things he thought she'd find useful. Bailey didn't stop to ask why he was helping her—as the resident nerd, she assumed he felt responsible for all things computer.

She turned to a new page in her pad and wrote *The Case of the Questionable Art Dealer*. Below that, she created a list.

CLUES
- *Local trader (unknown) ... bought / stole paintings from warehouse.*
- *Danny Douglas ... stole painting from antique shop and art gallery.*
- *Mr Lancaster ... stole painting from his own home.*
- *Doogie ... who is he and what role did he play?*
- *Dodgy art dealer ... drives expensive red Mercedes. To be avoided if possible.*

Further down the page she created another.

ACTIONS
- *Identify the local trader.*
- *Talk to Danny Douglas.*
- *Find Doogie.*
- *Locate the red Mercedes.*
- *Recover the missing paintings.*

As Bailey perused the list of items, wondering where to start first, her eyes were drawn to her mobile phone vibrating across the desk.

Its face illuminated the words *Unknown Caller*.

She stood and stared.

It buzzed.

And buzzed again.

Get a grip girl. It could be your father.

She reached for it slowly, accepted the call, pushed the phone to her ear and listened.

Breathing. A male breath. Deep and heavy.

She swallowed. 'Hello.'

The breathing faltered and resumed.

She switched the phone to her left hand and picked up a pen. 'It's Bailey here, who's this?'

A volley of rapid breaths, a laugh and then, 'Bailey Kelly. I remember you, princess. Isn't this nice?'

The gravelly voice had a thick Irish inflection. She listened.

'Have you got it?'

She didn't answer.

It said, 'Have you got it?'

'Dad?' She held her breath until it hurt.

'I'm not your daddy, princess.' It sneered. 'Do you know where Connor is?'

Its tone frightened her, but the mention of her father's

name angered her. 'Why do you want to know where my father is?'

'A little thing called retribution.'

'What if I *have* got it?' Bailey said, scribbling the word *retribution* in the pad.

'The key belongs to me. Connor owes me.' The voice paused. '*You* owe me.'

A net of fear enveloped her chest. And tightened.

'I'll be getting to your daddy soon, princess. But first,' the voice said. 'I'm coming for you.'

Bailey ended the call to the malevolent sound of rich, baritone laughter.

Episode Four

Bailey Jacobs
and the
Dealer's Den

Prologue

A fat man closed the boot of a red Mercedes and massaged his knuckles. 'She was heavy,' he said.

Smoke billowed from the mouth of an older man in tweed. 'Take her to Kensington and put her with the others.'

The fat man nodded.

'But first, come and say *hi* to Janet. She's made quiche.'

The fat man straightened his tie and followed the dogs into the house.

Chapter One

Rain spilled from leaden clouds to bruise the grass and buckle the willow tree in an unyielding assault. A stretch of patio concealed by puddles, danced in the deluge of bullets from above. Bailey stared through the glass doors, wiping crumbs from her mouth as she watched the clash unfold.

Retribution.

It had been three days since her telephone conversation with the gravelly-voiced Irishman, and each day had brought rain.

I remember you, princess.

She had been so excited by the prospect of speaking with her estranged father—nervous about what to say, yet thrilled at the thought of hearing his voice after so many years. But the man she had spoken to wasn't her father. And he had scared her.

I'll be getting to your daddy soon, princess. But first ...

She had been stupid to give her name.

I'm coming for you.

That night she'd slept badly and when Friday morning finally arrived, the last thing she wanted to do was go to work. After twenty minutes discussing, arguing and pleading with her mother to take the day off, she had agreed to go, but only if a taxi took her there and back again. So at five past nine on Friday morning, with Smeak waiting for her with his clipboard, she had arrived late for work again.

The day had dragged. Christine—new best friend and waitress at the coffee shop—hardly stopped talking. Bailey struggled to pay attention to the girl as she nattered away, pausing only to breathe. Washing up was a mundane job, but it made it easy for Bailey's thoughts to wander and what she had wanted to do that day was focus on her father and the Irishman—Christine's constant interruptions made that impossible. By the time Bailey collected her jacket at five o'clock, the only thing she had clear in her mind was that she still had a lot to think about.

When she arrived home that evening, Bailey had been disappointed to count her wages and discover half of it deducted to pay for the window she'd broken. The arrangement she had with Mr Smeak—the beak-nosed coffee shop manager—was that she'd work to pay off a £200 debt incurred when she stopped a thief by pushing him through the shop window. Even though her heroic act had brought the shop a lot of publicity at the time, Smeak demanded she cover the insurance excess and that meant she would have to work for at least four weeks to pay off the debt.

She had spent most of Saturday researching her father on her new laptop, only to find a string of useless leads that did nothing more than waste her time. *Connor Kelly* seemed a popular name and searching through the results gave her a headache.

Although she'd studied a hundred different *Connor Kelly* faces, none had compared to the photo she had of him. Her dad had dimples in both cheeks, just like her. He had blue eyes, big brows and thick black hair, just like her. Taken a few weeks before he apparently *died*, the picture of him on a motorbike was the only one she had and it resembled none of the people who showed up in her search.

She hadn't forgiven her mother for fabricating his death. Bailey understood why she'd done it, but knew it would be a while before she forgave her. Being the *wrong sort* didn't seem reason enough to let your children grow up thinking their dad was dead.

Deciding whether or not to tell Timothy was a problem. She didn't like her brother, but felt he had a right to know. Timothy had been a baby when their mother fled to Farnham and she doubted he had any recollection of the man they escaped.

The Irishman's threat weighed on her mind. *A little thing called retribution.*

She hadn't left the house since Friday evening and now, as she watched the rain ruin Sunday, home seemed the safest place to be. But she knew that tomorrow would bring new challenges—the start of another week grafting in the kitchen for the intolerable Mr Smeak.

She despised Smeak. He had a lanky frame, pinched eyes and mouth set to the first curl of a sneer. Work was bearable, Smeak was not. And his wife was just as bad. When she first started working there a week ago, Bailey had been pleased to learn Mr Smeak had a day off, but horrified to know his wife filled in for him. The woman was creepy—she had a villainous drawl on her vowels and hissed when she spoke. She made Bailey's skin crawl.

A shadow fell across the dining table and she jumped, dropping her toast.

'Weirdo,' her brother said, sitting with a bowl of cereal.

She watched milk dribble down his chin as he spooned

flakes into his mouth, hardly pausing to chew. 'You're such a disgusting pig.' She threw a crust of toast that hit his face and dropped into the bowl.

'Oi,' he yelled, picking it out.

'Well learn to eat properly.' She lifted her plate and left the room and as the lounge door closed behind her, she heard his muffled reply.

'Creep.'

Bailey ducked into the kitchen and pushed past her mother to drop her plate in the sink. She was almost out the door when she felt a hand on her arm.

'What's going on?' her mother asked. 'Have you upset your brother again? I don't know what's got into you lately, you're so angry all the time and ... well, just not yourself. Please, darling,' her mother's voice softened, 'take one of the tablets.'

Bailey felt her anger flare and die between breaths. 'No,' she said. 'I don't want any more of those things.'

'You promised you would.'

Having suffered from mood swings for most of the year, Bailey had been diagnosed with chronic low-grade depression. Whilst a failed relationship and lost job were contributing factors, she felt the problem went deeper. But she'd improved in recent weeks, thanks in part to her new job and new hobby as amateur sleuth. She knew there was hope for the future, she just had trouble seeing it sometimes.

'What's wrong, Bailey Bee. Come on, you can talk to me.'

'Really?' Bailey's tone suggested venom and her mother recoiled. 'About Dad? The fact you're still married? What about your other secrets? The men in the black car. Can we talk about them too?' Her mouth felt sticky and she wiped the back of her hand across it. 'You know it's funny, but the person I love the most is the one I trust the least.'

'But I …' her mother said, reaching out.

'Forget it.' Bailey turned and left, her bare feet thudding the stairs on the way to her bedroom.

* * *

Mr Lancaster's list was tucked inside an A4 pad on her desk. It detailed six paintings and six artists, but none of the names were familiar to her.

He'd given her the list last week when they discussed the theft of a painting from his house—a break-in he had carried out himself. When she'd told him she knew that *he* was the thief, he was quick to unburden himself of information. Apparently, three boxes of paintings had been procured from a warehouse and distributed to local dealers. When someone realised six of the paintings were originals, the race was on to recover them by whatever means.

Mr Lancaster had acquired the list of paintings from Doogie—the nephew of a friend. Doogie knew a dealer willing to pay a good price should any of the paintings find their way to him. He didn't know the dealer's name, but said he drove a classy red Mercedes.

Bailey flipped the pad open to the page titled *The Case of the Questionable Art Dealer* and read on.

CLUES
- *Local trader (unknown) … bought / stole paintings from warehouse.*
- *Danny Douglas … stole painting from antique shop*

and art gallery.
- *Mr Lancaster ... stole painting from his own home.*
- *Doogie ... who is he and what role did he play?*
- *Dodgy art dealer ... drives expensive red Mercedes. To be avoided if possible.*

ACTIONS
- *Identify the local trader.*
- *Talk to Danny Douglas.*
- *Find Doogie.*
- *Locate the red Mercedes.*
- *Recover the missing paintings.*

Things were beginning to get complicated and she didn't know what to do next. Should she search for the local trader or find Danny Douglas? On top of everything else she had to deal with at the moment, the lack of progress on this case was severely testing her patience.

She flipped to a page marked *The Case of the Resurrected Father*.

Bailey was thrilled her dad was alive. Having spent the last fourteen years believing him dead, it excited her to know he was still out there somewhere, probably thinking of her, probably looking forward to the day they would meet again. But apprehension was never far away and finding him made her nervous—her mother had moved countries to be away from him, so why was it a good idea for Bailey to track him down now?

And then there was the Irishman—a chilling voice on the phone with threats of retribution. She'd had to look the word up and hadn't liked what she found.

Retribution ...
Requital according to merits, especially for evil.

She'd also looked up the word *requital*.

Requital ...
A retaliation for a wrong or injury.

None of it sounded good.

The phone number on the back of her dad's photo had put her in touch with the Irishman. He'd asked about a key. But what key? And what did it open?

She lifted the lid of her laptop and loaded Google. The cursor blinked aggressively at her, waiting for her to type. But she had nothing. She'd searched her father's name countless times before and always drawn a blank. So what next?

She returned to the pad and read the page again.

ACTIONS
- *Find Dad.*
- *Talk to Aunt Liz.*
- *Research Connor Kelly (Dad).*
- *Identify Dad's motorbike.*

One item on the list stuck out above the others: *Talk to Aunt Liz*.

Bailey hadn't seen or spoken to her aunt in five years —not since being banished to live with her after setting fire to her brother's bedroom. That had turned out to be a magical summer: driven to an unknown destination to spend time with an aunt she hardly knew. She remembered the cars, so big and imposing. The smart chauffeurs were enough to impress any twelve-year-old. Hopping out of one, into the next, being whisked away like royalty.

Aunt Liz smoked constantly, drank a lot and swore at the telly. When they first met, twelve year old Bailey had been fascinated to find a woman who looked just like her mother, but with a more adventurous vocabulary.

Bailey tried to recall the last time her mother had spoken to Aunt Liz, but couldn't. As far as she knew, the sisters didn't talk often, even though they'd been close growing up. Born and raised in Portsmouth, they'd played together, schooled together, even dated boys together. So why were they distant now and why did Aunt Liz never visit them in Farnham? Whatever the reason, she wasn't going to let the past spoil the future.

Bailey's thoughts turned to her mother who had been acting unusually mysterious of late. Whilst she was close to her mother and wanted desperately to be able to trust her, every day it was getting harder to do so. She couldn't understand why her mother was so guarded about her own activities and what she could possibly have to hide. For the last few days, Bailey had been planning to uncover her mother's secrets, and now felt like a good time.

Creeping across the landing to the top of the stairs, she stopped to listen. She could hear her mother in the kitchen and the television in the lounge where she guessed Timothy was watching something nerdy. Dressed in grey pyjama bottoms and a long, black t-shirt, she tiptoed to the end of the corridor and eased open the door to her mother's bedroom.

A large, uncluttered room with double bed and built-in wardrobe, it smelled of lavender. The neatly made bed sat centrally and Bailey headed towards a small side-table.

She stopped to listen again before opening a tiny drawer.

It contained a paperback book, a tube of cream, a half-eaten bar of chocolate and a packet of yellow earplugs. In the cupboard below she found two further books—neither looked interesting or noteworthy.

The mirror-fronted wardrobe stretched the length of one wall. It slid open with a begrudging whine that seemed loud enough to carry through the house. She held her breath and waited. When she heard her name called, she darted onto the landing in time to see her mother climbing the stairs.

'Is everything all right up there?'

'Fine,' Bailey said. 'I'm just doing some stuff.'

Her mother took another step up. 'What was—'

'Any chance of more toast?' Bailey took a step down. 'I'm ravenous?'

'You're not—'

'And a glass of Coke? Thanks, Mum. You're ever so good to me.'

Her mother paused for an uncomfortable length of time and as her face hesitated between doubt and concern, Bailey thought she was on to her. But then she smiled, turned and headed back downstairs. 'Of course,' she said as she descended. 'Anything for my favourite child.'

When her mother disappeared into the kitchen, Bailey continued her search. She knelt to rifle through a row of shoes on the bottom shelf of the wardrobe, then stood to fondle piles of folded clothes along the top. Her fingers touched a box at the back and she pulled it down. Plain, brown and scuffed on the edges, it looked like an old shoe box, but not one she recognised.

She fumbled the lid off and gasped.

Ignoring a pile of passports, she reached for a wedge of

bank notes and flicked through them slowly, enjoying the musky smell as she tried to count. She had never seen so much money in one place before. There must be thousands.

Her hands shook as she lowered the bundle back into the box and picked up the passports. Bailey Jacobs. Timothy Jacobs. Valerie Jacobs. The name on the fourth passport was Valerie Kelly. She was about to leaf through them when something shiny caught her eye. Nestled in the corner of the box, was a key. She picked it up and passed it between her fingers, studying the scratch-marks along its golden length as she wondered if it belonged to the Irishman.

At the bottom of the box was a folded piece of paper with what looked like a mobile telephone number written beneath the name *Morgan*.

Curiouser and curiouser, she thought. Her mother's mysteries were getting deeper and darker, and ever so interesting.

She returned everything to the box and replaced the lid, then put the box back on the shelf, closed the wardrobe door, extended a final glance around her mother's bedroom, and left.

'What were you doing in there?'

Bailey jumped. 'Shhh,' she said, closing the door with a soft click.

'Why were you in Mum's room?'

'Shhh,' she said again.

'Why are you sneaking around like this?'

'I can't tell you,' Bailey whispered.

Timothy started for the stairs. 'Then I'm going to tell Mum.'

'Wait.' She grabbed his hand and pulled him into her

bedroom then closed the door. They stood in the middle of the room facing each other, eyes twitching like a fencer's sword. 'I've got something to tell you,' she said. 'It's not going to be easy to hear.'

'What?'

'It's about Dad.' She dragged back a lock of hair and cleared her throat. 'He's alive.'

Timothy folded his arms and sighed.

'He's alive,' she said again. 'And I think he's looking for me.'

'So,' Timothy said, pushing his hands firmly into his pockets. 'She told you then? It's about time.'

'You knew already?'

His face twisted into a bitter smile. 'For about six months. Some policeman-bloke came round last Christmas and told us Dad was getting out.'

Bailey took three long breaths to process the information. Had her father been in prison all this time? That would go someway to explain why he hadn't been in touch. 'When was he released?'

'Earlier this year.'

'When?'

He shrugged.

'Don't you know?'

'Why should I care?' he said. 'I never knew him. Mum hated him. Why should I be interested in a dick like that?'

She stiffened as a wave of anger swelled. 'Because he's your father.'

Timothy shrugged again. 'Fuck him.'

'No,' Bailey said, swinging a fist that caught his nose with a crunch. 'Fuck you.'

Chapter Two

Through the kitchen window, Bailey watched the taxi pull away, its break lights glaring as it slowed at the top of the road before accelerating out of sight. She sighed.

Sounding like a caught pig, Timothy's squeals had quickly brought her mother running and she flew into hysterics when she saw the blood spilling from his nose. She had covered his face with a towel and led him into the bathroom, shouting instructions as she went. Bailey had been charged with phoning for a taxi and after an argument with the taxi firm over how long they would have to wait, she was satisfied when one screeched to a stop outside the house ten minutes later.

Timothy had milked the attention for all he could, moaning like a child as her mother fussed around tending to his every need. They had stumbled out of the house together, Timothy holding tissue to a bent nose that flared red against an ashen face.

Now, as the taxi disappeared behind a privet hedge on its way to the emergency ward of the local hospital, Bailey pulled her mother's green address book from the pocket of her pyjamas and leafed to the entry for Elizabeth Jacobs. There were two numbers listed: one land, one mobile.

Using the phone in the lounge, she dialled the landline with a trembling hand, remembering the last time she'd made a call when things didn't turn out too well.

She waited for the line to purr into life and was

surprised when someone picked it up on the first ring. Cautious since her brush with the Irishman, she let a wall of silence build before impatience tore it down. 'Hello.'

There was definitely someone at the other end—their muted breath agitated the stillness.

'Hello,' she said again. 'Aunt Liz?'

Then came another sound, a familiar sound, the tapping of fingers across a keyboard.

Bailey slammed the phone down and stared at it, unsure what had just happened. She thought twice about trying the second number, but tapped it in anyway and waited for the line to connect. When it did, it took four rings for someone to pickup.

'Hello,' Bailey said, ready to end the call if she had to.

Nobody spoke at the other end, but Bailey heard movement. And a more erratic level of breathing.

'Aunt Liz?'

A moment of quiet before, 'Bailey? What's happened?'

Having not spoken to the woman for so long, Bailey thought she wouldn't recognise her voice, but she did. Similar to her mother's it had a husky undertone. 'Aunt Liz, I—'

'What's wrong?'

Aunt Liz was more abrupt than Bailey expected her to be. 'Nothing.'

'Then why the hell are you phoning? How did you get this number?'

'I …'

'Does your mother know you're calling me?'

'No.'

'Then you shouldn't be. You have to go.'

'Wait!' Bailey screamed into the phone, louder than

she intended. 'Please wait.' She listened, unsure if her aunt was still there, only continuing when the silence was punctuated by a sigh at the other end. 'Did you know my dad's alive?'

A single breath and then, 'Yes.'

Bailey felt her legs weaken. Did everyone know except her? 'Please,' she said. 'Tell me about him.'

As the voice at the other end of the phone loosened and flowed, Bailey pulled up a chair and sat, making notes in a pad about her father, her mother and the role Aunt Liz played in putting them together.

Chapter Three

Bailey sketched her father's face into the pad. She greyed his hair, puffed his eyes and hallowed his cheeks, then she sat back and reviewed her work.

An avid artist at school, she hadn't done any drawing since leaving, but found it came back to her quickly. Her art teacher had said she could be good if she applied herself, but that's what most of the teachers had told her at one stage or another and she was yet to prove any of them right.

Pretty good, she thought as she held the pad up and looked at the face of her now aged father. She leaned the pad against the wall and was about to compare it with the faces peering back at her from the laptop, when the front door opened. Muffled voices followed and someone climbed the stairs—it sounded like her brother. She expected him to stop outside her room to complain about his nose and explain how disappointed Mum was, but he didn't. And for a fleeting moment, when she heard the soft click of his bedroom door closing, she felt sorry for him.

Downstairs, she found her mother sorting through the medicine cupboard. 'What's up with dickhead?' Bailey said.

Her mother turned sharply. 'You broke his nose.'

'Oh.'

'They tried to realign it, but they don't think it will ever be quite the same again. He was in so much pain.'

'I didn't mean to.'

'No,' her mother said. 'You never do. Why did you hit him in the first place?'

'Didn't he say?'

'No.'

At least he didn't snitch. 'We had a disagreement. Is he very upset?' She didn't expect a comprehensive reply but something more than a scowl would have been nice. 'Maybe I should pop up and see him?'

'No,' her mother said. 'Give him space. Give him lots of space.'

Bailey withdrew the address book from her pocket. 'Here,' she said. 'In all the confusion I forgot to put this back in your bag.'

Her mother took it. 'Did you happen to …'

'What?'

'Nothing. I guess you'll be getting your things ready for work soon.'

'Yeah,' Bailey said. 'Guess I will.'

In her bedroom, Bailey continued sifting through the Connor Kelly photos on her laptop, but stopped when she heard a strange noise. She cocked her head until it came again.

Something was moving around in the loft.

Bailey didn't mind rats and mice, but she did mind being interrupted. She got up, stood on the chair and hit the ceiling with her fist. 'Shut up.'

The noise stopped for about twenty seconds and then came again. This time louder.

She stormed out of the room and onto the landing where she glared at the hatch in the ceiling. The loft was one place in the house she'd never been before. Confined spaces, locked doors and anywhere she couldn't exit

273

quickly, agitated her claustrophobia. She knew Timothy wouldn't want to help and her mother was way too squeamish—this one she would have to do herself. Removing a wooden pole from a hook at the end of the bannisters, she reached up and clicked the loft hatch open.

Metal steps unfolded with a groan and dust drifted down, settling on her face. She wiped it away.

A light switch on the landing illuminated the roof space, but it still looked incredibly creepy and not the least bit inviting. With one foot on the first step, she hesitated, wondering what possible outcome could make this a good idea. Then she heard it—the *meow* of a kitten —and she was half way up the ladder before she could stop herself.

A pocket of warm air surprised her as she eased her head through the hole and looked around. Cardboard boxes covered much of the floor—pushed to the edges, there was sufficient space for a person to crawl between them, and plenty of places for a cat to hide.

'Here, kitty.'

She locked onto the sound of scratching at the far end of the loft, then coughed and called again. The scratching stopped.

Stupid cat. Probably stuck. Definitely scared.

Against her better judgment, she climbed all the way into the loft and took to her hands and knees, the floor groaning as she edged along. Dusty air dried her throat and a cobweb wrapped her face. Her legs hurt and she caught a splinter in one hand. Her chest heaved and she wiped her top lip dry.

With less room than she first thought, she had to shoulder boxes out the way in order to reach the dark and ominous-looking chamber at the far end of the attic, from where the scratching had come.

The lightbulb blinked off and on.

What the hell was she doing? And why was it getting so hot?

Shadows danced as she moved and the further she crawled from the light, the darker they became. When she reached what looked like the last of the boxes, she stopped and squinted into the chamber beyond.

The scratching noise came again. So close now. So loud.

She pushed aside a box and reached into the dark, feeling around, expecting to find something soft and hoping it would be a cat.

The lightbulb blinked again and she grabbed a succession of dusty breaths.

Her fingers touched the edge of something hard and square. Slightly larger than her fist, it felt heavy for its size. She pulled and it came, but the shadows distorted its features and she held it close to her face to inspect it.

It was a hard plastic box, smooth and weighty, with a pale blue light emanating from one side.

The box spoke. 'Gotcha, creep.'

Behind her, metal groaned and pinged as the attic steps crashed back into place. Struggling to turn around, her heart-rate doubled.

From out of the box came laughter and the lightbulb blinked for a final time before darkness consumed her.

* * *

Sweat soaked the pillow and matted her hair in clumps. Her chest heaved with fierce breaths and a breeze chilled her arms.

She had dreamed of the field again: her mother crying as her father laboured through the mud, stumbling but never falling, baby Timothy in his arms.

Had she screamed before waking?

Light seeping through the curtains suggested it was morning. But which day? She rolled over and cried out as pain cramped her side. Switching on the table lamp brought another surprise: the room was a complete mess. Her blue carpet had turned grey, bits of plaster and fluff were scattered everywhere and the ceiling sported a hole large enough for her to crawl through. She stared at it blankly, wondering what the hell happened.

In the bathroom she lifted her shirt and winced. It was stuck to her skin and she peeled it off carefully, watching the flesh lift and separate as she pulled.

Abrasions covered all one side with a background of bruises. Someone had dressed the wound but the once white gauze was now thick with congealed blood. She flanneled it clean and headed downstairs with a towel tucked beneath her shirt, held in place by an elbow.

In the kitchen her mother offered her a chair, kissed her face when she sat and squeezed her gently. 'How are you feeling?'

Dazed and out of sorts, her eyes felt puffy and her body objected to the slightest movement. 'What happened?'

'I think you had an episode.'

'A what?'

Her mother filled a glass with water and handed it to her. 'Drink this.'

'Any Coke?'

'Water first.' She took something out of the cupboard above the fridge. 'And take one of these.'

Bailey looked at the tub of yellow pills and then back to her mother. 'There's a hole in my bedroom ceiling.'

'Don't you remember?'

'Should I?'

Her mother flipped open the lid and handed her a pill. 'Swallow.'

* * *

Bailey bound through the park with a cheerful stride, unconcerned by the ache in her side and the drizzle that covered her. She skipped over puddles, sidestepped people with a smile and even laughed as a big wet dog shook itself dry, covering her in spots.

There was no other explanation for it: she must have blacked out. She must have been in the attic and simply blacked out. But why couldn't she remember? And what possible reason did she have for going into the attic in the first place?

According to her mother—who seemed more upset than anyone—she heard a commotion and ran upstairs to find Bailey dangling through a hole in the ceiling, screaming manically at the top of her lungs and struggling to break free.

It didn't bother Bailey too much that she couldn't remember a whole chunk of yesterday evening. But if it were to happen again, and if something more serious were to take place, maybe she'd feel differently.

A dog's deep bark boomed behind her and she turned to see its owner struggling to drag it away from a tall man wearing a knee-length black coat. The man intrigued her, and not just because of his choice of clothes. He walked with careful, measured steps and hid his face beneath a black brimmed hat. As she watched, his pace slowed.

Was *he* the Irishman? She considered confronting him, but dismissed the thought as nonsense. Even if the Irishman did intend to track her down, could he do it so quickly with just a mobile phone number to work from? She thought not, but even so, she headed off at a faster pace. When she reached a line of trees at the edge of the meadow, she was pleased to see that the tall man in black had vanished.

Although the morning hadn't started well, she felt pumped and ready to tackle the day. Even the thought of spending time with Smeak didn't discourage her. Maybe a new week meant a new start? She would happily give him another chance.

Someone grabbed her shoulders and she turned with arms raised.

'Hang on slugger,' a man said.

Dressed in lycra bottoms and rugby shirt, she recognised the fitness fanatic who'd saved her from an upset Asian three weeks ago. He'd been pestering her ever since. 'Oh, it's you,' she said, before walking away.

He sidled up to her. 'Have you got time for breakfast?'

He had a strong face, she liked that. And thick blond hair. 'Sorry, no can do.'

'In a rush?'

'Work,' she said. 'Where are your women today?'

He laughed. 'My first class doesn't start until nine. What is it you do for a living?'

'Why?'

'Just curious.'

In truth she was a professional washer-upper, but she'd promised herself never to tell anyone. 'I work at a cafe in town.'

'Well,' he said. 'It seems to be working for you.'

'Why d'you say that?'

'Because you're looking great.'

Wearing a leather jacket, jeans, trainers and nothing more than eyeliner, Bailey guessed he was talking out of his arse. She grunted.

'Your hair looks lovely.'

She eyed him suspiciously and ran a hand over her head to check her ponytail was still in place.

'You've definitely got more colour in your cheeks as well.'

She hated her rosey cheeks—they made her look wholesome and young.

'And you're not wearing your rings.'

'That's where you're wrong.' She held up her left hand to show him the one ring she wore on her little finger.

'Cool,' he said.

Who the hell says *cool*? She stopped and placed a hand between them. 'Here's the thing, you seem nice enough …' The way he stood made him look incredibly buff. 'But you're just not my type.'

'Are you sure?'

'Of course I'm sure.'

'Oh, I get it,' he said with a nod and a smile that made his face glow.

'Get what?'

'You bat for the other side.'

She scoffed. 'I don't bat for any side. There's no batting. I just don't fancy you. Get over it.'

'That's a shame, because I think you're definitely an eight out of ten.'

'Only an eight?'

'Yeah, that's pretty good though. It means I think

279

you're lovely.

'You can't just go around telling people you think they're lovely.'

'Why not?'

'It's …' She searched for the word. 'Disturbing.'

'I bet some people would think it's nice.'

'Oh yeah, and you'd know would you?'

'No, but …'

Bailey pointed to three women dressed in bright sports clothing at the park entrance. They bounced around pulling stretches. 'Like them you mean?'

'Part of my nine o'clock class,' he said.

'Well …' She walked on. 'Best you get started.'

'By the way,' he called after her. 'My name's Matt.'

Without stopping she turned her head, waved a hand and said, 'Whatever.'

Chapter Four

Bailey slipped through the side gate at five past nine, went in the back door and up the stairs to the snug where she found Smeak sitting on the sofa with a clipboard on his lap.

He checked his watch and wrote something down. 'How many days have you been working here, Miss Jacobs?'

Bailey bit her lip and counted. 'Is this like the fifth?'

'Indeed.' Smeak cleared his throat. 'And how many days have you arrived late?'

Bailey removed her jacket and hung it up. 'It wasn't my fault, the traffic was—'

'Please don't,' Smeak said. 'There isn't an excuse that I haven't heard. The fact is, you're a slacker, Jacobs. And nobody likes a slacker.'

Bailey slipped an apron over her head and began tying it at the front. 'I'll definitely try better tomorrow.'

'No, Miss Jacobs. You'll try *harder*, tomorrow. *Better* is not a noun to be prefixed with *try*.'

She nodded.

'I'll not accept any further tardiness from you. Do we understand each other?'

Bailey wasn't sure they did, but nodded anyway.

'Good.' He stood and motioned to the door. 'Now jump to it, Jacobs. Work awaits.'

Bailey jumped, heading for the stairs and thumping each in quick succession. A tray of dirties waited for her in the kitchen and she pulled on a pair of yellow gloves before filling the sink with hot water and bubbles.

Moments later, the swing door swung open and she turned to see Christine carrying a single spoon. 'That's about all I can manage today,' Christine said, giggling as she dropped it into the sink.

'Tough weekend?' Bailey asked.

Christine nodded. 'Last night I went for a drink with Jill from class. She's split from her husband. You should see her drink. Her sorrows were properly drowned.'

'What class?'

'Art class.' Christine giggled. 'Every Wednesday night at the university.'

Intrigued at the prospect of developing her drawing skills and perhaps learning more about paintings and artists along the way, Bailey asked, 'Is there room for another?'

'Um …' Christine fidgeted with her apron. 'I'm not sure if it's your type of thing.'

'You don't know that. I like to draw and I was pretty good at school,' Bailey said. 'And it wouldn't be my first art class.'

'Um …'

'Can I go with you or not?'

'Okay. That's a date.'

'Well,' Bailey said, remembering the last time Christine invited her out. 'Not an actual *date*, like, you know.' She grinned. 'Just friends, right?'

'Sure,' Christine grinned back. 'Friends. By the way, it's £25 for five classes. You can pay on the night.'

'Right,' Bailey said, wondering where she was going to get the money from now that her mother had to pay for a new ceiling. 'Not a problem.'

* * *

When lunchtime arrived, Bailey peeled off her gloves, scraped back her hair and popped in one of Christine's mints.

'Going anywhere nice?' Arthur asked as he dried a stack of plates faster than she would ever be able to. 'Lunching with the man of your dreams perhaps?'

Arthur was at least sixty, but acted half his age. Had he actually been half his age she wouldn't have put it passed him to ask her out. Had he been half his age, six inches taller and better looking, she might not have waited for him to make the first move.

'Not exactly,' she said, hanging her apron behind the door. 'I've got a favour to ask someone and I'm not sure how he's going to respond.' In fact, she thought, I don't know if he's going to be at all happy.

Out through the side gate and onto the cobbled lane, Bailey pressed through the shoppers to the art gallery at the top of the courtyard. The gallery door tinged once as she opened it.

'Ah, Miss Jacobs.' Clemence's voice sailed across the gallery floor, sweeping past a well-dressed couple inspecting a gaudy sculpture of a child climbing a tree. 'My Guardian Angel. How may I assist you today?'

Bailey shuffled inside, careful to avoid anything that looked more expensive than she could afford to replace—which was pretty much everything. She offered her hand and Clemence took it in both of his, kissing it gently as he bowed.

'Come, my friend.' He turned to a red-haired lady in the far corner of the room. 'Miriam, tea for Miss Jacobs if you please.' He turned to Bailey. 'Or would you prefer something else.'

'Do you have Coke?'

'Of course. Miriam, A Coke for Miss Jacobs.' He took her by the arm and led her to a leather sofa positioned beneath an abstract green and yellow painting of equal width. 'Sit, please. And tell me, to what do I owe this pleasure?'

Feeling out of place and conscious that a very large and heavy-looking painting hung a couple of feet above her head, Bailey faltered, 'I …' Even though the room was cool and fresh, she felt herself crimson. 'You said that you would help me if you could.'

'It would be an honour,' he said, striking a fist across his chest. 'You went out of your way to help Clemence, so the least Clemence can do is help you in return. Anything within my power to give, is yours. All you have to do is name it.'

Ten days ago Bailey put an end to the escape plans of an art thief who had lifted a painting from Clemence's gallery. Clemence's appreciation extended to him offering to repay her kindness any way he could. Now she was ready to collect. 'I want to improve my art,' she said, delighting in the smile that stretched his face.

'Ah, you're an artist. A great thing indeed,' he said. 'What is your preferred medium?'

'Er,' said Bailey, making a raspberry sound as she shifted her weight on the leather sofa. 'Pencils.'

Clemence's smile didn't waver, but she could tell he considered his next words carefully. 'I can see,' he said, 'a certain beauty to be had using pencils.'

'I've used other things as well, paints and stuff, but pencils are easier, not so much mess and there's always one to hand. Anyway, I want to take an evening course at the art college, but I don't have the money to pay for it.'

'Problem be gone,' Clemence said, squeezing her hand. 'Clemence will take care of the cost. Present the bill and it will be settled.'

Miriam approached with a tray and two glasses. Bailey took the one nearest to her and sipped. 'The course costs £25 and I need the money up front.'

'For such a worthwhile course,' he said taking the second glass. 'That seems a trifle expense. Miriam, please remove £50 from the safe and bring it to me. Bailey is to embark on a voyage of discovery.'

'Thank you so much,' Bailey said. 'But I only need £25.'

He touched her knee. 'Then spend the rest on something else. But promise one thing,' he added. 'You'll return to see Clemence again soon. And bring your first completed work of art.'

Bailey nodded, wondering if she would. 'I promise.'

'So, let us drink …' He raised his glass. 'To a deal made between friends.'

Bailey smiled and sipped. 'Cheers, Mr C.'

* * *

By the time Bailey finished work she was hot, tired and irritable. Home seemed a long way away and she reached for her mobile to call a taxi, but the phone was dead and she swore at it before heading off on foot.

The park was busy as always and her thoughts turned to the money in her pocket and the art class it was going to pay for on Wednesday. She looked forward to an evening out, even if that meant a couple of hours with Christine in a classroom. Not until she reached the top of the park and saw a man disappear into a thicket of trees, did she think about the Irishman.

She jogged the rest of the way home and reached the front door out of breath.

Her brother passed her in the hallway without speaking. A pink mask covered half his face and she tried not to laugh as he scuttled upstairs.

Bailey dropped into a kitchen chair and took a moment to catch her breath. 'Coke,' she said, pointing to a new bottle on the worktop. 'Please.'

Her mother took an opened bottle from the fridge and poured a glass. 'What's up with you?'

Bailey didn't stop until the glass was empty. She smacked her lips and said, 'I think someone's following me.'

Her mother folded a tea-towel, seemingly unsurprised.

'There's a suspicious man in the park, Mum.'

'Suspicious?'

'Yeah,' Bailey said. 'Suspicious.'

'What did he look like?'

'All dressed in black. Black coat, black shoes, black hat. Suspicious-looking.'

Her mother peered through the kitchen window, seemingly distracted by something outside. 'Oh, I shouldn't worry too much about him.'

'That's why I need a new phone,' Bailey blurted. 'This one's knackered and if someone *is* following me …'

Her mother turned from the window. 'Don't you think you've had enough from me recently? The boots and the laptop, I've got to repair your bedroom ceiling, now this. I'm not made of money.'

Bailey bit her lip as she considered the money stashed away in her mother's bedroom. She refilled her glass, drank and waited for the tension to fade. Then she asked, 'Did Dad ever hurt Timothy?'

Her mother's face tightened. 'Why do you ask that?'

'I keep dreaming about something bad that happened, but it's not clear. Dad's got a baby in his arms—I assume it's Tim—they're in a field. You and I are watching from the car. I'm scared and you're crying.'

Her mother's eye twitched once and she turned her back.

'Mum?'

Staring through the kitchen window, her mother shook her head, but it was so prolonged and pronounced that Bailey wasn't sure whether it was intended for her or someone outside. When she crossed the room and dropped her glass into the sink, she saw the tail end of a black car driving away from the house.

'Sorry, darling,' her mother smiled meekly. 'What did you say?'

Chapter Five

The hazy morning sun, already several inches clear of Farnham's roof-tops, drifted in a dreamy-blue sky as Bailey crossed the park on her way to work. In town, she took the alley from Castle Street to Lamb Yard, passing a pub and a courtyard of offices. When she reached a cluster of industrial retail bins bordering the shopping area, she was surprised to see a man appear from between them.

Looking distinctly unkept and underfed, he rushed at Bailey and grabbed her by the shoulders as he pushed her against a wall. 'What did you tell the coppers?'

She smelled the heady mix of tobacco and alcohol. And a trace of sick.

'What did you tell 'em?'

Bailey placed a foot against the wall and levered herself forward, pushing his scrawny body back. 'Who the hell are you?' she yelled as he tripped and fell, hitting his head on the tarmac. He scrambled to his feet and it dawned on her that she'd seen him somewhere before. About two weeks ago when she pushed him through the coffee shop window. 'Danny Douglas,' she said. 'The Bird Thief.'

'So the papers say.' He massaged his head. 'Thanks to you.'

He stepped forward and she raised her fists. 'What do you want, Danny?'

'Not to fight with a girl, that's for sure.' He cleared his

throat and spat. 'The coppers are trying to fit me up with jobs I never done.' He produced a packet of tobacco and started rolling a cigarette. 'They say I stole more paintings than I did. Some from a warehouse in Aldershot and from my mate's house at the top of town.'

She lowered her hands. 'Your mate's house?'

'Yeah, Podge's place.'

'Where does he live?'

'Top of the park.'

'Brampton Road?'

'I dunno.'

She wondered if it was too much of a coincidence. 'When you say *Podge*, do you mean Mr Lancaster?'

Danny flipped open a lighter and drew his next breath from the end of the cigarette. 'Dunno. Everyone calls him Podge because he's fat.'

Bailey's brain purred with the speed it worked. She was looking for a man named Doogie, and if Mr Lancaster was affectionately known as Podge, did that mean Doogie was standing in front of her now? 'Does he know your name?'

'What sort of stupid question is that?'

'I mean does he call you Danny, or does he know you by something else like Doogie?'

'Yeah, that's it. *Doogie Fetch,* 'cos I've got a knack of retrieving. Get it?'

'Yeah, I get it,' Bailey said. 'But you didn't do a very good job of retrieving all the paintings.'

'Exactly. That's what I'm trying to tell the coppers. I didn't do the warehouse and I didn't do Podge's place.'

'I know you didn't do Podge's place, because he told me you talked him into breaking into his own house.'

'S'that what he said?'

'Not in so many words, but yes.'

Danny blew a balloon of smoke that filled the space between them. 'He was keen enough when I told him there was a chance to make some decent money. Who wouldn't be? All we had to do was find a few paintings and pass 'em on to this dealer guy and he'd let us know if they were any good.'

'So you made a list and started to track down the paintings?'

'*He* made the list.'

'Who?' Bailey asked.

'The dealer guy. He drives a fancy red Merc. Very nice. He'd given the list to a mate of mine who'd done some business with him before. My mate gave me a copy. I already knew who had the paintings from the warehouse so I thought it was easy money.'

'Who was it?'

Danny squinted.

'Who had the paintings from the warehouse?'

'Fella from Green Hill bought 'em off a security guard. Unofficially of course. He passed 'em on to some of the local traders and I called round to get 'em back. I was half way to getting clean away from that nobby gallery when you pushed me through the window.'

It all made sense, she thought. A petty thief trying to earn some easy money, but going about it like a blundering clown. 'So, what do you want me to do about it?'

Danny shifted his weight between feet. 'You can tell the coppers I didn't do the other jobs.'

Even if should could help, Bailey didn't understand why he thought she would. 'What makes you think I can help?'

'You're tight with 'em.'

'Tight?' she said.

'Yeah. In the lockup, they were talking about you as if you're something special.'

'What?'

'One said he'd like to teach you a thing or two, the other told him he couldn't 'cos you're a *special case*.'

'Do you mean like I'm stupid?'

'Far from it. I got the impression she meant you were significant.'

'She?' Bailey asked.

'Yeah. The other one was a bloke. I couldn't see their faces.'

Tierney, Bailey thought. It had to be him. The creep of a policeman who hated her for no good reason and went out of his way to let her know. 'Danny,' Bailey said. 'Tell me about the Dealer? The one who drives the red Mercedes.'

'You don't wanna go down that road, missy.' Danny sucked in the last of the cigarette and stamped it out on the ground. 'Not if you know what's good for you.'

* * *

The conversation with Danny made her late for work again and Smeak was there to record it with a familiar sneer.

The day dragged and she crawled with it, switching to automatic as she washed and dried and made small talk when needed. She laboured the hours away, smiling at Arthur's jokes and nodding at Christine's excited account of their upcoming art class. And all the while, Bailey escaped to other places.

The Dealer had a property in Bentley, a small village a few miles from Farnham. Danny had told her what he knew about him, which wasn't much. He said he had his fingers in a lot of holes, not just art but collectables as well—and he didn't mind if it was legit. There was talk of him having dealings in London, something big but Danny didn't know what. One thing Danny was sure about though: he didn't like the look of him—he had an edge, something nasty.

None of that bothered Bailey, if she planned it properly then infiltrating the Dealer's premises would be a breeze. It was all about not being caught. Danny was a blundering clown—she would be a ghost in the shadows.

Smeak was away for most of the day, but he returned to the coffee shop in time to collide with Bailey as she rushed out of the building at a minute after five.

'Sorry,' she said, not stopping to see what happened to the contents of the cup he'd been holding.

There was no sign of the Irishman and Bailey made it home in record time. By half past five she was sitting at her desk with her laptop open, using Google Maps to survey the Dealer's address in Bentley.

A chill crept through the hole in the ceiling and she shuddered. Had she really gone into the attic of her own accord? That didn't seem like her at all, but she was certain the memory would come back to her at some stage.

According to her virtual drive-past, the Dealer's place in Bentley was an isolated farmhouse surrounded by fields and separated from the road by trees and a very high wall. It had a number of outbuildings, one as large as the house.

Bailey circled Bentley train station and the Dealer's

premises on a map, then she drew a line along the road that joined them. Spreading her hand between the two points, she guessed the distance to be about a mile.

Her plan was to catch a mid-morning train for the five minute journey to Bentley, locate the Dealer's place, confirm the presence of the stolen paintings and update Constable Mundy. If everything ran smoothly, she'd be home in time for tea.

Unlike Constable Tierney, Wendy Mundy was courteous and approachable, and Bailey felt they had an understanding. She trusted the policewoman—even liked her.

She folded the map and slipped it inside her jacket. A gust of cold air made her shiver and she glanced at the broken ceiling.

Enough, she thought as she pushed her chair beneath the opening and climbed up. Using the edge of the hole to steady herself, she tiptoed on her chair to get a better view inside. Cardboard boxes were stacked everywhere and she reached for the nearest one, but it was too heavy and her grip too slight for her to move it.

She got down, collected a handful of bird books and a dictionary, and stacked them on the chair. Then she gingerly climbed back up, pushed her head and shoulders through the hole and reached for the box with both hands. This time it moved and a smaller box on top moved with it. She pulled again and they edged closer until catching on a lip in the attic floor. Bailey thought if she reached in further she could get a better grip and tug it free. So she tried … and it all happened very quickly after that.

As she pulled, the front of the box remained caught and the rear of the box lifted, tilting the smaller box on top towards her. She raised her hands to protect her face against the objects spilling from it, but lost her balance and felt the books on the chair slide beneath her feet. Instinct took over and she reached out to stop herself falling, but was unable to find anything solid to hold onto.

Her scream—although loud and piercing—was hidden by the sound of a huge chunk of ceiling crashing to the carpet, along with two boxes, their scattered contents and a monsoon of dust.

She coughed and wiped her face as the commotion died and the dust plumed and settled around her.

The sound of hurried footsteps on the stairs forced her up and across the room where she closed and locked the bedroom door.

Someone knocked. 'Are you okay in there?'

'Fine, Mum.'

'What on earth was that noise?'

Bailey's attention was drawn to the items laying on the floor at her feet. 'Nothing,' she said, spitting dirt from her mouth.

'Why is there so much dust out here?'

'Is there?'

'Are you sure you're okay?'

She nudged a piece of plaster with her toe to reveal a pile of photographs. She cocked her head to get a better look at the top photo and the man standing next to her father. 'Yeah,' she said. 'Couldn't be better.'

* * *

Among the various photos of cars, buildings and scenery that she didn't recognise, Bailey found one showing a snow-white dog and some children playing in the front garden of a terraced house. She identified herself and her dog, Powder, but the house and the other children meant nothing to her.

There was a photo of her mother wearing a nightie, looking rosy-cheeked and carrying a bundle which Bailey assumed to be her baby brother. And there were three photos of her father. She lay them on the desk and pulled her jacket tight against the chill coming through the even larger hole in the ceiling.

She'd only ever seen one picture of her father and she consumed these new ones eagerly. He looked so handsome. In one of them he stood beside a blond-haired man of similar size and build, they both wore leather jackets and broad smiles, but only one had dimples. She pulled a face and felt the clefts in her own cheeks. Definitely her father's daughter.

Having sifted through both boxes and put back everything of little interest, she was left holding two items: a charm bracelet and a fluffy rabbit the size of her hand. The rabbit smelled of damp and she tossed it across the room onto her bed where it rolled in the dust. Then she turned her attention to the bracelet and inspected the charms. There were three in total—one for each birthday her father had been *alive*. That had been his special gift to her—every year he'd buy a new charm for her bracelet. She wondered what the fourteen missing charms looked like and where they were now.

It was after midnight when Bailey slipped into bed. With her head consumed by thoughts of her father, the Irishman and the Dealer in Bentley, she hoped for sleep but feared the worst.

Chapter Six

Bailey woke to a high-pitched scream and sat up shaking.

Her mother stood in the doorway, eyes wide with one hand over her mouth, the other carrying a tray. 'What happened?' She stared at the hole in the ceiling. 'You must have been freezing.'

'Maybe a little,' Bailey said, pulling the duvet to her chin.

'Why didn't you say something?'

'I didn't want to …'

'You didn't want to make a nuisance of yourself after that silliness with Timmy.' Her mother blew dust from the desk and put the tray down. 'You poor thing. You've got such a good heart.'

Bailey shrugged.

'Here,' her mother said. 'A glass of Coke and a biscuit will cheer you up. And there's another tablet for you to take as well.' She hovered over the photos. 'Where did you get these?'

Bailey couldn't remember which photos she'd left on top, but from the tone of her mother's voice, she guessed it was the ones of her father. 'I found them in a box in the attic.'

'Were you snooping around up there?'

'I wasn't *snooping*. I was trying to use the boxes to block the hole to stop the wind getting in. That way you wouldn't have to buy a new ceiling.'

'He was a good-looking man, your father.'

Bailey got out of bed and joined her. She picked up the glass and pointed to the photo of her dad standing next to the blond-haired man. 'Is that Quinn Maguire?'

'Yes, how do you know that?'

'Aunt Liz. I spoke with her when you took Tim to the hospital.'

'You spoke with Elizabeth?'

Bailey drank, wondering how much trouble she was going to be in.

'How is she?'

She tried to think. In the time she'd spent on the phone with Aunt Liz talking about her father and Aunt Liz's role in introducing him to her mother, Bailey hadn't bothered to ask how she was doing. 'Don't know. But she said that she and Quinn were the ones who introduced you to Dad. Is that right?'

'Yes. Elizabeth was going out with Quinn long before I met your father. She pestered me for ages for a double-date. I eventually gave in and fell for him that first night. He was ever so handsome.'

Bailey spoke with a mouth full of custard cream, 'He's a funny looking man.'

'Quinn?' Her mother laughed. 'Quinn was a charmer. He could talk his way into and out of anything. He had such a lovely voice. Deep and gravelly.' She laughed again. 'Like a sack of rocks.'

'What?'

'Elizabeth used to say he had a voice like a sack of rocks being dragged along the ground.'

Bailey studied Quinn's face. Was he the Irishman with the baritone voice? He looked more comical than threatening. 'Why doesn't Aunt Liz visit us?'

Her mother picked up another photo and ran a finger

across it. 'This is me,' she said. 'Just back from hospital with your brother.'

Bailey opened the large cardboard box that had come through the ceiling, and retrieved a yellow blanket. 'I think it's the one in the picture.'

'Oh yes,' her mother said, holding it to her face.

Bailey saw a tear crown in her mother's eye and she squeezed her arm. 'Mum, why doesn't Aunt Liz visit?'

'I don't know, sweetheart. We just grew apart. Here, take your pill.'

'But you're twins. You told me you were so close.'

'We were once, but these things happen sometimes. Take your pill, get dressed and I'll fix you something nice for lunch. Do you know where the bacon went?'

'Don't you mean, breakfast?'

Her mother patted her hand and smiled. 'At eleven thirty? Here, swallow.'

'Shit, no time for that,' Bailey said, pushing her mother aside. 'I need to get going. I'm investigating a very important case today.'

* * *

Damn, damn, damn, damn, damn.

Bailey hurried through the park, bootlaces whipping around her ankles, rucksack over one shoulder and sweat rolling down the small of her back.

Damn.

Her one day off and she had slept in.

She'd planned to spend the morning investigating the crooked art dealer in Bentley. But oh no, sloppy head had struck again.

Bugger.

Avoiding a triage of ladies gathered around a pram, Bailey stepped onto the grass and felt something soft squelch beneath her boot. 'Don't mind me,' she said as she limped passed, prompting one of the women to mumble something in return that she didn't understand.

Back on the path, she stopped to check her boot which, from the hideous smell, had landed on a fresh pile of dog poo. Using the edge of the grass to scrape the worst off, she saw something out of the corner of her eye. Without making it too obvious she was checking him out, she snatched a glance back along the path and recognised the tall stranger she had seen in the park recently. He was closer this time and although she couldn't see his eyes, he was heading straight for her.

She panicked, took a breath and bolted across the field, trying not to lose her footing on the damp grass. Without turning round, she headed for the benches at the top of the golf course where the figure of an old man sat. Even from behind, she recognised the Colonel—his white hair and thin shoulders were easy to spot. She reached him out of breath and doubled over. When she found the strength to look up, all she could do was point.

The Colonel followed her finger across the field and frowned.

'I think,' she said between pants. 'Someone's following me.'

He seemed concerned, but said nothing.

'That telephone number.' She wheezed. 'From the code we cracked. I rang it. And I spoke with a man.'

'Your father?'

'Irish, yes. But not my father.'

'What did he say?'

Bailey sat and put the rucksack between her feet. She

pushed back a lock of wet hair and fanned her shirt to cool her stomach. As her breathing eased, she told the Colonel everything. She told him about the Irishman's telephone threat. She told him about contacting Aunt Liz and her role in putting her parents together. And she told him about the contents of the box she found in her mother's wardrobe.

He seemed unsettled. 'Do you trust your mother?'

'What kind of question is that?'

'It's a question that has more or less bearing depending on what answer you give. Do you trust her or not?'

'Of course. She's my mother.'

'And the bad man in Ireland is your father, but something tells me you trust him rather less.'

Bailey hesitated. Did she really trust her mother? With all the secrets between them, she wondered.

The old man reached across and placed a wrinkled hand on her arm. 'Come to my house.'

'What?'

'Come to my house. I have something to give you.'

Four weeks ago his proposition would have resulted in a slap or at least a verbal assault. But now? She hardly knew the Colonel and yet she respected him more than any man alive.

'Find your way to Granny's Antiques at the top of Pine Hill. Turn right onto Ridgeway, walk past the play area and I am on the left. Look through the oak trees for a yellow bay-fronted house. That will be mine.'

'Right,' said Bailey, thinking it must be a big house if it had more than one oak tree in the driveway. 'Will do.'

The Colonel turned and waved to a blonde-haired lady standing at the edge of the car park. 'I have to go,' he said.

'Shit, I mean, so have I.' Bailey stood but the Colonel didn't. She saw him kiss two fingers and lay them on the bench, taking a moment to close his eyes as his lips moved to words she couldn't hear. 'Why do you do that?'

'Kiss her bench?'

'Whose bench?'

'Did you never notice the plaque?' He stood and pointed to a mottled bronze plaque set in the back of the bench.

Maggie Baxter. My love. My life.
Col. Baxter (2008)

'This was our spot,' he said. 'We were married forty-two years and almost every Sunday we strolled through the park together, coming to rest here beneath the tree. We'd look out across the fields to Farnham and make plans for the future. That was long before they built the golf course.'

'Your wife's dead?'

He nodded.

'Then who's that woman?'

'Annie? She's a friend.'

'I've seen you kiss her.'

'A good friend.' He chuckled. 'With benefits. Now go, little bird. Be on your way, but promise to come and see me soon and please …' He took her arm and squeezed until her eyes settled on his. 'Keep your wits about you.'

* * *

Pushing through a crowd on the corner of Castle Street, Bailey crossed the road with less care than her mother taught her, resulting in the belch of a car's horn and stares from passers-by.

Having ducked into bushes, doubled back and at one stage hidden in the children's play area, it had taken longer than normal for her to reach the town centre. As far as she could tell, her manoeuvres had worked because the Irishman was nowhere to be seen.

Ducking into the alley between the bank and the shoe shop, she hurried on. She knew she had left it late, but if the trains were running in her favour and luck was on her side, she could still get everything done in time.

As she weaved across the busy car park a scruffy little dog skipped alongside her.

Duncan.

She looked around for its owner and sure enough, saw a man dressed in brown sitting beneath a tree eating a sandwich. She walked over to him. 'Hey,' she said. 'Still here then?'

The man stood and pocketed the sandwich. 'Seems so.'

Bailey had grown fond of Jack and was getting used to bumping into him around town over recent weeks. He was a tramp, he lived on the street and her mother wouldn't approve of them being friends, but there was something endearing about him that she liked. He had made plans to leave Farnham, and she was going to miss him when he eventually did. 'What were you before … all this?' She dropped her rucksack on the ground and the dog sniffed it.

'Before becoming a man of leisure?' He laughed. 'I worked in a bank. In London.'

Bailey nodded, realising she was late and wished she hadn't asked the question.

'I had one shitty customer too many and decided to

pack it in and travel. That was just over a year ago.'

'Been anywhere nice?'

'Canterbury was lovely. That's where my travels started. I'm trying to do as many of the cathedral cities as I can. Chichester was all right, but Guildford was way too busy. After that I stopped in Farnham and never got going again. But I think we'll be setting off for Winchester soon. Duncan's not fussed as long as he gets his breakfast.' Jack pulled the dog away from the bag. 'What's in the bag?'

Bailey moved the rucksack behind her legs. 'Just a few essentials.'

'How's your new job?'

'Don't ask. When there's more time and less drama, I'll tell you about it.'

'That bad?'

She puffed.

'What about the search for your dad?'

'Some progress,' she said. 'That Shakespeare quote you weren't able to decipher, turned out to be an encrypted phone number.'

'Really?'

'Yeah, but it wasn't as helpful as I hoped.'

'How so?'

'I think I spoke with one of my Dad's old friends. You might think that's a good thing, but I'm not so sure. He sounded pretty scary.'

'Too bad,' Jack said, lifting his hat, combing a main of brown hair with his fingers and resetting it. 'So that's the end of that?'

'No. But it means I need to take a different tac.'

'Which is what?'

'My Auntie, I'm softening her up. Did I tell you she

and Mum are identical twins?'

'No.' He sounded surprised.

'Yeah, I'm sure she knows more than she's saying and I'm going to find out what. Plus,' Bailey said. 'I've got another case on. A dodgy art dealer. I'm going to visit him now.'

'Good luck with that,' Jack said. 'Do you want some company?'

'Not really.' His face dropped. 'But you can walk me to the station.'

They set off at a slow pace and by the time they reached the river at the meadow on the south side of town, Bailey had caught Jack up with almost all the latest news.

'And tonight,' she said as they sat on a bench watching a man teach a young boy how to launch a kite. 'I'm starting art class.'

'I never took you for an artist. Are you any good?'

'Used to be.'

The man ran backwards furiously pulling a string and the boy squealed as the kite bounced along the grass.

Bailey took out her mobile and the screen blinked on to let her know she had left it too late. There was no way she could get to Bentley, find the Dealer, solve the case and get back home in time for tea. She stretched. She may as well not go now. She may as well stay and enjoy the moment: Jack's company, the meadow and the debut launch of the challenging kite.

She turned to the tramp. 'Smeak's still being a dick.'

Chapter Seven

Standing outside the boxy building on Faulkner Road, listening to students mix banter with profound statements as they trickled in, Bailey felt her stomach churn with the twist of regret at not having gone to college. Things seemed so much easier at school—and she would have no problem fitting in with this lot.

She scanned the evening shadows in search of the Irishman. Nothing.

A bright girl with a good future, but disillusioned at the time, Bailey had jumped at a job instead of furthering her education. As it turned out, the chicken factory wasn't a great move for her because that's where she met Paul and fell in love. And within six months, she'd lost a baby and he'd lost her trust. It still hurt to think about it, but every day that passed was making it easier to do so.

Now, as she stood in front of a sign for the Farnham University of Creative Arts, she longed to have the reassuring arms of a school around her.

Someone brushed past and she flinched. A tall boy sauntered to the building, a bag over one arm and a folder under the other. As he disappeared through the college doors, something poked her in the back and someone giggled.

'Hello, new girl.'

Bailey smelled cigarettes and turned to see Christine's pale face alive with smiles. She had done something with her hair and her skin looked incredible clear. 'Hi.'

'Got your war paint on then,' Christine said.

Bailey had decided not to leave the house that evening without a full spread of makeup. If the Irishman was going to tackle her, he'd get her looking her best.

'I love the lips. Black is so sexy.'

Bailey wet them, blew her a kiss and cracked a smile.

'Remember,' Christine said playfully. 'We're just friends, not lovers.' She set off in the wake of the tall boy.

Bailey followed her into an airy, air-conditioned reception with sand-coloured marble tiles that sucked at the soles of her boots. They walked along a bright corridor with art-covered walls and a ceiling interrupted by skylights. A group of people passed by, excited by a conversation Bailey couldn't follow.

'This way,' Christine said as she turned into another corridor and slowed until Bailey drew level. 'Have you been here before?'

'Once,' Bailey said, recalling the time last September when her mother insisted she visit before accepting the job at the chicken factory.

'Did you meet, Giovanni?'

'Who?'

'The art teacher. Giovanni Palumpo. He's Italian.'

'Palumpo?' Bailey imagined a sweaty fat man with greasy skin. 'What's he like then?'

'Um ...' Christine said with a glint in her eye. 'You'll see.'

Up ahead, restless voices hummed behind a set of double doors. The volume increased as they pushed through into a bright industrial room where alternating desks and easels circled a table. A dozen people stood talking in groups and their faces turned for the briefest moment. Bailey spotted a man in mauve, but he didn't look Italian. The rest were a mix of females of different ages, some as old as her mother.

Christine led Bailey to the far corner. 'Do you want a desk or an easel? I prefer a desk, but go for what ever you want.'

'Can we sit together?' Bailey asked.

'If you want an easel, yes. Take that one.'

There was a slight chill in the room but Bailey removed her jacket anyway, rolling it into a ball and setting it beneath the easel next to Christine's desk. She wore a black t-shirt covered with a pirate's head and a background of smoke and flames.

Christine organised her desk with a large pad and an assortment of pastels. 'I didn't bring anything to draw with,' Bailey said. 'Or on.'

'What do you prefer using?'

'Not fussed.'

Christine pointed to a workbench along the far wall with doors beneath. 'You should find something in those cupboards.' She checked her watch and said, 'But do it quick because he'll be here soon.'

Who? Bailey thought. The plump Italian?

She found what she wanted in the second cupboard and laid out a block of paints and three brushes on a stand next to her easel. As she filled a beaker of water and settled down on the stool, the studio doors burst open and the room hushed.

Christine giggled and a woman whimpered.

'Buona sera, tutti.' A slender man with curly black hair marched inside and his aura ignited the room. He clapped his hands together twice with extravagant grace. 'To your seats. Velocemente.'

Christine fidgeted in her chair and sat up. She turned to

Bailey, mouthed the word *Giovanni* and giggled again.

Oh, Bailey thought, he's not fat at all.

Dressed in blue jeans and white shirt opened at the front to reveal a shiny chest, he cruised around the room, gesticulating as he spoke. 'Benvenuto, ladies … and gentleman.' He nodded to the man in mauve and the girls either side of him laughed. 'How are you today?'

Some replied in murmurs, but one women held up her hand and let out a high-pitched squeak.

He pointed at her. 'Si, Annabella.'

Annabella fidgeted on her chair as he neared. 'I was practicing with my boyfriend at the weekend,' she said, 'in oils.'

'Molto bene, Annabella.' He touched her arm and moved on. 'Anybody else?'

Apparently, nobody else had. Or at least, Bailey thought, they weren't willing to let on.

The girl on Bailey's left had red hair and a large chest that she made the most of with the help of a tight jumper. Giovanni ran a finger along the front of her desk and flashed a smile as he passed. And then he noticed Bailey.

'Ah, impressionante.' He stopped beside her easel and exaggerated his gaze.

She took a breath and savoured his musky scent. Clean shaven with rich olive skin, he hardly seemed old enough to be taking the class. But there was a devilish glint in his big brown eyes that told her this was a man, not a boy. She quivered. 'Hello.'

'Bella signorina, come ti chiami?'

The weight of stares from the rest of the class unsettled her. 'Pardon?'

He touched her arm and his fingers felt hot. 'I ask, what is your name?'

'Bailey,' she said, only breaking contact with his eyes to delight in his smile. 'Bailey Jacobs.'

'Ah, Miss Jacobs. How are you today?'

'Okay, I suppose.'

'Please ... stand.'

'What?'

He took her elbow. 'Let me regard you.'

Bailey edged herself off the stool and stood before him.

He seemed to trawl her body with his eyes, grazing on her features. 'Eccellente,' he said. 'You're very welcome to my class.' Then he turned and walked to the table in the middle of the room and every face followed him. 'This evening I promised you something very special.'

A buzz of excitement spread.

'But the model, he is unable to join us.'

Christine caught Bailey's eye, her mouth had sagged like a wet rag.

'So, let me ask if anybody here wishes to take his place.' Giovanni moved around the room again. 'Ah, bella Christina, will you share your gifts with us?'

'Um,' Christine's face blistered and she shook her head vigourously.

'No? Then perhaps our ripest member, Bailey Jacobs. Will you share your gifts with the class?'

Bailey didn't understand what he meant. 'Sorry,' she said. 'I don't have any gifts.'

People laughed.

'Ah, signorina is too modest. Or perhaps too shy or even afraid.'

'No I'm not,' Bailey said before catching sight of Christine waving her arms behind Giovanni's back in the universal sign that means *don't do it*. 'I'm not afraid of anything. I just, don't have anything to share.'

Laughter again and some of the class pointed. She glared at them.

'Muscle was promised and muscle you will have. So, Giovanni will model for you this evening.'

The news excited the class and an escalating murmur threatened to choke the room until Giovanni removed his shirt and there was silence.

Bailey peered around the side of the easel and watched him reach for his shoes. She felt herself being drawn forward, leaning so far that she almost fell off her stool. As he unbuckled the strip of leather around his waist and pulled it clear, she was conscious that she'd stopped breathing.

He released the poppers on his jeans and let them fall and Bailey, along with several other people, exhaled.

Giovanni stood in front of them wearing only a pair of tight, white boxer shorts that contrasted his olive-skin. He knelt to retrieve his trousers, folded them neatly and placed them on top of his shoes. Then he tucked his thumbs inside the edge of his shorts and pushed them to his ankles.

The room gasped.

Bailey managed a sideways glance to Christine who didn't notice because she had her eyes trained forward.

Giovanni lifted a stool onto the table and leapt up with a single bound. He sat and shuffled himself comfortable. 'Class,' he said. 'Begin.'

It was a while before Bailey managed to break free of her trance and when she eventually did, the rest of the class had already started.

She couldn't believe it—a naked god-like creature sat just ten feet away, a teasing smile parting his lips.

Her eyes welded with his.

Had he winked at her?

A warm glow blossomed inside as she selected a brush, wet the tip and began.

* * *

Chasing Christine outside, Bailey sprinted from the college building. 'Wow,' she said, catching her at the curb. 'That only cost me a fiver.'

Christine giggled. 'I thought you'd enjoy it.'

For almost the entire class Giovanni had been on display, sharing his machismo with the group, the fluorescent lights illuminating every inch of his sculpted, hairless body.

'You gave him a green willy.'

Although happy with progress on her unfinished piece, Bailey wasn't sure she had got his skin tone right. 'I know,' she said. 'And it was too big.'

'What? Yours or his?'

'Both.'

Christine lit a cigarette and offered the packet across.

'I didn't know you smoked,' Bailey said as she took one. 'But then you always smell minty.'

'Good job too. Mum doesn't know and Mr Smeak hates the habit.'

A handful of students exited the building behind them and loitered in a group. Their voices faded in the night air the further from the University Bailey and Christine walked. Street lamps provided pockets of amber light along the quiet back-road and Bailey quickened her pace between each one, eyeing the shadows with distrust.

'Um, drink?'

'After that experience …' Bailey took a long drag on her cigarette and spluttered. 'I could do with a stiff one.'

Having walked past it almost every day to get to work, Bailey knew where the Hop Blossom pub was, but had never been inside. A typical Farnham building, it looked old and curious and fronted by flowers. Nothing like the Excelsior Club Paul insisted they go to every Wednesday and Saturday to play snooker and watch football.

She followed Christine through the front door and an open fire welcomed her like an old friend. It wasn't overly crowded and some of the faces flicked their way, but none settled. A happy-looking fat woman stood behind a wooden bar, her breasts resting on the counter. Her smile dropped as they approached.

'IDs please.'

Christine handed over a driving licence which the woman duly checked and returned. Then she looked at Bailey. 'Got some ID on you?'

'I did have, but my bag was stolen. Everything taken.'

The bartender's eyes narrowed. 'How old are you?'

'Nineteen,' Bailey said without hesitating.

She scoffed. 'When were you born?'

'Fifteenth of March 1999. What about you?'

'What was number one that Christmas?'

'Dunno, I was too young to notice. But while you're jabbering, fix me half a pint of Carlsberg will you?'

She stiffened. 'You look familiar. Do I know you?'

'Would you like to?' She could see her luck fading as the bartender's patience ebbed. 'Look, I reported the theft to the police—Constable Tierney if you must know—call them if you don't believe me. And when you do, ask them if they've found it yet. My whole life was in that bag.'

'Hmph.' The bartender hesitated long enough for

Bailey to think she was going home without a drink, then she picked up a glass and started to fill it.

'That was a close one,' Christine said as they positioned themselves around an inconspicuous table near the fire. 'You've obviously done that before.'

Bailey nodded as she drank, then wiped her mouth. 'Fat people don't like me. Anyway, I thought you were seventeen?'

'I am,' Christine said. 'But my sister's not, and she looks just like me.'

'That's handy.' Bailey drank some more. 'Why didn't you tell me it was a life class?'

Christine put down her gin and dabbed her mouth with a finger. 'I did.'

'Did you? Maybe I wasn't listening. That was great though. How long have you been going?'

'About six months.'

Bailey took another gulp, picturing Giovanni's naked form. 'Have you ever?'

'What?'

'You know, have you ever been tempted?'

'With Giovanni? No. I mean, I wouldn't *say* no. Just that he's never made a move. But he seemed to like you.'

He did, Bailey thought as she raised her glass again. And I wouldn't say no either.

'I can guess what you're thinking,' Christine said. 'Do what you like, but Giovanni's a bit of a player.'

'What d'you mean?'

'Let's just say that he likes women. He *really* likes them. He's flirted with half the class at one time or another, even the men, and lots of them never come back. That reminds me, Jill wasn't there tonight.'

'Your friend who split from her husband? Was she

Giovanni's latest conquest?'

'Probably,' Christine said.

'Well, I guess some people are worth doing regardless of the consequences.' Bailey emptied her glass and held it up. 'Fancy another?'

Christine nodded. 'But you'd better take it easy. You've got work tomorrow and Thursday means you'll have Smeak's wife to deal with.'

'In that case,' Bailey said. 'This time, I'm going to ask my fat friend for a pint.'

Chapter Eight

The taxi screeched to a stop at a junction, the shrill sound of its brakes raking through Bailey's nerves. Then it sped off and she lurched to one side as it rattled along, veering this way and that as the road turned.

'Open the window if you're going to puke, love.'

Piss off and don't call me love. Her stomach spasmed and she heaved a pocket of bile-infused air, releasing it through tight lips. 'Hurry,' she said, her face slapping the window as the taxi sped around Farnham's streets. When it eventually stopped, she climbed out, slammed the door and groaned. How the hell was she going to make it through the day?

She didn't remember much about the previous night. There'd been drink—lots of it—and laughs too. According to her mother, the *brouhaha* began just after one in the morning when Bailey arrived home singing a Sinéad O'Connor song. Unable to open the front door, she ended up banging on it loud enough to wake the neighbours. Although Timothy helped, getting her upstairs was an ungainly and awkward process that resulted in Bailey laughing so much she fell over three times.

Now, as she pushed open the side gate and felt her way along the wall to the rear entrance of the coffee shop, it was all she could do not to vomit. She fumbled the back door open, stepped inside and heaved as she breathed coffee. Her face chilled, her stomach rose and she gagged as she stumbled upstairs holding her mouth.

If not for the presence of Mrs Smeak blocking her way at the top of the stairs, Bailey might have made it to the toilet before being sick. However, as the meddling boss's wife tried to question her lateness, Bailey let loose a flow that spewed four feet into the air, catching the side of Mrs Smeak's face and all of one shoulder.

Bailey pushed past the hysterical woman and rushed to the toilet. 'Sorry,' she mumbled as she stuck her head into the lavatory bowl and held her nose against the intense smell that greeted her. She took a chance and opened her eyes and saw the residue of the previous occupant's deposit still floating in the water. She vomited again, covering the contents with a creamy layer.

Through the pain, she heard someone pounding up the stairs and a moment later there was a duet of shrieks. Bailey guessed it was Karen and tried to turn her head to see, but it hurt too much when she moved. She hurled again and continued retching until she could hardly breathe. By the time the spasms stopped and her head cleared, the room had darkened and she felt the press of the closed door against her feet.

'No,' she slurred to anybody listening. 'Leave it open.' She reached for tissue and wiped her mouth then tried to rise, the hand basin groaning as she pulled herself up. Then she opened the door.

There was nobody on the landing, just a patch of glistening, yellow sick soaking into the carpet. Doing her best to avoid the mess, she limped towards the snug where she found Mrs Smeak at the sink with her top off, a collection of moles on her bony back contrasting the white straps of her bra.

'Sorry,' Bailey said, trying not to drawl. 'I had a bit to

drink last night.'

Mrs Smeak didn't turn around.

'Can I help with anything?' Bailey asked.

'Don't you think you've done enough?'

'I feel a bit better now. Maybe I could—'

Mrs Smeak swivelled. 'You have just two things to do today, Jacobs.' Her nostrils flared and she blowed like a bull about to charge. 'Clear up that mess in the hall.'

'Sure, no problem. I'll get right onto it,' Bailey said. 'What else?'

'Simple …' Mrs Smeak snorted and it reminded Bailey of her husband. 'Go home. You're fired.'

* * *

'Fired?'

Bailey rubbed her temples, wondering if the ache would ease when her mother stopped shouting.

'You've had the job less than two weeks and you've been fired?'

The Coke soothed her throat, but didn't help her focus and the paracetamol was taking its time to kick in. She'd anticipated her mother's eruption, but didn't think there would be quite so much discharge.

'You're seventeen, you've had two jobs and you've been fired from both of them.'

Ten minutes, Bailey thought. If she kept her mouth shut and let her mother finish her rant and tire herself out, she could be tucked up in bed within ten minutes.

Her mother slumped at the kitchen table with her head in her hands. 'I'm at my wits end, Bailey. You exhaust me.'

Maybe five.

* * *

After three hours sleeping, Bailey took a shower, dressed in a pair of baggy jogging trousers and jumper, and nestled into the armchair facing the telly. She found the least offensive channel and turned the sound down, losing herself in the images.

Her mother joined her before the programme was over and Bailey sighed, shrugged and smiled all at the same time. 'Sorry, Mum.'

'It's okay, sweetie. I'm sorry too.'

They watched the programme in silence until Bailey spoke several minutes later. 'What is it with men?' Her mother raised a brow. 'I mean, how do you know when you've found a good one?'

'I wish I knew,' her mother said.

'You thought Dad was decent when you met him, right?'

'Yes. But love's a funny thing.'

'How so?'

'You can love someone so much that you don't see who they really are. You can be so infatuated that everything else gets overlooked.'

'Was that what it was like for you and Dad?'

'Yes. I was besotted by him.'

'So why did you leave him?'

'I eventually came to my senses and saw the man for who he really was.'

Bailey leaned forward on her chair. 'Was it worth it?'

'What?'

'Him. Meeting him. Marrying him.'

'Of course,' her mother said. 'I had you.'

'And Timothy.'

Her mother nodded. 'Why do you ask?'

'Because I think I've met someone.'

'Oh, do tell.'

'It's early days yet,' Bailey said, turning in the chair to face her.

'What's he like?'

Since waking from her second sleep that morning, Giovanni had dominated her thoughts. Not just her excitement at seeing his perfect naked form, but his voice, his hair, his entire being. She shivered. 'He's lovely.'

'Handsome?'

'Ever so.'

'How old is he?'

Bailey wasn't sure how old he was, but Christine had thought somewhere in his late twenties. 'Just a bit older than me, I think.'

'Did you meet him at the pub last night?'

'No,' Bailey said, wondering how much she should tell her already on-edge mother. 'Art class.'

'That's nice. I'm happy for you, darling. So,' her mother said in a softer, smoother tone. 'Are you completely over Paul now?'

'Yes, I guess I have been for a while.' Bailey wondered why there was a hesitant look on her mother's face. 'Why?'

'Because I saw him getting into a fancy car with a leggy-blonde,' she said. 'They seemed to be very close.'

They'd only been going out for six months. He was a cheating dickhead and although she didn't care he had found someone else, she was pissed off he had done it so quickly. 'A lucky escape for me,' she said. 'I'm moving on to better things. Cup of tea?'

Chapter Nine

Beware of the dogs.

Seven foot high and twice as wide, imposing gates blocked Bailey's path—an ominous introduction to the Dealer's farmhouse. She peered between iron bars to the grounds beyond where a gravel drive snaked its way through the shadow of a hundred trees.

There was no sign of movement—canine or otherwise.

The route from Bentley train station to the Dealer's house consisted of a short road followed by a long lane which had taken fifteen minutes to walk. Although she could be no more than five miles from Farnham, there was so much countryside around that it felt more like fifty. She had passed a few houses along the way, but no cars and no people. The Dealer's place was creepily quiet and now she faced a warning sign that suggested getting eaten alive was a distinct possibility.

Turn back or go on? She bit her lip and studied the grounds again.

A blanket of tall grass and swollen ferns crowded the space between the trees—perfect cover for any four-legged beast lying in wait. Unconvinced by the apparent stillness, she let out a long, loud whistle, dangled a strip of bacon through the bars and waited.

A desperate urge to pee made her fidget and squirm. She was about to break into someone's house—not just *someone's*, a *criminal's*. The newspaper headline loomed large before her.

Plucky Girl Outsmarts Criminal Mastermind
A spirited Farnham girl with no A-levels, made fools of
local gangsters ...

When she was sure it was safe to move, she returned the bacon to the rucksack and climbed the gate.

Having recovered from her drinking adventure the evening before, she'd eaten a light lunch and walked into town to catch the train from Farnham to Bentley. Wearing her mum's blue anorak, a baseball cap, sunglasses and no makeup, she had moved with a confident air, satisfied that her inconspicuousness wouldn't attract attention from the wrong sort.

She'd taken a window seat at the end of the train where she could observe the platform and everyone who got on. Only a handful of people did, and none looked like the Irishman. But just because she hadn't spotted him, didn't mean he wasn't out there somewhere looking for her. As the train pulled away, she relaxed.

On her lap sat a rucksack filled with items to aid her quest: a torch, a claw-hammer, a cigarette lighter, half a dozen cable ties, two bin liners, a can of hairspray and a family packet of bacon. Prepared for every eventuality she could think of—and thanks to the drive-past on Google, that included aggressive guard dogs—she was confident she could infiltrate the Dealer's home and recover the paintings.

She dropped to the ground on the other side, pushed the rucksack over one shoulder and ducked into the undergrowth, approaching the property in stealth-mode. Her heart pounded so hard she thought it would burst.

Through the branches, a red-brick house loomed. White lattice-windows peppered the building, but none showed any sign of life inside. An empty car-port stood to the right and she edged towards it, careful not to break cover from the trees. She checked the windows again before making a run to the corner of the house.

What the hell was she doing?

She pressed against the wall to steady her breathing.

Mum would take a squint if she found out.

She approached the first window and looked inside.

A sofa and armchair sat in front of a stone fireplace. Beyond that a dining table, chairs and patio doors to the back yard. She was about to try the next window when something caught her eye.

Had something moved inside the room?

She ducked down and held her breath, ready to run if she had to. But a minute passed and then another, and impatience gave way to curiosity. She pushed her face to the window, cupped her hands around her eyes and scanned the room again.

Whatever it was must have—

A face full of teeth lunged at the glass.

She pulled back, fell to the ground and looked up to see a dog fogging the window with its breath. Its mouth dripped saliva as its jaws quivered, releasing a low, relentless growl.

Trespasser Eaten Alive
The shredded remains of a local do-gooder were
discovered today ...

Bailey scrambled along the ground to the side of the house and waited. She expected someone to come tearing out with a shotgun, or worse still, a shotgun and a dog. But nothing happened. There were no raised voices and no signs of human activity. Even the dog quietened.

Christ, she thought, holding her chest to stop it exploding. Was this really worth it? The heady rush of adrenaline pumping through her body told her it was.

Gravel continued down the side of the house and she followed it to the backyard where it gave way to concrete and a series of outbuildings. There was a tin-topped barn as long as the house, a row of brick stables and a wooden garage big enough for four cars.

The dog stared at her through the patio doors, only now it had a companion and they both watched as she navigated the yard. The second dog looked identical to the first—thickset and angry. She felt their eyes on her back as she tiptoed to the shed, prised apart the crooked doors and slipped inside.

The smell of oil and metal greeted her, and another smell, something foul. A shaft of light through the doors behind her split the room in two, but it was still too dark to see. She retrieved the torch from the rucksack and a rat scuttled ahead of its beam as she swept the room—its long tail flicked hard before it vanished beneath a sheet of cardboard. Although unruffled by any rodent she had encountered to date, this one took her breath away.

A wooden work bench ran the length of one wall with tools and equipment spread across in no particular order. At the rear, a sheet covered something large and she crossed the room towards it, sidestepping an open pit in the floor. Beneath the canvas sheet the torch revealed a green car with metal bumpers and black cloth roof. She let the cover fall back into place and inspected the rest of the garage, but nothing took her interest.

Outside, she noticed the guard dogs had abandoned their post. Had they been released? And if so, by whom?

With ears and eyes honed for anything that might suggest an attack, she hurried across the yard to the stables. There were three in all, each with a corrugated roof and a two-part door. Carefully, she pushed open the top half of the first door and recoiled at the smell of manure that assaulted her senses. Straw covered the floor and a barrel of water stood in one corner. A net of hay hung from a wall, but there was no horse. She retreated and coughed her lungs clear.

The second door was secured by bolts at the top and bottom and her anticipation mounted as she slid them back and pulled it open.

Boxes of different sizes covered the floor, the largest as tall as her waist. She rushed to the first one, delved inside and removed something heavy that shone like brass in the torch light. She dropped it back and covered it over. From the next one she pulled a silver tray and a candlestick.

Damn, she thought. Expensive and probably stolen, but not what I'm after.

Turning her attention to the larger boxes along the far wall, she opened one and gasped. With the torch between her teeth, she lifted out a painting and reflections off its gilt-edged frame filled the room with a golden glow. There were three other paintings in the box and after inspecting each in turn, she decided they all looked genuine.

Amateur Sleuth Finds Old Masters
Art-loving teenager Bailey Jacobs, had a brush with death ...

'Well done, girl,' she said through a grin as she reached

for her mobile and cheered when it suggested a thirty percent charge—should be plenty.

After photographing the paintings, the boxes, the stable and the house, she found Constable Mundy's number on speed-dial. The phone pulsed in her ear and she bounced from foot to foot waiting for it to connect.

'Constable Mundy's phone.'

Bailey stiffened at the sound of Tierney's voice. She paused on the edge of *hello*.

'Constable Mundy's phone,' Tierney repeated.

She switched the mobile off, slipped it into the back pocket of her jeans and exited the stable. The last thing she wanted to do was speak to Constable Dickhead. Instead, she would inform the police another time, when there was a bit more distance between her and the Dealer. She closed the door and was ready to leave, but the third stable beckoned.

No good investigator left a job half finished.

The top part of the third door had been pinned back against the wall. As she drew closer, something disturbed the shadows inside. She pushed the torch in first, then followed with her head.

The beam settled on the face of another dog, but this one was far from scary—it had a big head, floppy ears and a lovable expression. It jumped up when it saw her, placed giant paws on the lower door and wagged its tail madly as a pink tongue lapped the air in front of her face.

Definitely a Bernese Mountain Dog, she thought, stroking its ears.

Bailey loved dogs and had researched this particular breed after Mrs Chatterington lost hers during the case of the disappearing dogs. This one was just as she described: waist-height, black and white with brown markings, and the most adorable eyes.

'I wonder,' she said. 'Are you Mrs Chatterington's dog? The one she calls Bailey?' The dog's ears pricked. 'Bailey,' she said again, and the dog barked. 'Shhh … I guess you are.' She reached for a leather lead hanging inside the door and fastened it to the dog's collar.

Heroine Finds Loot and Saves Dog
Animal-loving Bailey Jacobs recovered beauty with the booty …

She'd be a local celebrity—that would please Mum. Too bad Tierney wouldn't be so happy. She sniggered.

She was about to release the dog when she heard the sound of gravel crunching beneath the wheels of an approaching vehicle. She dropped the lead inside the stable and looked around.

To her right, the tin barn beckoned, promising a dozen places to hide. Then she remembered the canvas-covered car and ran to the garage. The dogs had returned and they watched as she raced across the yard and slipped between the garage doors. She peered through the crack in time to see a shiny red car pull into the carport.

The Dealer's Mercedes.

Her heart hammered. Her breathing faltered.

Get a grip girl. Calm head and clear thoughts.

A car door slammed shut and then another. She couldn't see the men who got out, but she heard voices and shortly after that, dogs barking.

Avoiding the pit, Bailey hurried across the garage to the car at the back. Her foot caught and she fell, stifling a yelp as pain exploded in her knee. She scrambled to her feet, found the edge of the tarpaulin, snuck underneath and climbed inside the car. With the rucksack on the passenger seat, she massaged the pain from her knee.

It was cold in the car, and it smelled of mould. The side window was half open and the handle slipped when she tried to turn it. She forced the glass up with the palm of her hands, but only so far and there was still a sizeable gap between the glass and the flimsy cloth roof.

The dogs snuffled in the yard outside, and there were voices too—deep and menacing. The tarpaulin shrouded her like a widow's veil and she could see nothing but eerie shadows through it. Then light bathed everything as the garage doors groaned open.

The dogs were onto her straight away, snorting as they poked around the car.

'Away from there,' a man called.

But the dogs didn't. One pushed its head beneath the cover and tried to climb into the car, snarling as it eyeballed Bailey, its hot, stinky breath making her heave. She reached into the rucksack, grabbed a fistful of bacon and threw it through the window. The ball of meat fell to the floor and both dogs were on it, snapping at each other as they squabbled.

'Leave it,' the man called again.

Something clattered, the man whistled and a shadow fell across the tarpaulin.

'Get out.'

Bailey froze as one dog yelped and the other squealed. Their scrabbling paws faded and the commotion died as the shadow of the man grew smaller. She heard him mutter as he went. Something about rats.

When the garage doors closed, darkness descended and Bailey breathed. But the quiet that followed was fractured by the muffled sound of her mobile ringing in the back pocket of her jeans. Unable to reach it, she adjusted her position in the small car, but her knee caught beneath the steering wheel. As she fought to free herself, the phone continued ringing, only now it was getting louder. A final pull and her knee wrenched clear, she reached behind and fumbled the phone out of her pocket. Covering the speaker with one hand, she read the name on the screen: *Constable Mundy.*

'Constable Mundy,' Bailey whispered into the phone. 'Thanks for getting back, I so need your help.'

'Is that you Jacobs?'

Tierney's gruff voice made her want to scream. Where the hell was Mundy? 'Yes,' she said. 'It's me.'

Tierney didn't speak.

'Are you there?' she asked.

He grunted. 'What do you want?'

'I need your help. I've found the stolen paintings, but I'm trapped in a car. There are dogs and some men. I think they'll hurt me if they find me. Can you come?'

'Piss off, Jacobs.'

'I'm being deadly serious. Please. I know you don't like me and that's fine, but I'm in trouble and I really need your help.' As a policeman sworn to uphold the law, she expected him to put their differences to one side—she would give him the address, he would turn up with an army of colleagues and together they'd close the case. What she hadn't expected, was silence. 'Hello? Constable Tierney?' The phone trembled in her hands as she stared at the words on the screen: *Call Ended.*

She didn't know how long it was before the rage ebbed away and she felt composed enough to leave the car—a few minutes, maybe more—but when she did, the only sound was the wind in the eaves and dirt grinding beneath her boots. With rucksack under arm, she crept to the doors and put her eye to the crack.

She could see the carport, the car and the lane along the side of the house, but not much more. There were no dogs, no people, no particular noises or movement of any kind. But she could smell tobacco and wondered for a moment why it was so potent.

She pushed her head between the doors and looked around.

Two men stood watching her.

One puffed on a cigar with the dogs at his heel.

The other directed a punch.

Chapter Ten

Bones ached from head to toe and a searing pain shot through her jaw as she licked crusted saliva from her lips.

Deathly quiet and suffocatingly hot.

She opened her eyes, then tried to open them again.

The darkness was utter.

She couldn't see, she couldn't feel her hands and her legs demanded to stretch. Her right arm felt numb beneath her body and she tried to roll back to release it, but her movement was confined. With her left arm, she reached out and felt a wall around her. Inches from her face, it had a fur-like touch and held fast when she pushed it.

Her shoulders quivered and stomach knotted and she started to convulse. Stealing three quick breaths—and ignoring the acute protest from her jaw—she screamed.

Bailey pounded and struggled and kicked and pushed as her screams muffled and died against the prison walls.

Terror took control and she struggled in its grip, thrashing to be free at any cost.

* * *

Bailey shook herself awake. Hot and sweaty, she desperately wanted to stretch. Dank air tasted old and stale and the short half-breaths she managed to snatch, only weakened her. With her left hand, she wiped a drizzle of snot from her nose and pushed sticky hair from her wet face.

Tremors surfaced and she fought to control them.

The Colonel—an image of the old man came to her, his serene face, perfect teeth and comforting smile—what would the Colonel do? He'd be rational. He'd be calm and in control. He'd start with the things he could influence and work from there.

She tried to force her breathing to calm, but all she could think about was breaking free. Reaching beneath her body, she pulled her right arm clear and massaged it back to life. Then she tried her legs. Half bent to her chest, they felt heavy and difficult to move. They ached when she flexed them against the wall and panic found an edge again.

She bit through an emerging scream and swallowed it silent.

Her mother's face appeared, soft and smiling, mouthing something undistinguishable as she morphed into Christine and then Giovanni. The local newspaper flashed in front of her and Bailey read the headlines of her own death with a picture of Smeak and Tierney laughing together on the front page.

Fuck them.

She took a long, slow breath.

Exhaled.

And calmed.

Carefully and methodically, she investigated the walls again, feeling for an edge, a purchase, anything she could work with.

The tips of her fingers touched a ridge and she forced them in behind, then pulled until it hurt. But with hardly any grip, her fingers slipped and pain erupted when a nail caught. She tasted blood as she rolled her tongue over the raised nail before pushing it into place with a grunt.

She slowed her breathing and attacked the ridge again.

With fingers wedged behind some kind of fur-covered board, she encouraged it free little by little, pulling and pushing, straining until the bones in her hands howled and pain brought tears to her eyes.

She rested, calmed and tried again.

Something ripped and tore free and she pushed it aside to reveal a tiny strip of light filtering through the smallest crack. It reminded her of a nightmare and she shuddered with the fear of it coming true—suffocating in a place where no one can hear you scream.

She pushed her face to the crack and sucked in a mouthful of clean air.

With fingers secured around another piece of the wall she was ready to pull again, but stopped when she heard footsteps on gravel.

The noise grew so loud and so close she felt the person must have passed over the top of her. The box moved, it rocked gently up and down and she steadied herself against the walls.

A click and a whir and the lid of the box opened.

Sucking in clean air, she closed her eyes against the light and shielded her face from whatever attack was imminent.

But none came.

She forced her eyes open and squinted into the face of the Irishman.

Too frail to fight, she was unable to prevent him reaching in and taking her.

* * *

Confused and weak, Bailey opened her eyes to a bright,

fuzzy room. A low hum of surrounding conversation stopped when a woman gasped. Something touched Bailey's cheek and she turned to see a face out of focus.

'It's all right, darling,' the face said. 'Take it easy.'

'Margh.' Pain in her jaw turned her words to a moan.

'Shhh. Rest now.'

She closed her eyes and drifted.

Chapter Eleven

Bailey turned to the front page of the *Farnham Echo* and read it again.

Heroine Exposes Criminal Network
Seventeen-year-old Bailey Jacobs risked her life in
pursuit of justice ...

No matter how many times she read it, it thrilled her. And the fact it was written by the *Echo's* pain-in-the-arse reporter Lawrence Williams, made it doubly enjoyable. He must have chewed his tongue as he wrote it.

'You've got a visitor.'

Bailey looked up to see Constable Mundy standing there, her policewoman's hat in one hand, a bunch of flowers in the other.

'I'll make some tea,' her mother said, leaving the room.

Bailey unfolded her legs from the armchair and tried to smile.

'Don't get up,' Mundy said, looking around. 'I bought the heroine flowers, but it seems I'm not the first.'

In the forty-eight hours since leaving hospital, Bailey had received nine bouquets of flowers, three boxes of chocolates and a bottle of gin. She didn't recognise all the names attached to the accompanying notes and get-well cards, but she vowed to find out and thank them all personally. Even Smeak had arranged a collection of carnations from the team at the coffee shop. He'd also sent a note offering her job back at an increased hourly rate.

Bailey pointed to the sofa. 'Sit,' she said through wired teeth.

'How is that working for you?' Mundy asked, pointing to her mouth.

Bailey shrugged. It didn't hurt if she didn't move, but sleeping was a problem and she had to drink her meals. Still, she guessed things could have turned out worse. 'It's okay,' she said.

'Constable Mundy—'

'Please, call me Wendy.'

Bailey nodded and pulled a lock of hair free from the metal in her mouth. 'Wendy,' she said. 'Tell me about the dog?'

'It's definitely Bailey, Mrs Chatterington's dog. They scanned his microchip at the station. She's ever so pleased to have him back.'

Bailey felt a tear roll the length of her nose and she wiped it away. 'I know,' she said, pointing to an extremely large bunch of flowers sitting in the centre of the dining room table. 'Those are from her.'

'She wanted me to extend her thanks to you again,' Wendy said, 'and to let you know you're welcome to visit the manor at any time.'

Bailey thought she would like that. Although initially wary of Mrs Chatterington's forceful and somewhat pompous nature, the two-hundred pound cheque she attached to the flowers had swayed her opinion. And when she discovered Mrs Chatterington was married to one of the largest local landowners in the area—and considered by some to be local nobility—Bailey's views of the woman softened.

'I need to apologise to you, Bailey. My mobile, I left it on the desk. Tierney heard it ringing and—'

'It's okay,' Bailey said, seeing the discomfort on the policewoman's face.

'I reported him for failing to lodge your call.'

'He didn't tell you that I phoned?'

Wendy shook her head. 'Not until much later, when you were in hospital.'

'I pleaded with him for help,' Bailey said, 'but he hung up.'

Wendy exhaled and shook her head. 'Someone will probably contact you in the next few days to discuss that in more detail.'

'What will happen to him?'

'Tierney? If he's found negligent then he'll be disciplined, probably suspended. It's going to damage his career. He's got designs on being a detective. At least he did have. I don't know what he'll do now.'

'Oh,' Bailey said. 'I guess he dislikes me even more.'

Wendy looked up as Mrs Jacobs came into the room carrying a tray. She handed a cup to the Constable and a glass of Coke with a straw to Bailey. Then she left.

Bailey sucked at the straw, making gurgling noises. 'Sorry,' she said.

'How much longer do you have to wear that thing?'

'Four weeks at least. It's only been a couple of days and already I'm craving solid food.' She tried not to laugh.

'You know you were silly to do what you did?' Wendy said. 'Very brave, but very silly.'

'Mum's given me that lecture already. I take it you recovered the paintings?'

'We found a good haul of paintings and what looks to be stolen property from some other jobs. We haven't finished searching yet and we're still questioning Mr Anderson and his colleague.'

'Mr Anderson?'

'The owner of the property you trespassed on. We arrested his wife as well. She came at us with a kitchen knife when we dragged her husband away. A really nice lady.'

Bailey wondered if she might be prosecuted for trespassing.

'You realise you could be prosecuted,' Mundy said.

'For trespassing?'

'Yes. He might be a Governor in one of the most notorious Firms in the south, but he can still prosecute you if he wants to.'

'Firm?' she asked.

Wendy seemed surprised. 'Frank Anderson is a key figure in a London crime network. Thanks to you, he and his punch-happy sidekick have been arrested and their various interests are being looked into.' She sipped from her cup. 'We think you've started a lucrative investigation.'

'Oh,' Bailey said, trying to unstick the straw from her lips. 'That's good then.'

'Potentially it's very good.'

'Who do I thank for rescuing me? Was he one of yours?'

Wendy shook her head. 'Have you asked your mother about him?'

'She said he's a policeman, that's all.'

'He is, but he's not from around here.'

Bailey wondered why that mattered. 'So?'

Wendy paused with her mouth open, appearing to build her next sentence carefully. 'It's not for me to say. You should talk to your mother.'

I will, Bailey thought, just as soon as you leave.

'Tell me, Bailey. Have you thought what career path you'd like to follow when things go back to normal?'

'What do you mean?'

'You know, when you get better … I think you'd make an excellent police officer.'

Bailey felt herself blush. *Her*, a policewoman? She liked the sound of that—there must be some great perks to being in the police. Then she considered having to work with Tierney and his like. 'I haven't thought about it,' she said, playing with the straw.

'Well if you'd like to talk to me about it, don't hesitate to get in touch. We're not all like Constable Tierney. Most of us are like you: normal, average people who want to make a difference in the community.' Wendy stood and held out her hand. 'Have a think about it.'

'Thank you,' Bailey said, shaking it hard. 'I'll definitely give it some thought.'

The policewoman turned smartly and left and got as far as the front door when her mother pounced from the kitchen. Although she couldn't hear what they were saying, Bailey knew they were talking about her.

She folded into the chair and contemplated life as a policewoman. Would she get her own car? She'd have to learn to drive first. Perhaps she could be a dog handler, or a firearms expert? Did they get paid more than regular officers?

'How are you feeling, darling?'

She turned to her mother and nodded. 'Not so bad,' she said, lying through her teeth. 'Mum, who saved me from the car?'

'Ah,' her mother said. 'The lady Constable said you were asking about that.'

'I deserve to know.'

'I know you do, darling.' Her mother sat on the sofa with hands balled on her lap. 'I have some … important friends,' she said. 'In the police force. Special friends.'

Bailey wasn't sure what she meant and her face must have said so.

'They look out for us.'

'What d'you mean?'

Her mother flexed her fingers. 'Let's just say, they're the good guys and they're on our side.'

'So the man following me, the one who got me out of the car, was he one of your police friends?'

'Yes.'

'How long had he been following me?'

'A few days.'

'Why?'

Her mother dropped her head and didn't answer.

'Is he out there now?' Bailey said. 'Can we invite him in? I'd like to thank him.'

'No. They've agreed not to, I mean … he won't be following you any more.'

'Was he following me because of Dad?'

'Yes.'

Bailey ran her tongue over the metal brace. It tingled to the touch and she wanted to rip it off. The police had been following her since she'd found her father's telephone number. 'Did they think Dad was going to contact me?'

Her mother's eyes watered. 'Your father's in trouble.'

'What?'

'He's got himself into trouble.'

'Do you know where he is?'

'No, nobody does. He's not been seen for a few months. He was released from prison in January and the last contact the police had with him was early March … just before your birthday.' She swallowed and took an extended breath. 'Apparently, some of his old business partners are looking for him as well.'

Bailey couldn't be sure she understood. She'd only recently found out her father was alive and already he was missing. 'Can we help him? If he turns up here can we look after him?'

Her mother frowned. 'I don't think—'

'He could have my room,' Bailey said, feeling her jaw ache as her excitement grew. 'I could sleep in the lounge. We'd be like a safe-house for him.'

'I don't think it's going to come to that.'

'But—'

'No, Bailey. He's definitely not going to turn up here.'

'How can you be so sure?'

'Because he doesn't know where we are.' Her mother stood and adjusted her skirt. 'And for our own safety, it needs to stay that way.'

* * *

Sitting at her desk with the pad open to the page entitled *The Case of the Resurrected Father*, Bailey updated her notes.

CLUES
- *Lives in Ireland (probably).*
- *Released from prison in January 2018.*
- *Being hunted by former business partners.*

- *Cryptic message ... For all the times I failed.*
  02898417833. 21 Botanic.
- *Pictured with a blond-haired man (Quinn Maguire).*
- *Aunt Liz and Quinn introduced Mum to Dad.*
- *Irishman returned my call ... coming for retribution?*

ACTIONS
- *Find Dad?*
- *Avoid the Irishman.*

If she were serious about finding her father, the next logical step would be to travel to Ireland to continue searching for him. Would she be able to find him in a country she knew nothing about? Probably not. Should she at least try?

He was not a very nice man.

She closed the pad, put down the pen and stretched. Crippling joints and consuming tiredness were constant companions these days. She moved to the bed and lay down, studying the section of ceiling the builders had repaired during her stay in hospital. A gentle knock sounded on her bedroom door and her mother entered carrying something.

She held it out. 'To replace the broken one.'

Bailey turned the leather-bound photo frame in her hands. 'Thanks, Mum.' She sat up and they hugged. 'You know, when I was trapped in the boot of that car, I remembered one of the dreams I've been having.'

Her mother stiffened. 'The one about the field?'

'No. The one about being confined somewhere dark. I think it was the airing cupboard at our house in Ireland. It was warm and soft and dark, except for a strip of light beneath the door. I don't know how I got locked in, but nobody came when I screamed.' Bailey saw tears gather in her mother's eyes. 'Until finally, you let me out.'

'I …'

The tears bulged and fell and Bailey reached to her mother's face and wiped them away. 'Did you lock me in the cupboard, Mum?'

'No. I would never …'

'It's okay,' Bailey said, holding her hand. 'I forgive you. I'll always forgive you.'

'It wasn't me. I didn't …'

'I know,' said Bailey. 'But I guess that explains why I don't like confined spaces.'

Her mother sniffed. 'And why you're not keen on ironing.'

Pain prevented Bailey laughing.

'Will you accept Mr Smeak's offer?'

'To go back to work? I don't see why I should. He's not been very nice to me and anyway, with Mrs Chatterington's cheque I can pay off the money I owe for the broken window.'

'That reminds me.' Her mother got up, moved to the desk and turned the chair to face the bed before sitting. 'Mr Smeak showed me an invoice from the *Farnham Echo* for the cost of repairing one of their cameras … the one you broke during that scuffle with their reporter. Mr Smeak said the invoice should be passed on to you.'

Shit, Bailey thought, I'd forgotten about that. 'How much for?'

'Twelve-hundred pounds.'

She swallowed. 'I can't afford that.'

'No, but he said you can work it off.'

Twelve hundred. Even with a pay rise, that was going to take months to clear. And Mrs Chatterington's donation would hardly make a dent in it. She sighed. 'Could you lend me the money?'

Her mother shook her head.

'In that case, I guess I'm going to have to go back to work.' She picked at her wire-sewn teeth. 'But not just yet. Not until after this.'

Although she was keen to share her adventures with Christine and the Colonel, she wanted to see more of Giovanni and she was eager to say goodbye to Jack before he left on his travels, under no circumstances would she do so with a face full of scaffolding.

Having rescued a beautiful dog, broken the back of a major crime syndicate and come face to face with a terrifying death and survived, Bailey knew she deserved some time for herself. Time to recover, to regain her strength and to enjoy the positive attention of her new found fame—however long it lasted.

After all, she still had so much to do.

Her father was yet to be found and that would take planning. She had to reach him, to help him, to understand why he'd done what he did. With her support he might be able to turn his life around. She couldn't be sure, but she had to try.

And the Irishman? Perhaps his threat was fanciful. Part of her didn't care, the other part wouldn't let her sleep. Either way, his retribution was likely to pale against the hatred Tierney must have for her at the moment. She'd need to watch out for them both.

Tragedy had selected her that week, but she'd avoided it by the skin of her teeth—not unscathed, but still alive— and for that she was thankful. She had made new friends, learned new values and grown as a person. She'd also recovered lost memories, deciphered dreams and remembered what had tempted her into the attic.

Yes, Bailey thought as the word *retribution* flashed in front of her, she still had so much to do.

Bailey returns in
Episode Five

Bailey Jacobs
and
Tomorrow's News

An impossible newspaper predicts Bailey's death.

To stay up to date with the latest Bailey Jacobs
news and offers, register as a member
on the author's website …

https://www.vjbarrington.com